Paula Marshall

Oct '83

Praisesong for the Widow

Praisesong for the Widow

Paule Marshall

G. P. PUTNAM'S SONS
NEW YORK

The author gratefully acknowledges permission from the following
sources to reprint material in their control:

Atheneum Publishers for an excerpt from *The Woman at the
Washington Zoo* by Randall Jarrell, copyright © 1960 by Randall
Jarrell.

Amiri Baraka for an excerpt from "leroy," by Amiri Baraka
(LeRoi Jones), from *Black Magic Poetry 1961–1967*, copyright ©
1969 by LeRoi Jones.

Dodd, Mead & Company, Inc., for an excerpt from "Little Brown
Baby," by Paul Lawrence Dunbar, from *The Complete Poems of Paul
Lawrence Dunbar*, copyright © 1940 by Paul Lawrence Dunbar.

Folkways Records, Moses Asch, director, for an excerpt from the
lyrics of "The Big Drum Dance of Carriacou," Folkways album
#FE4011 recorded and annotated by Dr. Andrew C. Pearse.

Harper & Row Publishers, Inc., for an excerpt from "Children of
the Poor," by Gwendolyn Brooks, from *Selected Poems*, copyright ©
1949 by Gwendolyn Brooks Blakely.

Alfred A. Knopf, Inc., for excerpts from "I, Too" and "The
Negro Speaks of Rivers," by Langston Hughes, from *Selected Poems
of Langston Hughes*, copyright © 1926 by Alfred A. Knopf, Inc. and
renewed in 1954 by Langston Hughes.

Liveright Publishing Corporation for an excerpt from "Runagate
Runagate" by Robert Hayden from *Angel of Ascent: New and Selected
Poems*, copyright © 1975, 1972, 1970, 1966 by Robert Hayden.

MCA Music, A Division of MCA Inc., for an excerpt from the
lyrics of "Romance in the Dark," words and music by Lil Green,
copyright © 1940, 1958 by Duchess Music Corporation, New York,
NY. Copyright renewed.

Ivan Mogull Music Corporation and Rolls Royce Music Company

for an excerpt from the lyrics of "Four Women," words and music by Nina Simone, copyright © 1966 by Ivan Mogull Music Corporation and Rolls Royce Music Company.

Random House, Inc., for an excerpt from "Good Times" by Lucille Clifton from *Good Times*, copyright © 1969 by Lucille Clifton.

Viking Penguin, Inc., for an excerpt from "The Creation" by James Weldon Johnson from *God's Trombones*, copyright © 1927 by The Viking Press, Inc., and renewed in 1935 by Grace Nail Johnson.

Warner Bros. Music for an excerpt from the lyrics of "Jelly Jelly Blues" by Earl Hines and Billy Eckstine, copyright © 1944 (renewed) by Warner Bros. Inc.

The text of this book is set in 11 point Goudy Old Style.

Library of Congress Cataloging in Publication Data

Marshall, Paule, date.
Praisesong for the widow.

I. Title.
PS3563.A7223P7   1983   813'.54   82-13215
ISBN 0-399-12754-2

PRINTED IN THE UNITED STATES OF AMERICA

Third Impression

For my grandmother,
Alberta Jane Clement
("Da-duh")

I

RUNAGATE

. . . and the night cold and the night
long and the river/to cross . . .
           —Robert Hayden

I wanted to know my mother when she sat
looking sad across the campus in the late 20's
into the future of the soul, there were black angels
straining above her head, carrying life from the ancestors,
and knowledge, and the strong nigger feeling . . .
           —Amiri Baraka

1

With a strength born of the decision that had just come to her in the middle of the night, Avey Johnson forced the suitcase shut on the clothes piled inside and slid the lock into place. Taking care not to make a sound, she then eased the heavy bag off the couch onto the floor and, straining under her breath, her tall figure bent almost in two, hauled it over the thick carpeting to the door on the other side of the cabin.

A thirty-inch Pullman stood packed and waiting there. Quickly she deposited the second bag next to it, and after pausing to dart a nervous glance behind her, she slipped over to a long sectional closet which took up the rest of the wall beside the door.

From the storage space at the bottom she pulled out another suitcase. Her movements a whisper, she raised up and with her free hand began stripping the hangers of as many clothes as she could carry along with the bag. In seconds her arms were full, and she had spun around and was heading rapidly back across the dimly lighted room, moving like a woman half her age, her shadow on the walls and ceiling hurrying to keep up.

Over at the couch, with the suitcase laid open on top of the bedcovers, she made quick work of the clothes, tossing them helter-skelter into the bag without a trace of the neatness and order that were her hallmark. A minute later found her back at the closet, blindly reaching and snatching at whatever came to her hand in the darkness. Then, noiseless as a sneak thief, she was beating it back to the couch, her arms piled high again.

Perspiration was beginning to sheet her forehead despite the air-conditioning in the cabin. She didn't stop to wipe it. The determined look on her face had brought her underlip jutting forward, exposing the spillover of raw pink across the top which she always kept hidden. She let the lip stay as it was. The back pain she suffered with occasionally was threatening to flare up with all the bending and hauling. She closed her mind to it.

Her mind in a way wasn't even in her body, or for that matter, in the room. From the moment she had awakened in a panic less than an hour ago and come to the reckless decision, her mind had left to go and stand down at the embarkation door near the waterline five decks below. While she swiftly criss-crossed the room on her bare feet, spiriting her belongings out of the closet and drawers, her mind had leaped ahead to the time, later that morning, when the ship would have arrived at the next port of call. The huge door in the steel hull would be rolled back then and along with her fellow passengers going ashore for the day, she would step from the liner onto the waiting launch. For the last time. And without so much as a backward glance.

Avey Johnson's two traveling companions, with whom she shared the large deluxe cabin, were asleep in the bedroom on the other side of a divider with narrow shelflike openings on top and a long chest of drawers below, facing what was called the living area. Not to risk waking them, she had left off the lamps in the living area, where she always volunteered to sleep each cruise because it was more private.

For illumination she had opened the drapes at the picture window of a porthole and was making do with the reflection of the deck lights outside, along with the faint glow of the night-light filtering through the divider, which the woman, Thomasina Moore, always kept burning in the bedroom, like a child afraid of the dark. The pale satin sheen of the night-gown she had on added to the small pool of light, as did the subtle aura, unbeknown to her, which her dark skin had given off since birth.

Slipping back over to the couch, her feet struck a chair. Quickly she stifled her outcry, shook off the pain and kept going. When was the last time she had gone barefoot around the house? She paused a second, the clothes she was about to let drop into the suitcase suspended in her arms. Halsey Street? Had it been that long ago? Back then the young woman whose headstrong ways and high feelings Avey Johnson had long put behind her, whom she found an embarrassment to even think of now with her 1940s upsweeps and pompadours and vampish high-heeled shoes, used to kick off her shoes the moment she came in from work, shed her stockings and start the dusting and picking up in her bare feet. The pots on in the tiny kitchen. The 78s on the turntable in the living room: Coleman Hawkins, Lester Young, The Count,

The Duke. Music to usher Jay in the door. Freed of the high-heels her body always felt restored to its proper axis. And the hardwood floor which Jay had rescued from layers of oxblood-colored paint when they first moved in and stained earth brown, the floor reverberating with "Cottontail" and "Lester Leaps In" would be like a rich nurturing ground from which she had sprung and to which she could always turn for sustenance.

Avey Johnson hadn't thought of that floor in decades.

A bottom drawer became stuck in the chest of drawers below the divider where her underclothes were stowed. Grasping it between her hands she tried jiggling it back on its tracks, unmindful for a moment in her haste of the noise she was making until she heard her friend, Clarice, shift massively in her sleep. Poor Clarice. She always sounded as if she were wrestling with someone as large as herself on the narrow bed whenever she turned. There quickly followed a sound from the other bed, like the knocking in a radiator as the steam rises, as Thomasina Moore, her sleep disturbed, began an ominous implosive clucking at the roof of her mouth.

Her hands froze on the drawer. That was the last person she wanted to wake before she was done! Scarcely breathing, she remained bent double over the chest, perspiring, her back aching, holding herself rigid except once when she gave a fearful glance back over her shoulder—something she had repeatedly caught herself doing since yesterday.

Only when the two inside the bedroom had been quiet for some time did she try the drawer again. With a burglar's finesse this time she eased it back on its tracks, slid it open without a sound, and the next moment was darting across to the couch with the wealth of underthings she had scooped up, the drawer left open behind.

Her skirts, blouses and summer suits were done. The sweaters and stoles she drew around her when the weather on deck turned chilly had been packed after a fashion. Crowded into the wrong bag were the linen shirtdresses she wore on excursions ashore in place of the shorts and slacks favored by the other women her age on board, no matter what their size. Her shoes were in their special caddy. Her hats in their cylindrical box. And she had just disposed of the last of her underthings. All that remained were her ensemble dresses and evening gowns. She was down to the last of the six suitcases.

"But why six, Mother? Why would anyone in their right mind need to take this much stuff just to go away for a couple of weeks?"—Marion, Avey Johnson's youngest, the morning she had come to drive her mother to the pier before her first cruise three years ago. Entering the house, Marion had stopped short at sight of the half-dozen bags neatly lined up in the downstairs hall, had stood staring at them for the longest time, trying to contain her exasperation but failing. When she finally looked up it had been all she could do, from her expression, not to reach out and grab her mother by the shoulders and shake her the way she might have one of her pupils in the small community school she helped to run in a church in Brooklyn. To shake sense into her. Around the face which bore Jay's clear imprint, her hair had stood massed like a raincloud about to make good its threat. And the noisy necklace of cowrie shells and amber she had brought back from Togo her last visit had sounded her angry despair with its rattle each time she breathed.

"Why go on some meaningless cruise with a bunch of white folks anyway, I keep asking you? What's that supposed to be about? Couldn't you think of something better to do on your vacation? And since when have you started letting Thomasina Moore decide how you should spend it? You don't even like the woman. What the hell's gotten into you?"

Avey Johnson's own mother would have slapped Marion down long ago had she been her child—and never mind she was twenty-eight and a woman already married and divorced. She would have raised a hard palm and with a blow to set her ears ringing put her in her place: "Girl, where you get off talking to *me* like that?"

And the Avey Johnson of thirty, forty years ago would have done likewise. She had been quick then to show her displeasure, her bottom lip immediately unfolding to bare the menacing sliver of pink and then her mouth letting fly with the words. But she had grown away from such high-strung behavior, and over the years had developed a special silence to deal with anyone the likes of Marion. With her daughter she simply acted as if nothing unpleasant was being said, that Marion was still, as she had once been, the most polite and tractable of her children.

"Here last summer I begged you to go on that tour to Brazil, and on the one, the year before that, to Ghana . . ." The voice hung unrelenting at her ear as she made the final hurried trips between the closet again and the couch. "And all I got for an answer was either 'we'll see' or that infuriating silence of yours. Yet here you are willing and eager to go off on some ridiculous cruise. Could you have thought of anything more banal!"

Banal? For a second before she quickly checked herself the word had threatened to overturn the rock of her calm. Did Marion know that the closest she had ever come to a cruise in her life had been the annual boatride up the Hudson to Bear Mountain as a child? What did she know?

". . . Why can't you be a little imaginative, for God's sake, a little independent, and go off on your own somewhere. Learn something!"

Marion had been the only one of Avey Johnson's three children to oppose the trip. Sis, the eldest, in her weekly phone call from Los Angeles, had urged her mother to go, reminding her that she and her husband, a systems programmer at Lockheed (the only one his color in his division), had sailed to Hawaii the previous year, taking their two boys and had enjoyed it.

Annawilda, interning at Meharry Hospital at the time, had written to say it was just what she needed, adding: "It'll take your mind off Daddy." It had been 1974 then, and Jerome Johnson had been dead only a little over a year.

And they, it turned out, had been right and Marion wrong. Because whatever doubts she had managed to sow in Avey Johnson's mind vanished the moment she saw the *Bianca Pride* that first time in her berth at West Fortieth Street and the river, with the flags and pennants flying from all her stations, her high bow canted toward the sun. All that dazzling white steel! Her hull appeared to sweep clear across to New Jersey. The precision and power of her lines! The ship's turbines, she had read in the brochure they had sent her before sailing, produced enough heat and light to run a city the size of Albany! And on a group tour of the bridge that first trip she had seen the huge Ferranti computer that monitored all operations on board. Her group had stood awestruck and reverent before the console with its array of keyboards, switches and closed-circuit television screens.

There had been no resisting it! Thomasina Moore had no sooner suggested a return trip the following year than she had accepted. And Marion, seeing her resolve, began keeping her objections to herself. Her eyes had carefully avoided the suitcases the last two times she had come to drive her to the pier, and on the way into Manhattan she had talked only of her pupils, most of whom had been rejected by the public schools as being impossible to teach. Her "sweetest lepers," Marion called them, from a poem she was always urging her mother to read.

The last of the evening gowns lay where she had just flung them on top of the final pile of dresses in the fold-over garment bag. They had graced their last dinner in the Versailles Room; they had attended their last Captain's Ball. As if sealing a tomb, Avey Johnson zippered the long flap into place over them, and still working feverishly, like someone pursued, folded the bag over on itself, latched the two halves together, and seconds later was dragging it across the cabin to join the others.

The marathon packing was done. On an armchair over near the window lay the clothes she had hastily set aside to wear. The suitcases, all six of them along with the shoe caddy and hatbox, stood assembled near the door, ready for the steward. Giving the apprehensive glance over her shoulder, she immediately headed toward them, not even allowing herself a moment to rest her back or wipe the perspiration from her face— or to consider, quietly and rationally, which was normally her way, what she was about to do.

Outside the glow of the deck lights was slowly being absorbed by a pearl-gray light that was both filtering down from the clearing sky and curling up like mist from the sea. And the sea itself had become a wide, silvertoned sheet of plate metal, which was already, out near the horizon, reflecting the subtle mauve and rose and pale yellows of the day.

Amid the burgeoning color stood the liner—huge, sleek, imperial, a glacial presence in the warm waters of the Caribbean. The long night run completed, it had come to rest and drop anchor a short time ago in the same smooth and sound-less manner with which it had moved over the sea.

From its decks could be made out the faint, almost insub-stantial form of an island across the silvery moat of the harbor. The next port of call.

Avey Johnson had finished in good time.

2

"What you doing up and dressed so early?"

A pair of grayish eyes with the unblinking watchfulness of a bird's were peering through the divider's narrow openings. They were like eyes at the slot of a speakeasy door.

Seconds later, wearing a sheer frilly dressing gown that looked meant for a bride (it even had a slight train), Thomasina Moore stepped curiously around the divider into the living area.

She was a thin-featured woman in her early seventies with a lined and hectic brow, what used to be called "good hair" covered over with a sleeping net, and the first signs of a dowager's hump across her shoulders: old age beginning to warp the once graceful curve of her back. She could still, though—she liked to boast—kick her legs as high as when she had danced in the chorus line of the Cotton Club back in the twenties. (At least she claimed it had been the Cotton Club. Which might have been true. She had the color to have qualified: black that was the near-white of a blanched almond or the best of ivory. A color both sacred—for wasn't it a witness?—and profane: *"he forced my mother my mother/late/ One night/What do they call me?"*).

She almost collided with the suitcases at the door.

"And what're your bags doing sitting here by the door? What's going on around here?"

Avey Johnson, gazing out of the window on the other side of the living area, didn't turn to her immediately. After quickly showering and dressing, she had gone to wait out the time till morning watching the island across the way gradually take shape in the growing light. A dark mass of coastal hills with a darker foil of mountains behind had been the first to appear. Then, as the sun rose fully, lighting the hills one after the other the way an acolyte would candles in a church, the town had become sharply visible: a pretty seaport town of pastel houses with red tiled roofs crowding down to the harbor and perched like tick birds on the flanks of the hills.

She had found the sight soothing, reassuring. The town, the hills, the distant mountains, the morning sunlight, all not only applauded her decision, it seemed, but assured her there would be a plane to New York later in the day with a seat for her on it.

So that as she turned to Thomasina Moore after making her wait almost a full minute, she scarcely felt the need to steel herself against the tirade she knew would follow. Indeed, it was as if she had already heard the woman out and had left. Part of her had already stepped on board the launch and was planing swiftly over the morning sea toward the island and the waiting plane.

She had decided, she said, to cut short the cruise and go home. She kept her gaze on the middle distance.

"You decided to do *what*? What you say?"

She knew it must come as a shock, her leaving on the spur of the moment like this, but it couldn't be helped. She had ignored the woman's outcry. The cruise itself she didn't think was to blame. Nor was she sick, although she hadn't been feeling herself the last couple of days. It was nothing she could put her finger on. She had simply awakened in the middle of the night and decided she would prefer to spend the rest of her vacation at home. It didn't make any sense, she knew, but her mind was made up. If she was lucky she might get a flight out today . . .

While she was saying all this, the words terse and final, her manner calm, Thomasina Moore started slowly toward her across the living area, her dumbstruck gaze taking in the emptied-out closet and the drawers, all of which stood sprawling open. She faltered to a stop in the middle of the floor, and from there, with a child's open-mouth disbelief, she examined the dressy two-piece ensemble Avey Johnson had on, the stylish but conservative pumps on her feet, and the straw hat she was already wearing, whose wide brim curved down to hide most of her face.

The pocketbook she had placed on a chair beside her also drew the woman's stricken gaze—a handsome bag of navy-blue straw to complement the muted beige and navy print of her dress, and draped over it a pair of mesh summer gloves with a single crystal button at the wrist.

Here her eyes came to focus and for the longest while she gazed at the buttons as if in her shaken mind they were tiny crystal balls which could tell her whether she was hearing right. Until finally, with a sound like that of a bewildered

mute struggling desperately to speak, her head jerked back
over her shoulder and she was calling toward the bedroom,
"Clarice! Clarice! Get on out here! *Clarice* . . . !"

She continued to summon Clarice even when the latter,
sleepily trying to pull a robe around her bulk, appeared from
behind the divider.

At fifty-eight Clarice was six years Avey Johnson's junior
and the youngest of the three women. Where the bones of her
face pressed up through the fleshiness, her skin—black with
an admixture of plum that spoke of centuries of sunlight—was
as smooth as a girl's. Yet she tended to look as old or older
than Thomasina Moore because of the worry lines furrowed
deep around her mouth and the downcast, burdened expression she never completely abandoned even on those rare occa-
sions when she laughed.

"Did you hear this?"

"No," she said, still struggling with the robe. "What's happened?"

Clarice asked but she really didn't want to know. She had
already, in a single apprehensive glance around the room,
taken in the suitcases by the door, the ransacked drawers and
closet and her two friends, one agitated and close to anger in
the middle of the floor, the other calm and enveloped in that
special intimidating silence of hers over by the porthole; and
she had resigned herself to the worst.

"What d'you mean what's happened? This one's leaving,
that's what. Walking out on the cruise. She all of sudden feels
she'd rather spend what's left of her vacation at home and is
going back today. Just like that. Without a word to anybody.
You ever heard anything like it . . . ?"

"Is that true, Avey . . . ?" Clarice's reluctant gaze sought
the tall figure across the room.

"What d'you mean if it's true?" Thomasina Moore's voice had risen sharply. "Don't you see her bags all packed over there near you? Don't you see the way she's dressed? Hat, gloves, the works. Do you think she'd be all dolled up like that if she was just going sightseeing with the rest of us today? She's leaving, I'm telling you. Quitting the cruise after only five days and taking a plane home!"

The shock of it was still so great she fell speechless again, and in the small charged silence left by her voice Clarice tried asking Avey Johnson what had gone wrong. Had something happened on board? Or had she come down with something? Was she perhaps feeling sick . . . ?

"Do . . . she . . . look . . . sick . . . to . . . you?" Her colors, as Thomasina Moore called them, were up: anger like a battery of flags being rung up all at once in a strong wind. ("Look out you don't get my colors up," she was always warn- ing. Or: "These white folks around here must be trying to get my colors up"—this on their first cruise, when they had been assigned a table in the dining room which she felt was too close to the service entrance. She had promptly had it changed.)

"Do she look sick to you, I ask?" Though furious, her voice was pitched low: despite her anger she was being mindful of the public corridor just outside the door. "Ain' not a thing wrong with her. Talking 'bout she ain' been feeling herself these past couple of days. Well, what's ailing her? What's her complaint? If she was sick she would have gone to the doctor, wouldn't she? That's what he's here for. No, she can't fool me with no excuse like that . . ."

Suddenly, the grayish eyes with their unblinking intensity narrowed, becoming more acute, more suspicious. "But I should've known somethin' was up the funny way she was

22

acting yesterday. Keeping to herself all day. Not showing up till dinner and then scarcely touching the food on her plate. Hardly talking to anybody. I should've known somethin' was up. And now come this morning here she is dressed back, ready to walk off the ship for good. All of a sudden like this! And without a word as to why! 'It's nothin' I can put my finger on.' Who she thinks she's kiddin'? A person would have to have a reason for doing a thing like this. No, somethin's behind this mess. Somethin' deep. She can't make me out for no fool!"

There would be a taxi waiting for her on the wharf of the little pastel town. Or one would arrive the moment she stepped off the launch. The driver would inform her that, yes, there was a plane to New York today, a nonstop flight scheduled to leave shortly. No, it was unlikely to be filled, this being May and the off-season. She was certain to get a seat. The airport would turn out to be only a short drive away, on a wide safe plain between the hills fronting the sea and the mountains she had glimpsed in the distance. They would reach there in ample time for the flight.

". . . And what about the money? Have you heard her say anything about all the money she's gonna be losing . . . ?" Thomasina Moore swung with this toward Clarice, the violence of her movement sending up a shower of scented dust from the bride's dressing gown, and causing the daylight inside the cabin, which was only an hour old, to waver like a used-up lightbulb.

"Have you, I'm asking!"

Clarice, backed up against the tall wooden support to the divider, numbly shook her head. She had assumed the pose characteristic of her whenever there was trouble, her eyes lowered, her thick shoulders sloping down, and the burdened look adding years to her face. It was a look that went back

23

decades, dating from her endless difficulties with her husband before their breakup, her mother's long demanding illness and death, and her disappointment in her only son who had suddenly, after years of being a straight A student, dropped out of the predominantly white college he had been attending. With each crisis her weight had increased, the fat metastasizing with each new sorrow. Now, under the robe she had finally managed to pull around her, her flesh with the pierced heart at its center had opened to absorb this latest tragedy. For wasn't she, Clarice, somehow responsible for what was happening? Wasn't she in some way to blame? Her dullness, her rampant flesh, her blackness . . .

"Gonna forfeit the fifteen hundred dollars she paid for the cruise and then turn around and spend more money to take a plane home! Now what kinda sense do that make, will you tell me? She must be out of her mind . . . Wait, that's it! She's done gone and lost her mind . . . !"

The lined face, the color of old ivory, came thrusting forward as the woman tried surprising the insanity under the turned-down hat brim. She was met instead by the underlip Avey Johnson had left thrusting forward slightly so that the knife edge of raw pink was still visible, and by the expression in her eyes of someone who had already left the cabin and the ship and was well on her way somewhere else.

"Gots to be," she muttered, drawing back, "out of her cotton-pickin' mind."

The taxi driver had been right. The plane was far from full. She had the three seats in her row all to herself. They had already reached cruising altitude, so that the only thing visible when she looked down was the hazy undifferentiated blue of the sea far below. And with the flight under way everything had come right again. She no longer caught herself giving the little fearful involun-

24

*tary glance back over her shoulder, and the odd unpleasant sensa-
tion in her stomach that had plagued her off and on for the past two
days was gone. Down the aisle the stewardess was taking orders for
drinks before lunch. She would have a glass of white wine to
celebrate.*

"'. . . If I'm lucky I might get a flight out today.'" The
words, spoken in the low-pitched shout, were a scathing par-
ody of Avey Johnson's. "Just listen to her! Who told her she's
gonna find a plane going to New York today? Who's guaranteed her a flight right away? Why, some of these little islands
don't see a plane going anywhere but maybe two, three times a
week. She might be stuck for days. And in some place that
probably won't have a decent hotel to its name. She'll wind
up having to stay in some dump where the mosquitoes'll eat
her alive and the food—or what passes for food—won't be fit
for hogs.

"And forget about drinking the water! Remember that
place we stopped at last year?"—she half swung toward Clarice again with the same violent movement that jarred the
light—"Cartarena or Cartarana or whatever they called
it . . ." (It had been Cartagena, Colombia, where, to Avey
Johnson's disgust, the woman had abandoned them to dance
in a carnival parade they were watching with other passengers
from the *Bianca Pride*. Had gone off amid a throng of strangers
swishing her bony hips to the drums. With the slight hump
like an organ grinder's monkey begging pennies from her
shoulders. And with their fellow passengers watching. White
faces laughing! White hands applauding! Avey Johnson had
never been so mortified. And she had returned, the woman,
laughing proudly, with the jumpsuit she had on soaked
through under the arms, and in her laugh, in her flushed face,
something of the high-stepping, high-kicking young chorus

25

girl she had once been. "Girl, those drums *got* to me! Where's some water?")

". . . Remember the water they gave me to drink there? You could see the bugs swimming around in it clear as day. Well, just let this one here go running around eating and drinking on her own. She's gonna come back with her stomach all *tore* up!" (With her colors up she said "tow.") "A girlfriend of mine went to Mexico for a week and was laid up in the hospital for two months straight when she got back just from drinking a glass of water down there . . ."

The drive from Kennedy to their small section of North White Plains was over. The airport limousine had deposited her at the door and departed. Before leaving, the driver had helped her take the suitcases into the front hall. She could glimpse them through the archway to the dining room where she had gone to sit for a moment in the welcoming dark, at the great oval-shaped table. Where the light from the hall fell across the table's polished surface, the cherry wood glowed like a banked fire that had awaited her return. Over on the buffet the coffee service on its chased and footed tray was a study in silver and black in the semidarkness. Everything was as she had left it: her special crystal in the china closet, her silver-plate—all eighty pieces—in its felt-lined case. It was her favorite room, the dining room. She was right not to go back on her promise to Jerome Johnson and sell the house as Marion kept nagging her to do. (According to Marion, the house had served its purpose.) Later, she would make herself a cup of tea and drink it here at the table in the half-light.

". . . Packing her things in the middle of the night like some thief . . . no reason . . . no explanation . . . good money gone . . . gots to be crazy . . . no plane for days . . . gonna run into all kinds of trouble . . ."

Caught in the riptide of her anger, Thomasina Moore was powerless to stop herself.

". . . Here the three of us suppose to be traveling together and she just ups and leaves, ruining the rest of the trip for the two of us. And after all the time I spent seeing to it everything would be just right!" (Which was true. The woman devoted the better part of the year to planning for the cruise—which each year took them to a different set of islands. She had the time, not having worked since her show business days. Her dead husband, a dentist, who had been taken with her color, had indulged her shamelessly, treating her as if she were all the children they had never had.)

". . . No decent person'd do a thing like this. Why she's no better come to think of it than some bum on a Hundred Twenty-fifth Street, never mind the airs she gives herself. But she never had me fooled. Oh, no, this is one boot she couldn't play for a fool. I could tell her airs were nothing but a front. Always knew she had it in her to pull somethin' mean and low-down like this. Knew it!

"That's why," she cried, her suppressed fury at a new high, her breath sucked deep into the bony wells at her throat, her eyes convulsed. "That's why if I've said it once I've said it a thousand times: it . . . don't . . . pay . . . to . . . go . . . no . . . place . . . with . . . *niggers!* They'll mess up ever' time!"

Unhurriedly, Avey Johnson bent and picked up first her gloves and then her pocketbook from the chair beside her. To her surprise she found she was smiling. A little faint, pleased, self-congratulatory smile, as if, instead of the insult, the woman had said something complimentary. It didn't make sense. Yet there the smile was, its warmth stealing across her face, its gentle pull easing the strain from the held-in lip that had become a permanent part of her expression over the years. To hide the smile she was forced to remain bent over the chair longer than necessary.

Then, with the pocketbook on her arm and her gloves in hand, she was stepping around the still raging figure in the center of the room: ". . . somethin' deep's behind this mess. You can't tell me different . . ." She gave her a wide berth, the way she might have some mildly demented bag woman railing to herself on the city's streets.

Her unhurried step led her across to Clarice at the divider. She had intended apologizing privately to her friend. Had meant to say, her voice low, her back to Thomasina Moore, that it was wrong of her to leave in this manner, but that she hoped Clarice would not hold it against her. It was just that something—she couldn't say what—had come over her the past couple of days. She couldn't explain it. She could make no sense of it. Anyway, they would see each other back at work once their vacations were over and everything would be as usual. (They both worked for the State Motor Vehicle Department, Avey Johnson as a supervisor and Clarice as a Grade Five clerk.) Their first day back they would splurge and have lunch at the seafood restaurant near the office.

She had it in mind to say something on this order crossing the room, to assure Clarice that she was in no way to blame. But the moment she drew up in front of her friend and saw close-up the familiar burdened slope to her shoulders and the expression of mute acceptance on her face, her tongue balked. For the first time in the twenty years they had known each other, something about Clarice both frightened and offended her. She found herself wanting to back away from her as from something contagious; or to make a sign (if she had known one) to ward off some dangerous hex. At the same time her hand ached to reach out and lift that bowed head, force it up. She wanted to shout at Clarice the way her father used to at her long ago whenever he caught her slouching, "Pull your back up, girl!"

Instead all she said, quickly moving away, was, "I'm going to arrange with the purser about my leaving. I'll be back with a steward for my things."

In seconds she made her way around the suitcases to the door, and was opening and hurriedly closing it on the voice which continued choleric and unflagging from the middle of the floor.

". . . no reason . . . no explanation . . . trying to play people for fools . . . !"

3

Could she have dared mention as one possible reason the parfait they had had for dessert two nights ago? Or the dream she had had the night before that? Avey Johnson considered this as she hurried down the long passageway from their cabin to the bank of elevators that would take her to the purser's office midship. A few early risers passed her on their way to breakfast or a jog around the promenade deck, but with her mind given over to the thought she scarcely noticed them.

No, any mention of the parfait or the dream would only have made matters worse. They sounded too illogical and absurd. Thomasina Moore would have been quick to use them as proof positive that she had indeed lost her mind. *"Walking out on a seventeen-day cruise after only a week because of dessert! Forfeiting fifteen hundred dollars because of a dream! Now I KNOW she's out of her cotton-picking . . ."* She could just hear her.

Yet, ridiculous as it sounded, the two things were linked, she sensed, in some obscure but profound way, with her decision to leave.

There had been the dream three nights ago, to begin with. As a rule she seldom dreamed. Or if she did, whatever occurred in her sleep was always conveniently forgotten by the time she awoke. It had been like this ever since the mid-sixties. Before then, she had found herself taking all the nightmare images from the evening news into her sleep with her. The electric cattle prods and lunging dogs. The high pressure hoses that were like a dam bursting. The lighted cigarettes being ground out on the arms of those sitting in at the lunch counters. Her dreams were a rerun of it all. The bomb that exploded in the Sunday School quiet of Birmingham in '63 went off a second time in her sleep several nights later. And searching frantically amid the debris of small limbs strewn around the church basement she had come across those of Sis, Annawilda and Marion. And it was the Sunday in the dream when Sis was to have recited "The Creation" in the annual program. She had learned all twelve stanzas by heart: ". . . *And God said I'm lonely still . . . I'll make me a man . . . !*"

Avey Johnson had ceased dreaming after that.

And then three nights ago the old habit returned. Tired after a long day spent ashore on Martinique, during which she and her companions had traveled overland for hours to visit the volcano, Mount Pelée, she had gone to bed early that evening, only to find herself confronted the moment she dropped off to sleep by her great-aunt Cuney.

The old woman, who had really been her father's great-aunt, was someone Avey Johnson couldn't remember ever having dreamed of before. She had scarcely thought of her in

31

years. Yet there she had been in her sleep, standing waiting for her on the road that led over to the Landing. A hand raised, her face hidden beneath her wide-brimmed field hat, she was motioning for her to come on the walk that had been a ritual with them during the Augusts she had spent as a girl on Tatem Island, just across from Beaufort, on the South Carolina Tidewater.

At least twice a week, in the late afternoon, as the juniper trees around Tatem began sending out their cool elongated shadows, her great-aunt (who resembled the trees in her straight, large-boned mass and height) would take the field hat down from its nail on the door and solemnly place it over her headtie and braids. With equal ceremony she would then draw around her the two belts she and the other women her age in Tatem always put on when going out: one belt at the waist of their plain, long-skirted dresses, and the other (this one worn in the belief that it gave them extra strength) strapped low around their hips like the belt for a sword or a gun holster.

"Avatara."

There was never any need to call her, because Avey, keeping out of sight behind the old woman, would have already followed suit, girding her nonexistent hips with a second belt (an imaginary one) and placing—with the same studied cere-mony—a smaller version of the field hat (which was real) on her head. To protect her legs from the scrub grass and brush along the way she was made to wear wool stockings despite the heat and her high-topped school shoes from last winter, which her mother always sent along for her to finish out the summer in.

Thus attired, they would set out, her great-aunt forging

ahead in her dead husband's old brogans, which on her feet turned into seven-league boots, while Avey, to keep up, often had to play a silent game of Take a Giant Step with herself: *"Avey Williams, you may take two giant steps." "May I?" "Yes, you may."*

The first leg of their walk took them along the road which bordered the large wood belonging to their neighbor, Shad Dawson. The wood, dark even on the sunniest day because of the Spanish moss hanging in great silver-gray skeins from the oaks, was a place filled with every kind of ha'nt there was, according to the children she played with in Tatem.

Once past the wood which Shad Dawson was to lose eventually to the white man in Beaufort whom he had entrusted to pay his taxes for him, came the one church in Tatem, set in a bare yard, a decrepit listing clapboard structure that also served as the school. A cross and an open book painted on the front window marked its dual purpose. In its lopsided stance the church looked as if it had never recovered from the blow dealt its authority one evening long ago when Avey's great-aunt had raged out of its door never to return.

The old woman (she had been young then) had been caught "crossing her feet" in a Ring Shout being held there and had been ordered out of the circle. But she had refused to leave, denying at first that she had been dancing, then claiming it had been the Spirit moving powerfully in her which had caused her to forget and cross her feet. She had even tried brazening it out: "Hadn't David danced before the Lord?" Finally, just as she was about to be ejected bodily, she had stormed out of the circle and the church on her own. The ban had been only for the one night, but outraged, insisting still on her innocence, she began staying away from the Ring

Shouts altogether. After a time she even stopped attending regular church service as well.

People in Tatem said she had made the Landing her religion after that.

Some nights, though, when they held the Shouts she would go to stand, unreconciled but nostalgic, on the darkened road across from the church, taking Avey with her if it was August. Through the open door the handful of elderly men and women still left, and who still held to the old ways, could be seen slowly circling the room in a loose ring.

They were propelling themselves forward at a curious gliding shuffle which did not permit the soles of the heavy work shoes they had on to ever once lift from the floor. Only their heels rose and then fell with each step, striking the worn pineboard with a beat that was as precise and intricate as a drum's, and which as the night wore on and the Shout became more animated could be heard all over Tatem.

They sang: *"Who's that riding the chariot?/Well well well . . ."*; used their hands as racing tambourines, slapped their knees and thighs and chest in dazzling syncopated rhythm. They worked their shoulders; even succeeded at times in giving a mean roll of their aged hips. They allowed their failing bodies every liberty, yet their feet never once left the floor or, worse, crossed each other in a dance step.

Arms shot up, hands arched back like wings: *"Got your life in my hands/Well well well . . ."* Singing in quavering atonal voices as they glided and stamped one behind the other within the larger circle of their shadows cast by the lamplight on the walls. Even when the Spirit took hold and their souls and writhing bodies seemed about to soar off into the night, their feet remained planted firm. *I shall not be moved.*

It wasn't supposed to be dancing, yet to Avey, standing

beside the old woman, it held something of the look, and it felt like dancing in her blood, so that under cover of the darkness she performed in place the little rhythmic trudge. She joined in the singing under her breath: *"Got your life in my hands/Well well well . . ."*

With the church behind them on the walk, they came to the last few houses in the small settlement. There was the drab-gray, unpainted bungalow of "Doctor" Benitha Grant, which she had enlivened with a crepe myrtle bush—all red blossoms—at the door and a front yard bright and overflowing with samples of the herbs she used to treat the sick and ailing. During Avey's first summer in Tatem she had instantly stopped the pain and swelling of an insect bite on her arm with fennel picked fresh from the yard.

Next along the road stood the frame dwelling belonging to Pharo Harris and his wife, Miss Celia. There not a single flower or herb or blade of grass was to be seen out front. Instead he and his wife had piled their dusty yard and the porch to the house with all the rusted washtubs, scrubboards and iron kettles from the years she had taken in washing and all the broken plows, pitchforks, hoes and the like from his sharecropping days. Pharo Harris had even dragged out the worn traces and reins from his mules who had died and flung them on the heap. All of it left there for anyone passing to see, while they—old and bent now—kept busy in their vegetable garden out back. A Tidewater gothic amid the turnip greens and squash.

The two walking seldom saw the Harrises, but their neighbor, Mr. Golla Mack, whose greater age made them seem almost young, was always visible. The moment they rounded a bend in the road they would spot him, a short, thick-set old man with unseeing eyes the milky blue of a play marble, seated in monumental stillness on his tumbledown porch. Propped against his chair was one of the walking sticks he had been known for making before going blind, a snake carved up its length.

In his stillness there on the porch, in the shadow cast by the overhang, Mr. Golla Mack scarcely seemed a living breathing man, ordinary flesh and blood, but a life-size likeness of himself fashioned out of some substance that was immune to time, the August heat and flies and the white folks in Beaufort.

"Miz Cuney, is that that little ol' sassy gal from New York I sees with you?"

Mr. Golla Mack! They stopped to pay their respects on the way both to and from the Landing.

His was the last house. Beyond it all semblance of a road vanished, the trees and plant cover disappeared and the countryside opened into a vast denuded tract of land that had once, more than a century ago, been the largest plantation of sea island cotton thereabouts. *"War is cruelty and you cannot refine it"*: General William Tecumseh Sherman on his march of blood and fire up from Atlanta. The huge field had fallen victim to the pillaging and had never been replanted.

It took Avey and her great-aunt—the old woman never slackening her pace—over a half-hour of steady walking out under the sun just to cover one section of it. Almost the same amount of time was then spent picking their way down a rocky incline of high thistle grass and scrub that led to another ruined field at the bottom, this one a soggy, low-lying rice field that had been more recently abandoned.

Here her great-aunt always put to practical use the second belt girding her hips. Stopping briefly she would draw the top of her skirt up over it until the cloth lay in a fold around her and her hem stood clear of the sodden ground. The next moment she was striking out across the rice field toward a small pine forest at its edge.

The forest marked the final leg of their journey. Moving over the footpath the old woman knew by heart they were treated to the cool resinous smell of the pines, the soft, springy padding the needles formed underfoot, and the salt drift from the nearby marshes. And soon, coming to meet them like an eager host through the trees, there could be heard the bright sound of the river that was their destination. And over it, farther off, the distant yet powerful voice of the sea.

It was only a matter of minutes then before they were standing, the forest behind them and the river at their feet, on the long narrow spit of land, shaped like one of Mr. Golla Mack's walking sticks, which marked the point where the waters in and around Tatem met up with the open sea. On the maps of the county it was known as Ibo Landing. To people in Tatem it was simply the Landing.

"It was here that they brought 'em. They taken 'em out of the boats right here where we's standing. Nobody remembers how many of 'em it was, but they was a good few 'cording to my gran' who was a little girl no bigger than you when it happened. The small boats was drawed up here and the ship they had just come from was out in the deep water. Great big ol' ship with sails. And the minute those Ibos was brought on shore they just stopped, my gran' said, and taken a look around. A good long look. Not saying a word. Just studying the place real good. Just taking their time and studying on it.

And they seen things that day you and me don't have the power to see. 'Cause those pure-born Africans was peoples my gran' said could see in more ways than one. The kind can tell you 'bout things happened long before they was born and

37

things to come long after they's dead. Well, they seen everything that was to happen 'round here that day. The slavery
time and the war my gran' always talked about, the 'mancipa-
tion and everything after that right on up to the hard times
today. Those Ibos didn't miss a thing. Even seen you and me
standing here talking about 'em. And when they got through
sizing up the place real good and seen what was to come, they
turned, my gran' said, and looked at the white folks what
brought 'em here. Took their time again and gived them the
same long hard look. Tell you the truth, I don't know how
those white folks stood it. I know I wouldn't have wanted 'em
looking at me that way. And when they got through studying
'em, when they *knew* just from looking at 'em how those folks
was gonna do, do you know what the Ibos did? Do you . . . ?"

"I do." (It wasn't meant for her to answer but she always did
anyway.) "Want me to finish telling about 'em? I know the
story good as you." (Which was true. Back home after only
her first summer in Tatem she had recounted the whole thing
almost word for word to her three brothers, complete with the
old woman's inflections and gestures.)

". . . They just turned, my gran' said, all of 'em—" she
would have ignored the interruption as usual; wouldn't even
have heard it over the voice that possessed her—"and walked
on back down to the edge of the river here. Every las' man,
woman and chile. And they wasn't taking they time no more.
They had seen what they had seen and those Ibos was stepping! And they didn't bother getting back into the small boats
drawed up here—boats take too much time. They just kept
walking right on out over the river. Now you wouldna
thought they'd of got very far seeing as it was water they was
walking on. Besides they had all that iron on 'em. Iron on
they ankles and they wrists and fastened 'round they necks

38

like a dog collar. 'Nuff iron to sink an army. And chains hooking up the iron. But chains didn't stop those Ibos none. Neither iron. The way my gran' tol' it (other folks in Tatem said it wasn't so and that she was crazy but she never paid 'em no mind) 'cording to her they just kept on walking like the water was solid ground. Left the white folks standin' back here with they mouth hung open and they taken off down the river on foot. Stepping. And when they got to where the ship was they didn't so much as give it a look. Just walked on past it. Didn't want nothing to do with that ol' ship. They feets was gonna take 'em wherever they was going that day. And they was singing by then, so my gran' said. When they realized there wasn't nothing between them and home but some water and that wasn't giving 'em no trouble they got so tickled they started in to singing. You could hear 'em clear across Tatem 'cording to her. They sounded like they was having such a good time my gran' declared she just picked herself up and took off after 'em. In her mind. Her body she always usta say might be in Tatem but her mind, her mind was long gone with the Ibos . . ."

She always paused here, giving the impression she was done. A moment later though would come a final coda, spoken with an amazed reverential laugh: "Those Ibos! Just upped and walked on away not two minutes after getting here!"

"But how come they didn't drown, Aunt Cuney?"

She had been ten—that old!—and had been hearing the story for four summers straight before she had thought to ask.

Slowly, standing on the consecrated ground, her height almost matching her shadow which the afternoon sun had drawn out over the water at their feet, her great-aunt had turned and regarded her in silence for the longest time. It was to take Avey years to forget the look on the face under the field hat, the disappointment and sadness there. If she could have reached up that day and snatched her question like a fly out of the air and swallowed it whole, she would have done so. And long after she had stopped going to Tatem and the old woman was dead, she was to catch herself flinching whenever she remembered the voice with the quietly dangerous note that had issued finally from under the wide hat brim.

"Did it say Jesus drowned when he went walking on the water in that Sunday School book your momma always sends with you?"

"No, ma'am."

"I din' think so. You got any more questions?"

She had shaken her head "no."

And then three nights ago, in the dream, there the old woman had been after all those years, drawn up waiting for her on the road beside Shad Dawson's wood of cedar and oak. Standing there unmarked by the grave in the field hat and the dress with the double belts, beckoning to her with a hand that should have been fleshless bone by now: clappers to be played at a Juba.

Did she really expect her to go walking over to the Landing dressed as she was? In the new spring suit she had just put on to wear to the annual luncheon at the Statler given by Jerome Johnson's lodge? (He was outside the house this minute waiting for her in the car.) With her hat and gloves on? And her fur stole draped over her arm? Avey Johnson could have laughed, the idea was so ridiculous. That obstacle course of scrub, rock and rough grass leading down from the cotton field would make quick work of her stockings, and the open-toed patent-leather pumps she was wearing for the first time would never survive that mud flat which had once been a rice field.

Glancing down, she saw they were already filmed with dust just from her standing there. Her amusement began to give way to irritation.

From a distance of perhaps thirty feet, the old woman continued to wave her forward, her gesture exhibiting a patience and restraint that was unlike her. And she was strangely silent, standing there framed by the moss-hung wood; her voice, unlike her body, had apparently not been able to outfox the grave.

She kept up the patient summons; and from where she stood on the unpaved country road, Avey Johnson ignored it, growing more annoyed each time the hand beckoned. If she could have brought herself to it, she would have turned and walked away and left her standing there waving at the empty air. But such disrespect was beyond her. She would stand her ground then! Refuse to take even a single step forward! To ensure this, she dug her shoe heels into the dirt and loose stones at her feet. A battle, she sensed, had been joined.

They remained like this for the longest time, until finally, the old woman, glancing anxiously at the declining sun, abruptly changed her tactics. Her hand dropped and, reaching out with her arms, she began coaxing her forward, gently urging her, the way a mother would a one-year-old who hangs back from walking on its own.

It was behavior so opposed to the Aunt Cuney she had known, Avey Johnson stood there mystified, and then was all the more annoyed. She swung away her face, telling herself, hoping, that when she looked back, she would find that the old woman had given up and gone on the walk alone; or better yet had returned to her grave in Tatem's colored cemetery.

But not only was the tall figure still there when she looked around again, the coaxing had become more impassioned.

Her body straining forward as though to bridge the distance between them, she was pleading with her now to join her, silently exhorting her, transformed into a preacher in a Holiness church imploring the sinners and backsliders to come forward to the mercy seat. *"Come/O will you come . . . ?"* The trees in Shad Dawson's wood gave voice to the old invitational hymn, speaking for her. *"Come/Won't you come . . . ?"*

What was wrong with her? Couldn't she see she was no longer the child in scratchy wool stockings and ugly high-top shoes scrambling along at her side over the wrecked fields? No longer the Avey (or Avatara as she insisted on calling her) she had laid claim to for a month each summer from the time she was seven. Before she was seven! Before she had been born even! There was the story of how she had sent word months before her birth that it would be a girl and she was to be called after her grandmother who had come to her in a dream with the news: "It's my gran' done sent her. She's her little girl."

Great-aunt Cuney had saddled her with the name of someone people had sworn was crazy, and then as soon as she turned seven had ordered her father to bring and deposit her every August in Tatem, which he had done over her mother's unceasing objections: "My child comes back here looking like Tar Baby from tearing around in the sun all day behind that old woman!" And there year after year had filled her head with some far-fetched story of people walking on water which she in her childish faith had believed till the age of ten.

Moreover, in instilling the story of the Ibos in her child's mind, the old woman had entrusted her with a mission she couldn't even name yet had felt duty-bound to fulfill. It had taken her years to rid herself of the notion.

Suddenly Avey Johnson drew herself up to her full height, which equaled that of the tall figure up the road. The whole ridiculous business had gone on long enough. She was leaving. Let the old woman think what she will! Reaching over, she straightened the fur stole on her left arm, took a deep defiant breath, and was about to turn and walk away when a sudden eruption of movement up ahead caused her to stop, confused, in her tracks. Before she could take in what was happening or think to complete the turn and run, she saw her great-aunt charging toward her over the thirty feet between them like one of those August storms she remembered would whirl up without warning out of the marshes around Tatem to rampage over the land. In seconds a hand with the feel of a manacle had closed around her wrist, and she found herself being dragged forward in the direction of the Landing.

How could her flesh still be so warm and her smell the same homey mix of brown washing soap and the asafetida she wore in a sac pinned to her undershirt to ward off sickness? How could she still be so strong?

To have been treated before like a year-old baby who needed to be coaxed and now as if she were a balky mule to be hauled off somewhere against its will! The indignation which filled her lent her a strength equal to the older woman's, so that quickly digging in with her shoe heels again, bracing herself, she brought their headlong movement to a halt. The older woman immediately tried pulling her forward again. Grimly Avey Johnson resisted, and a locked, silent tug-of-war began between them, which saw them evenly matched and equally determined, and neither of them giving ground. The struggle went on for what seemed hours, and only once in all that time did Avey Johnson feel herself weaken, and then only briefly. It was when her great-aunt, who had kept her back turned all along, suddenly swung around, and she saw for the first time the face under the wide-brimmed hat.

The fury she saw there—fury at being defied—had so distorted the features, it was scarcely the face she remembered from her childhood. Oddly enough though, the eyes held none of her rage. They were filled instead (and this was what caused her to feel the sudden weakness) with the same disappointment and sadness that had greeted the thoughtless question she had asked as the ten-year-old long ago. In them was reflected also the mute plea: *"Come/Won't you come."*

In answer, she gave the arm the old woman was holding an abrupt, violent tug, hoping to catch her off guard and break her grip. But as if her great-aunt had expected the move, the hand around her wrist tightened its hold.

All her wrenching movement succeeded in doing was to dislodge the stole draped over that arm. Up it flew in a burst of pale mink, and for a second appeared to hover in the air at the exact level of their gaze before falling with a sound like an expiring breath to the ground.

For a moment, her mind blank and unaccepting, Avey Johnson simply stared down at it lying there, like some furry creature from the nearby wood that had been wantonly slain and flung in the dirt at their feet. The next moment, her outraged cry broke the silence, and she was raising her free hand, the fist tightly clenched, and bringing it down with all her force on the old woman. Wildly she rained the blows on her face, her neck, her shoulders and her great fallen breasts—striking flesh that had been too awesome for her to even touch as a child.

Her great-aunt did not hesitate to hit her back, and with the same if not greater force. While firmly holding her wrist with one hand, she began trading Avey Johnson blow for blow with the other. Moreover, as if the fallen stole had also triggered a kind of madness in her, she began tearing at the spring suit, the silk blouse, the gloves. The tug-of-war was suddenly a bruising fist fight, which Avey Johnson saw to her horror, glancing around, had brought her neighbors in North White Plains out on their lawns. There they were, a long row of neat dark family clusters, each in its square of green.

Worse, among the black faces looking on scandalized, there could be seen the Archers with their blue-eyed, tow-headed children, and the Weinsteins. The only ones for blocks around who had not sold and fled. An uncharitable thought surfaced amid the shame flooding her. Could it be they had stayed on in the hope of one day being treated to a spectacle such as this: *at any moment the beast may spring, filling the air with flying things and an unenlightened wailing . . .* It was something Marion was always quoting.

The fight raged on. Brawling like fishwives! Like proverbial niggers on a Saturday night! With the fur stole like her hard-won life of the past thirty years being trampled into the dirt underfoot. And the clothes being torn from her body. The wood of cedar and oak rang with her inflamed cry. And the sound went on endlessly, ranging over Tatem and up and down her quiet streets at home. Until suddenly, jarring her, her cry was punctuated by the impatient blast of a car horn.

The luncheon! The Statler! And this year they had been scheduled to sit on the dais, Jerome Johnson having been made a Master Mason. The thought of the ruined day brought her anger surging up anew, and ignoring the look of anguished love and disappointment in the old woman's gaze, spurning her voiceless plea, she began hammering away at her with renewed fury there on the road to the Landing, with the whole of North White Plains looking on.

4

There was the strange, unsettling dream one night, and the next day, before she had a chance to recover, the equally disturbing business of the parfait they had had for dessert at the evening meal.

She had gone to dinner as usual with her two companions in the Versailles Room where they had their table. Of the three dining rooms on board, the Versailles with its Louis XIV decor and wealth of silver and crystal on the damask-covered tables was the most formal. Passengers who ate there were required to dress accordingly—the men in dinner jackets, the women in gowns—for the evening meal.

One look their first cruise at the chandeliers, wall sconces and gilt-framed mirrors filling the room, and the tapestries depicting life at court during the period, and Thomasina Moore had immediately signed them up for a table there. "This is one boot don't believe in letting these white folks keep the best to themselves."

46

"Versailles . . ." Marion had echoed despairingly when Avey Johnson had made mention once of the name. *"Do you know how many treaties were signed there, in that infamous Hall of Mirrors, divvying up India, the West Indies, the world? Versailles"—repeating it with a hopeless shake of her head.*

That evening as the main course dishes were being cleared away, Avey Johnson let her gaze drift out across the huge room. She was still vaguely troubled by the dream. It was the strangest thing but that morning her body had felt as sore when she awoke as if she had actually been fighting; and all during the day, in the dim rear of her mind, she had sensed her great-aunt still struggling to haul her off up the road. Even now her left wrist retained something of the pressure of the old woman's iron grip.

Absently her eyes wandered over the fifty-odd tables, each, it appeared, with its own glittering chandelier overhead and its group of five to six diners. They were like islands, it suddenly occurred to her, and she felt oddly chilled; each table an island separated from the others on the sea of Persian carpeting that covered the room.

She idly scanned her fellow diners. As usual, even those who sat directly facing her at the nearby tables somehow gave the impression of having their backs turned to her and her companions. It had to do with the expression in their eyes, which seemed to pass cleanly through them whenever they glanced across, and even, ironically, with the quick strained smiles some of them occasionally flashed their way.

It was the kind of thing Avey Johnson had trained herself not to notice, or if she did, not to feel anything one way or the other about it. There were some things in this life, she once tried explaining to Marion, she simply refused to let bother her.

Beyond the tables and the heads of the diners, in an alcove at one end of the room, the dinner orchestra was playing a subdued version of "Begin the Beguine," and for a time she half-listened, although for some reason tonight she found the music tepid, insipid even. Finally her wandering, abstracted gaze was caught and held by a reflection in one of the huge gilt-framed mirrors which had all been hung so that they leaned forward slightly over the room; a distant reflection of three carefully groomed, older women sitting at a table to themselves.

There, in a pair of long, Pucci-print evening culottes, was Thomasina Moore, her face under a hairstyle that rivaled any to be seen in the room, blending easily with the hundreds of other faces at the tables. Opposite her Clarice was wearing the rose-colored gown she favored with beadwork at the collar and a wide A-line skirt. She easily recognized them both in the distant mirror. But for a long confused moment Avey Johnson could not place the woman in beige crepe de Chine and pearls seated with them.

This wasn't the first time it had happened. On occasion, shopping in her favorite department store she would notice a black woman of above average height with a full-figured yet compact body coming toward her amid the floor-length mirrors down the aisle. And in the way she always did she would quickly note the stranger's clothes. The well-cut suit, coat or ensemble depending on the season. The carefully coordinated accessories. The muted colors. Everything in good taste and appropriate to her age.

Another glance, swifter than the first: she did not want to be caught staring, took in the composed face with its folded-in lip and carefully barred gaze. She was clearly someone who kept her thoughts and feelings to herself.

But more than the woman's clothes or figure or face was her bearing as she made her way along the aisle. Her Marian Anderson poise and reserve. The look of acceptability about her. She would never be sent to eat in the kitchen when company came!—*I am the darker brother/They send me to eat in the kitchen/When company comes . . .*—lines from the poem Jay used to recite to her and Sis on Sunday mornings in Halsey Street would come to mind.

All this she would record in a swift glance or two before realizing who it actually was reflected in the mirror up ahead.

Other times the same stylishly dressed matron surprised her from the dingy windows of the train to and from work. She confronted her in the plate glass exteriors of stores and restaurants and the simonized bodies of cars parked along the curb as she walked past. One morning she even accosted Avey Johnson in her bathroom mirror as she raised up from washing her face.

When she mentioned it once to her doctor he had laughed; a sure sign, he had said, of money in the bank.

The parfait, a long-handled spoon beside it, was sitting waiting for her on the table as she turned away, frowning slightly, from the reflection in the mirror. *Peach Parfait à la Versailles* was the name given it on the menu. And it had been done to perfection in keeping with its name, with layers of sliced and sweetened peaches alternating with syrup, whipped cream and peach sherbet up the length of the tall fluted glass. A large dollop of cream shaped like a spiraling dome covered with chocolate sprinkles provided the finishing touch.

Her frown vanishing, she picked up the spoon. She had eaten sparingly earlier in the meal in order to treat herself to at least part of the dessert tonight, a few sinful spoonfuls.

Eagerly she started to nudge aside the cream topping to get at the first layer of peaches, only to have her hand, as if stricken with a sudden paralysis, come to a stop.

At the same moment she became aware of the heightened sound in the room. With the appearance of the parfait, the usually muted talk and laughter had risen sharply, spurred by the comments and exclamations over the dessert and the clinking of the hundreds of spoons against the glasses.

Puzzled, she sat for what felt to be a long while, listening to the noise around her and gazing at her immobilized hand holding the spoon. Her slight frown had returned. Until finally, without her having anything to do with it, her hand suddenly came alive again with a jerk, and she found herself firmly placing the spoon back down on the table. Her heart was beating thickly. Her stomach, her entire midsection felt odd.

"What's wrong, Avey? Don't you like it?" Clarice. She had already finished her parfait, scooping it down in the swift, almost furtive way she ate everything, and her eyes had been drawn helplessly to the untouched glass across the table.

"Not like it! How could anybody in their right mind not like it?" An abstracted Thomasina Moore had been slowly savoring each spoonful while humming under her breath to the music. But now the gray eyes with their unblinking intensity came sharply to focus. "This thing's delicious. The desserts this year are better than ever."

She waited, daring them to dispute this, ready to take offense. As the one who made the decisions as to where they ate, slept and how they spent the time on board, she took it as a veiled criticism of her planning whenever they voiced even the slightest complaint.

"What is it, Avey?" Clarice had grown anxious.

"I don't know," she said and she was genuinely puzzled. "Seems I have a little indigestion, although I don't see how, I hardly ate anything. I should be all right in a minute. I'd better skip the dessert though, as tempting as it looks." She slid the fluted glass across to Clarice: "You're welcome to it."

But the peculiar sensation lingered, troubling her off and on until the long meal was finally over and they left the dining room. To her relief it disappeared during their customary after-dinner stroll around the promenade deck, and there was no sign of it at the nightly game of pinochle which followed. Later, though, at the eleven o'clock floorshow in the Sky High Room on top deck, it flared up again the moment the waiter appeared to take their order for drinks and placed the usual tray of complimentary canapés on the table.

At its mildest it felt to be nothing more than a little trapped gas. At its worst, it seemed as though she had foolishly gone ahead and not only eaten the parfait but all the things she had omitted earlier in the meal: the pâté de foie gras appetizer and the cream of mushroom soup, the brioche pastry around the Beef Wellington that had been the main course and its thick gravy, the delmonico potatoes and succotash that had accompanied the beef, and the small mountain of bread and rolls in their silver wicker basket. Even the shamefully rich petits fours she always refused which came with the coffee at the end.

She might have gorged herself on all that only to have her system break down under the overload, leaving the mass of undigested food stalled not only in her stomach but across the entire middle of her body. At its worst it felt like that. Oddly enough there was no nausea or pain, nothing to suggest seasickness or—the terrifying thought had instantly crossed her mind—the first signs of a heart attack. She felt perfectly all right otherwise. There was only the mysterious clogged and swollen feeling which differed in intensity and came and went at will.

The floor show over, they were on their way to the midnight buffet which was served in a dining room other than the Versailles, when there it was again, this time worse than ever: it felt like a huge tumor had suddenly ballooned up at her center. She found herself stopping abruptly and announcing in a voice whose anxiety she could only barely control that she was tired and was going to turn in early, and before her companions had a chance to question her, she was hurrying away.

Once in the cabin she took an antacid (it might only be indigestion after all) and went immediately to bed.

The following morning—which had been yesterday and her last full day aboard the *Bianca Pride*, although she hadn't known it then—the odd discomfort was still there.

True, for the first minute or so after she awoke it appeared to have gone away. She had felt nothing lying there on the couch in the early morning light. But the moment she began puzzling over the events of the evening before and her thoughts touched on the parfait, there it was again, the vaguely bloated feeling she could in no way account for.

Moreover, when she got out of bed some minutes later and stood somewhat unsteadily on her feet, her head aching all of a sudden, she thought she felt the liner rolling and pitching ever so slightly around her, as if it too had fallen victim to the same strange malaise.

Did they feel it, the slight turbulence, she had called through the room divider. It had only been 6:30 and Clarice had still been asleep, but Thomasina Moore, who rose early like herself, had promptly answered from the bedroom in a voice ready to take umbrage: "What you been drinking this morning? This ship's steady as a rock. Always is."

It was then she decided to spend the morning alone. She needed some time to herself, a respite not only from her companions and the usual morning round of breakfast, cards and browsing in the huge shopping arcade midship but from the other passengers as well. A few hours completely to herself in a deserted spot on one of the upper decks, with the soothing blue sky overhead and the salt breeze that could cure anything drifting up off the sea, and the peculiar sensation in her stomach would vanish. The sudden headache would go its way. The impression of the ship floundering around her would cease. She would come right again.

Before the two in the bedroom were up and about, she had showered and dressed—moving quickly despite her vague discomfort—and was on her way out the cabin. She didn't feel like breakfast and was going up on deck for a while. She'd see them at lunch, saying it over her shoulder as she was halfway out the door.

Yesterday, unhappily, was a day the *Bianca Pride* spent entirely at sea, on the long run between San Andres just off Nicaragua, which had been their last port of call, and the small island of Grenada in the eastern Caribbean, the next stop. So that with everyone on board for the day, everywhere she went over the course of the morning in search of a little privacy was taken. Some two, three or more of the ship's fifteen hundred passengers would have gotten there before her. This was true even for such solitary places as the fantail, which ordinarily remained deserted until late in the afternoon, and the ledge below the bridge, as well as the shaded area at the base of the funnel and certain cool unfrequented corners high on top deck—places she used as sanctuaries when she needed an hour or two to herself.

Or when she did find one of her favorite spots deserted, she wouldn't have it to herself for long. Some group just fresh from breakfast, or one of the many snacks served throughout the morning, would make its appearance only minutes after she had settled into a deck chair, drawn the light cardigan she had brought with her around her shoulders and closed her eyes. Their voices crashing into the dusky orange silence behind her lids. Their faces looming abnormally large and white for a second as her eyes opened.

Immediately her head would start to ache again, and there would be the mysterious welling up in her stomach. Moreover, each time she rose to leave, a tremor would sweep the deck under her feet for an instant as the liner gave the troubled heave and roll only she seemed to be aware of.

The whole thing might not have been so annoying, she might not have felt the need to flee each time had it been a lone passenger, someone in search of a little privacy like herself, who came and sat quietly apart, reading or napping; she wouldn't even have minded if it was someone like her neighbors in the Versailles Room whose backs appeared turned away even when they sat facing her.

But to her growing exasperation yesterday it was always a small mob who came barging in, bringing with them their voices and the lingering smell of food. "You don't mind if we park near you, do you?" "Hope we're not disturbing you." "Isn't this an ideal spot!" "The sky never gets this blue even in the summer in Iowa City." "Is this your first cruise?" "I should be taking a few laps around the deck instead of sitting, but what the hell"—a balding heavy-set man in plaid knee socks and matching shorts dropped into a deck chair a few feet away to the laughter and scolding of his friends. "Would you care to see today's paper?"—a woman nearly the size of Clarice in a halter top pressed the ship's newspaper on her. "I swore I wasn't going to eat breakfast this morning after last night's buffet and here I am stuffed again!" "You should see the lovely hand-carved tray I got for only two dollars yesterday . . ."

In the beginning, not wanting to appear impolite, she had forced herself to remain for a reasonable period after their arrival. But by midmorning, when she had been routed from at least half a dozen places, her frustration was such she no longer bothered trying to hide her annoyance. No sooner than some group came and encamped itself near her, she would gather up her sunglasses and purse from her lap—almost snatching them up in her irritation—and hurry away.

She knew it couldn't be, but after a time it seemed to be the same noisy band of four or five couples her age and older who kept descending on her wherever she went. She thought she recognized the outrageously youthful sports clothes they had on. The voices that shattered her brief peace, that seemed determined to draw her down into the hollowness of their talk, to make her part of it, began to have a familiar ring. They were the same voices she could have sworn she had sought to escape the last place she had been, as well as the place before that. Even their flushed and suntanned faces struck her as being suspiciously familiar.

To her further bewilderment, other bizarre things began happening as the morning wore on. At one point, in flight from a quiet section on the afterdeck which had just been taken over by what seemed the same group, she stopped on the observation platform above the sports deck to collect herself and to think of where next to go. The huge sports deck was crowded, and as she stood at the railing gazing down at the various games in progress below, something in her suddenly felt as exposed and vulnerable, as fated even, as the balls the golfers in their cleated shoes and gloves were slashing into the sea from their practice range at the port railing. A second later, as if her eyes were playing tricks on her, the numerous shuffleboard games she saw there seemed to turn for an instant into a spectacular brawl, with the players flailing away at each other with their cue sticks—just as in the hockey games she sometimes glimpsed on her television screen at home: the padded Neanderthal men clubbing each other with the murderous sticks while the crowd cheered. And in the quoit games being played just below where she stood the thud of the hempen rings being thrown to the deck reached her ears as the sound of some blunt instrument repeatedly striking human flesh and bone.

One night from their bedroom window above Halsey Street she and Jay had watched the pale meaty hand repeatedly bring the nightstick down on the man's shoulders and back, and on the head he sought to shield with his raised arms. The car he had been yanked from for what might have been a minor traffic violation stood pulled over at the curb, its door sprawling open. Under the rain of blows the man finally sank screaming to his knees, his blood a lurid red against his blackness in the light of the streetlamp overhead. Then he was being shoved into the back of the patrol car which quickly sped away. Unable either of them to go back to sleep afterwards, she and Jay had sat up the rest of the night till dawn, like two people holding a wake.

For a long minute she stood gripping the railing, trying to steady herself and clear her head. Where had that night surfaced from? How could she, after all these years, hear the thud and crack of the billy and the man's screams so clearly? Her ears, her memory seemed to be playing the same frightening tricks as her eyes. What had come over her all of a sudden?

But even as she stood there wondering at herself, her eye was caught by a sudden uprush of movement from the far end of the sports deck where the trapshooting was taking place. One of the clay pigeons had just been sprung from the trap, and the passenger whose turn it was to shoot, a frail-looking grandmother in shorts and tennis shoes, stood at the railing taking aim with the twelve-gauge, open-bore shotgun which looked too heavy for her. Behind her a long line of other passengers impatiently awaited their turn.

Her head raised, Avey Johnson followed the bird's stiff-winged trajectory into the bright midmorning sky. It appeared to be rushing in a straight desperate line toward the upper air, as far above the ship as possible. It struck her as being somehow alive despite the stiffness—as something human and alive—and she felt a sudden empathy with it. She almost heard herself call out a warning; and when the shot rang out a few seconds later, shattering it midair, she recoiled as violently as if the old woman with the gun had turned in the next instant and fired it at her; and then with the look of someone hallucinating she was rushing toward the companionway leading from the observation platform.

What was left of the morning she spent wandering the decks in a dazed, shaken state. She had abandoned the search for a quiet place to herself. She no longer wanted to sit or even to stand in any one spot for too long. Her eyes and ears might act up again, turning the ordinary and familiar into something surreal, and causing her to see the same faces everywhere she went.

She stayed on the upper decks, but confined herself to the

enclosed areas where the public rooms were located. Her restless steps took her past the lounges and crowded cardrooms,
the bars which were already filling up although it was not yet
noon, and the casino on the boat deck which opened at eight
in the morning on those days the ship remained at sea.

Rushing past the various rooms, Avey Johnson kept her
gaze fixed ahead, not knowing what she might discover if she
glanced inside. The same was true with the people she encountered in the corridors and on the companionways. She
avoided their faces. And they, seeing her troubled, disori-
ented look and the headlong walk that gave the impression
she was being pursued, stepped quickly out of her way.

Down on the quarter deck she caught herself heading toward the shopping arcade which took up most of the floor
there, and she stopped short. Her companions were certain to
be still there, browsing in the shops and boutiques before
going to lunch. Quickly she looked around for the nearest
door leading back outside.

She found herself the next minute out on the Lido with its
huge swimming pool and scores of elderly sunbathers. (*"Don't
you know that practically everyone who goes on these cruises is at
least a hundred years old! Moribund, Mother!"*) And as she
quickly made her way through the maze of deck chairs—
looking to neither her right nor left, again avoiding the
faces—she felt something grab her skirt, and looking down,
startled, she saw the shriveled old man with the toothy smile
who had stopped her. Wearing red-and-white striped trunks
that were as scant as a bikini and a cap with a blue plastic
visor, he was leaning forward on his deck chair holding the
hem of her skirt in one bony hand and motioning with the
other toward the empty chair beside him.

"Hey, where you going in such a big hurry? Have a seat.

Have a seat. Take the load off your feet. You look as if you need to sit someplace for a while. C'mon, I won't mind."

And before she could think to act, her eyes played another of their frightening tricks. In a swift, subliminal flash, all the man's wrinkled sunbaked skin fell away, his thinned-out flesh disappeared, and the only thing to be seen on the deck chair was a skeleton in a pair of skimpy red-and-white striped trunks and a blue visored cap.

The sharp cry—part horror, part outrage—that broke from her as she reached down and snatched her skirt from his grasp caused the elderly folk lying nearby to raise their heads in alarm. But before they could take in what had happened she was already halfway to the exit. All they saw was her swiftly retreating back and the cardigan she had draped over her shoulders flaring out behind her like a sail.

This time, moving at a near run, she did not stop until she came to Three Deck where the public rooms ended and the endless corridors of staterooms and cabins began. There, off by itself around a corner from the main passageway stood a glass-paneled double door. Through the glass could be seen a large quiet room of book-lined walls, comfortable winged-back armchairs and reading lamps. The library. Even on the days the *Bianca Pride* spent at sea it remained empty.

It was there she stayed until dinnertime, seated in one of the armchairs that faced away from the door. After some time when her breathing calmed and the shock and bewilderment of the morning eased from her face, she almost seemed herself again, except for her eyes, which retained the look of some-one in the grip of a powerful hallucinogen—something that had dramatically expanded her vision, offering her a glimpse of things that were beyond her comprehension, and therefore frightening. And every so often as she sat there, her head

59

would involuntarily wheel back over her shoulder, as if she expected to see bursting through the door the noisy band who had hounded her from place to place all morning or the crowd from the sports deck with their cue sticks, golf clubs and guns.

Had it been in the library yesterday that the idea of abandoning the cruise had first come to her? Had the thought without declaring itself quietly slipped in and taken root in a furrow of her mind during the long hours she remained in the armchair, her back to the door?

These and other perplexing questions Avey Johnson put to herself as she made her way to the purser's office midship.

5

By the time she met with the purser and went through the formalities of her leaving—after silencing the man's questions with the look that said she had already left and that the hat on her head and the gloves neatly folded in her hand confirmed—she was the only passenger taking the launch ashore, along with a few crew members. All those who had signed up to tour the island had already left.

Thomasina Moore and Clarice should have been with them. Yesterday, during her bizarre and frustrating morning on deck, they had attended the orientation lecture on the island and afterwards purchased their tickets for the tour, including one for her.

But when she returned with the steward to collect her bags after leaving the purser's office, it was clear that neither of them would be going ashore. Clarice, still stubbornly holding herself to blame for what had happened, had not moved from over near the divider. She had not even once raised her head in all the time she had been gone.

Thomasina Moore had abandoned her noisy platform at the center of the room. Avey Johnson opened the door to find her sitting in the armchair over by the window which had held her pocketbook and gloves earlier. The long harangue had taken its toll. She sat drawn and silent in the chair, her face drained of its little saving color and her slight frame with the budding hump across the shoulders looking overwhelmed by the frilly dressing gown.

The grayish eyes were unchanged. They held the same angry glint as before. Her "colors" were still up. But her anger was matched now by the look of helpless curiosity and even awe with which she fixed Avey Johnson during the short time she remained in the cabin.

How had she done it, the woman appeared to be asking herself. How had someone like her been able to simply pick herself up overnight and go, walk out? Where had she found the gumption to do something so unheard of? And what was behind it? *Somethin' deep's behind this mess. You can't tell me different.* Could it be she had misread her all these years and there was more to her than she suspected: a force, a fire beneath that reserved exterior that was not to be trifled with? Her wondering gaze focused on the underlip which was still slightly pursed to reveal the no-nonsense edging of pink she had never seen before.

At the end when Avey Johnson, before following the steward out the door with her bags, started toward her to say goodbye, she swung aside her face. But in the fraction of a second before she turned away, her eyes despite their unforgiving glare seemed to send out a mute appeal and her body strained forward imperceptibly, as though, if she could have brought herself to it she would have asked to be taken along.

On the launch planing swiftly over the late morning sea, Avey Johnson thought of the complex look the woman had bent on her, and was puzzled. Along with the expected anger and the hate even, there had also been—had she seen right?—a grudging respect, and then when she was about to leave a fleeting wistfulness, a reaching out . . .

She saw again the shrunken figure in the armchair, and on the other side of the room Clarice impaled on the divider. Clarice had not even been able to respond to her good-bye aside from a resigned nod of her bowed head. It suddenly struck her that the two of them might well remain like that, like children frozen into absurd poses in a game of statues, until the ship docked back in New York.

"_. . . ruining the rest of the trip for the two of us . . ._" It was true. The woman had been right. Conscience-stricken suddenly, she turned around in her seat inside the cabin of the launch as though to call an apology back over the water to them. She turned only to have her eyes assaulted by what looked like a huge flash fire of megaton intensity and heat, as the tropical sunlight striking the liner's bow and sweeping over the hull appeared to have set it ablaze. She could almost feel over the distance the heat from the fires on the decks. Then, abruptly, as she shifted her line of vision away from the glare, it all vanished, and there was the _Bianca Pride_ lying huge, serene and intact out in the deep water. Yet, as she turned away the retina of her eye held on to both images for a long moment, and one seemed as real as the other.

For the remainder of the brief run she sat with her body

tensed forward, as if trying to spur the launch ahead, and with her gaze trained on the cool, incredible green of the hills above the harbor.

There was no taxi waiting to drive her to the airport the moment she stepped ashore as she had envisioned there would be back in the cabin that morning, as she had stood over by the porthole trying to block out the sound of Thomasina Moore's voice.

No vehicle of any kind was to be seen on the narrow road-way that ran between the crowded dock area where the launch had just deposited her and the row of warehouses and custom buildings of weathered brick and stone that fronted the har-bor. A number of cobblestoned streets rose sharply from the roadway between each block of buildings, leading up into the town clinging to the hillside like a sunlit eyrie of pastel-col-ored houses and red-tiled roofs. But even on the one or two streets she could make out from where she stood, in the mid-dle of the wharf, nothing resembling a taxi was visible. They had all, she concluded, been taken by the passengers from the *Bianca Pride* who had landed before her. She took it as a bad sign.

Nor did she see, somewhat anxiously inspecting the people around her, any of the official tourist guides who were usually on hand, wearing an identifying cap or badge of some kind, whenever a cruise ship—especially one as big as the *Bianca Pride*—came into port. And where were the little ragtag boys who served as unofficial guides, who the minute you stepped ashore seemed to spring from the cracks in the pavement around you? For a quarter or fifty cents they would have pro-duced a taxi for her even if they had to scour every street of the hilly town. But not one of them had as yet made an appearance.

Where for that matter—she gave another puzzled look around—were all the other types she was used to seeing on the wharves in other places she had been—the noisy, sweating stevedores, the souvenir vendors peddling their cocoa bean necklaces and Zulu balancing dolls, the women hawkers with their trays of fruit, the droves of idlers and hangers-on you had to guard your pocketbook against, and, in some of the poorer places, the beggars who could be so persistent at times she would regret having come ashore. None of them were in sight.

Instead, assembled on the wharf, under the late-morning sun, was a crowd of perhaps two hundred men, women and children, who from their appearance—their clothes and the way they carried themselves—were clearly from the more respectable element on the island. Inspecting those passing near her, Avey Johnson saw large family groups, young couples with small children, any number of old people, teenagers laughing and chatting together, babies in their mothers' arms. They were all neatly dressed, the men in sport shirts and even suits, some of them; the women in what looked like new outfits they had made themselves. To shield them from the sun, many of the women, especially those with babies, were carrying umbrellas, whose bright colors and prints rivaled those of the clothes they had on.

They were not at all the kind of people ordinarily seen on the wharves, and curious, the taxi forgotten for the moment, she followed their movement past her. Carrying overnight bags and gaily wrapped packages that looked like gifts, they were heading in an orderly stream toward a long line of schooners and sloops that stood tied up from one end of the wharf to the other. While the people behind pressed forward, eagerly awaiting their turn, those nearest the water were moving in a steady procession up the makeshift gangplanks to the boats under the colorful panoply of umbrellas.

The boats were the kind used in local trade between the islands. At nearly every port Avey Johnson had visited she had seen them insinuating themselves with their scarred and peeling hulls and dingy sails among the *Bianca Pride* and the other cruise ships and freighters, their decks sagging under a cargo that might include anything from mounds of oranges or bananas to drums of fuel oil to somebody's cow tethered among the few passengers on board.

The harbor here was virtually a floating city of the decrepit craft. Her launch had had to run an obstacle course through them to reach the wharf. Now, the moment a boat being boarded was filled and under way, one of those waiting behind immediately took its place.

Why would the people around her on the wharf, as decently dressed and respectable-looking as they were, be traveling on these relics? Where were they going? Why as sensible as they appeared would they risk their lives and the lives of the children and babies with them on a string of boats that scarcely looked seaworthy? They were being as foolhardy as Thomasina Moore in St. Vincent on last year's cruise. On their day ashore there, the woman, along with a few other adventurous souls from the *Bianca Pride*, had blithely gone off on a hired sloop to visit the black sand beaches to the north of the island, which were inaccessible by car. It had been a sloop, Avey Johnson recalled, with a mainsail that looked so worn and flimsy the least wind might tear it apart and a hull that listed noticeably to port. When she and Clarice had refused to go along, the woman had fanned them down in front of everyone from the deck of the sloop and sailed away.

"Excuse me, do you know where I might find a taxi?"

The young man whom she stopped—suddenly again remembering the taxi—was wearing well-pressed navy-blue pants and a sport shirt of mixed reds, yellows and blues, the colors vivid against the sun-burnished blackness of his skin.

He turned to her with a polite smile and, pointing toward the empty roadway, spoke rapidly in Patois; seconds later, still smiling at her over his shoulder, he was moving away in the crowd.

She realized then with a start that everyone around her was speaking Patois. She had been so busy examining them she had failed to take in their speech. Or her ears had perhaps registered it as the dialect English spoken in many of the islands which often sounded like another language altogether.

But reaching her clearly now was the flood of unintelligible words and the peculiar cadence and lilt of the Patois she had heard for the first time in Martinique three days ago. She had heard it that first time and it had fleetingly called to mind the way people spoke in Tatem long ago. There had been the same vivid, slightly atonal music underscoring the words. She had heard it and that night from out of nowhere her great-aunt had stood waiting in her sleep . . .

She became very still, frowning to herself under the protective shadow of her hat brim. Had that fleeting impression perhaps set off the dream? Sometimes the least thing seen or heard during the day, or merely thought of in passing, could trigger a dream of people and events long-forgotten. Perhaps this was what had happened. The vaguely familiar sound of the Patois might have resurrected Tatem and the old woman. If so, she felt no wiser for the knowledge, no closer to understanding what had come over her since that night—why, for example, she was standing on this wharf at the moment under a broiling sun trying to find a taxi to take her to a plane home.

"Excuse me, do you understand English—?" This time, a growing note of urgency in her voice, she stopped an older man who was wearing a jacket over his open-neck white shirt. Like nearly everyone there he was carrying a colorfully wrapped package under his arm. "Taxi . . . ?" She jabbed a finger at the suitcases the crew members had deposited at her side before vanishing; she went through the motions of steering a car.

The man laughed at her antics, then broke out in Patois. He too pointed toward the roadway, and before turning to leave he stretched his hand toward her in a way that said for her to be patient.

She took him to mean that a taxi would eventually come. But when? All hopes of her being able to leave today appeared to be dimming fast.

Around her the crowd continued to press toward the boats, their odd speech filling the air. They were clearly in a holiday mood. Nevertheless, beneath the festive voices reaching her ears Avey Johnson thought she detected a sober, even solemn note. It was as if the bell of the large white-stoned church she could see dominating the steep little town was ringing in a way only those on the wharf could hear, sending a summoning call to them down through the overheated air. Everyone there seemed to be moving within its solemn ambience, even as they laughed and chatted and waved to friends they spotted in the crowd.

Many of them in passing greeted Avey Johnson. A young couple leading two little girls in matching sundresses between them smiled and waved at her. An elderly man looking formal in a dark suit and tie lifted his hat. A woman in a bright yellow print carrying a small suitcase not only waved but called out something to her in Patois.

Every minute or so while she stood there keeping an anxious eye on the roadway, someone would pause and greet her, and more often than not address a few words to her before moving on.

In return she waved her hand and smiled, and nodded politely to the brief one-way conversations she couldn't understand. They were being friendly, like most of the island people she had encountered elsewhere—but also (she couldn't help feeling) more than friendly. There was a familiarity, almost an intimacy, to their gestures of greeting and the unintelligible words they called out which she began to find puzzling, and then even faintly irritating the longer it went on.

The problem was, she decided, none of them seemed aware of the fact that she was a stranger, a visitor, a tourist, although this should have been obvious from the way she was dressed and the set of matching luggage at her side. But from the way they were acting she could have been simply one of them there on the wharf. Some in passing even gave her a quizzical look along with their smiles, as if questioning why she was standing in the one spot and not moving with them toward the boats.

Avey Johnson had been holding her gloves in her left hand. Now, she suddenly drew them on and kept her hands folded in such a way that the gloves could not escape notice.

Where was a taxi?

Although she had been conscious from the moment she landed of the blistering sun overhead, she had not been unduly uncomfortable. Her hat brim had protected her face and there had been a cool intermittent breeze off the water that somehow managed to reach her through the crowd. But all of a sudden now—from the moment she had put on the gloves— she was aware of it bearing down on her head. It felt to be slowly burning through the straw crown of her hat. And the breeze for some reason had died, so that there was no relief from the heat which the glare-filled sky above, the pavement under her feet and the bodies massed on the wharf kept pouring into the air.

To make matters worse, looking around her she saw that in the twenty or so minutes she'd been there the crowd had grown larger. She could scarcely make out the roadway anymore for the people thronging it. How would a taxi get through if it came? And those passing near to where she stood were being pressed closer in on her by the swelling numbers behind them. The small island of space she had managed to secure around herself and the suitcases was shrinking by the minute. She would soon be in danger of being trampled upon or even uprooted and swept forward in their midst. That might well be what they wanted, the absurd thought came to her: to take her along with them. Was this perhaps what lay behind their more than just friendly smiles and waves, and the brief musical string of words some of them continued to call out to her in passing? Her eyes began to take on something of the hallucinatory cast they had held yesterday in the library. She could almost see them carrying her off onto one of the shabby boats, while she desperately tried to make them understand that she was simply waiting for a taxi. For the first time in the three years that she had been coming to the islands, she experienced that special panic of the traveler who finds himself sealed-off, stranded in a sea of incomprehensible sound.

When would a taxi come?

By now it felt as if the sun had finished burning away her hat crown, leaving the top of her head completely exposed to its rays. The long-line girdle she had on with its bones and heavy latex was beginning to chafe her. Her armshields had soaked through. She regretted having worn a two-piece dress. Then suddenly in the midst of all these discomforts, she felt something tug at the straps of her pocketbook which she had hung as usual on her left forearm and was holding close to her side. She looked down alarmed, ready to wrest the bag away from whoever it was, only to find that the large curved handle of an umbrella an old woman passing near to her was carrying under her arm had accidentally hooked on to the straps. The woman, wearing a sunhat that provided as much shade as an umbrella, stopped, laughed when she saw what had happened, apologized: "Pa'don, oui." Then, after quickly extricating the handle she moved on, waving to her like someone who had known her all her life.

Minutes later found her leaning sharply back out of the way of a baby perhaps eighteen months old, who suddenly reached for her with an eager cry over his mother's shoulder as he rode past in her arms. The baby's eyes had lighted on the small gold pin in the shape of a cornucopia—complete with a spill of tiny jeweled fruit—she was wearing on the lapel of her jacket, and he was making a grab for it. (It was the way her children when they were babies used to grab for her earrings the moment she picked them up.) The small hand missed by a wide margin, but for an unnerving second she saw it fastened with that peculiar strength and tenacity of a baby's grip on the pin, and her being dragged along by mother and child until she ended up on a boat with them.

Then, suddenly: "Ida, doux-doux, qu'est-ce qu'il y a? Ma'ché! Ma'ché!"—a man's voice sounding just inches from her ear; and this time it was nothing imagined, a hand on her elbow was actually steering her out into the crowd. It even succeeded in moving her a half-step forward before she recovered her wits enough to snatch her arm free and turn.

She found herself facing a smiling broad-shouldered man of about fifty who was carrying his suit jacket over his arm because of the heat. He grew sober the moment he saw his mistake. "Pa'don, oui." Then, abruptly, he was smiling again, and saying with an amazed laugh, "But if you didn't look everything like a woman I know named Ida from the back. Is the same way she stands, oui. The same way she holds her head. You even look a little something like her from the front. Is twins if I ever saw it. Don' ever let anybody tell you, my lady, that you ain' got a twin in this world!"

She was so rattled and outdone, she failed to register that the man had spoken in English until he had disappeared still laughing in amazement and shaking his head.

Twins! The twin of some woman he knew named Ida! The indignation that swept her in a rush of heat felt almost like the hot flashes she had suffered through at the change. What was the matter with these people? It was as if the moment they caught sight of her standing there, their eyes immediately stripped her of everything she had on and dressed her in one of the homemade cotton prints the women were wearing, whose West Indian colors as Thomasina Moore called them seemed to add to the heat. Their eyes also banished the six suitcases at her side, and placing a small overnight bag like the ones they were carrying in her hand, they were all set to take her along wherever it was they were going.

That this was clearly the intention of the man she now saw heading toward her through a break in the crowd no one there could dispute, and she froze. He was younger than the man who had just disappeared, in his early thirties it looked like, and taller, much taller, with a body that was one long fluid reach of bone. His stride as he swiftly approached her seemed designed to cover an entire continent in a day, and there was a reddish, burnt ocher cast to the blackness of his face and his swinging arms. He might have stepped off the pages of the expensive photography book with the word "Masai" on its cover which Marion kept in her living room. A warrior without his spear and leaning stick, without his shield, wearing mirror sunglasses and a straw ten-gallon hat.

He came bearing down on her from the roadway with the smile that had the plan behind it. And unlike the man before, he didn't intend to simply herd her by the elbow out into the crowd. His elongated arms stood ready to scoop her up, suitcases and all, and make off with her to the nearest boat.

She saw the smile, the walk, the frightening arms and for an interminable moment could only stand there immobilized, envisioning the worst. Then she was diving frantically for the suitcases, thinking—thinking she didn't know what—to fling them in his path to block his way, to throw them up in a barricade around her . . . ?

She was still struggling to get a grip on the handle of the first bag when a long, lean, beautifully articulated hand reached down and gently took it from her. "Taxi, my lady," the man said. "You looks like you could use a taxi."

6

The one flight to New York for the day had already left, but there would be another tomorrow at four, he informed her. And she should have no problem getting a seat, this being the off-season.

She was safely inside the taxi, her suitcases stowed in the trunk and on the empty seat beside the driver; and the car, an old-model Chevy which the man had updated with a tape deck under the dashboard and a miniature pair of cowboy boots dangling from the rearview mirror, had started a labored climb up one of the hilly streets leading from the wharf.

She quickly asked him now about a hotel for the night, although not without some apprehension. She recalled Thomasina Moore's angry prediction earlier: ". . . *stuck for days in some place that won't have a decent hotel to its name . . . she'll wind up having to stay in a dump . . ."* The woman had seemed so certain.

74

"A hotel?" The man laughed. "Plenty hotels, oui. That's all we got in Grenada now. And only the best . . ." Looking up into the mirror he appeared to take a quick inventory of her from behind the shiny, blacked-out lenses of his sunglasses. Then: "I gon' take you to one to suit."

She had another question for him, but she waited before asking it until they had reached the top of the street, and the crowded wharf as well as the harbor with its flotilla of ancient boats lay some distance below them. "By the way," she said, "who were all those people on the wharf?"

"Out-islanders," he said, and went on to explain that they were people from the tiny out-island of Carriacou nearby who lived and worked in Grenada; and that once a year it was their custom to go home on a two- or three-day excursion.

"The Carriacou Excursion!" he exclaimed over the country-and-western music coming from the tape deck. "Is a serious business, oui! Every year this time every man, woman and child that's from the place does pick up themself and go. They don' miss a year. No matter how long they been living over this side, even when they's born here, come time for the excursion they gone. All today and tomorrow the wharf gon' be overrun with them rushing to take a boat. Out-islanders like peas! Down there does be so thick with them, everybody else stays away. You only catch me there 'cause I had one of them for a fare."

"I tried asking them about a taxi, but they all spoke Patois—at least that's what it sounded like . . ." She tried not to think of the man who had spoken English and the scare he had given her.

He nodded. "Oui, Patois, creole, whatever you want to call it," he said. "Is just some African mix-up something. You used to hear the old people 'bout here speaking it when I was a boy,

75

but no more. Only the out-islanders still bother. That's another thing about them. They can speak the King's English good as me and you, but the minute they set foot on the wharf for the excursion is only Patois crossing their lips. Don' ask me why. And the nice *nice* way they dress! The way they stepping! I tell you, you would think they was taking a boat—a decent boat—to go to America or England or someplace that's someplace instead of just to a little two-by-four island up the way.

"The Carriacou Excursion!" An annoyed frown appeared on the bit of his forehead visible between the hat with its wide curled up wings and his glasses. "Is a thing I don' understand, oui."

The harbor had dropped from sight by now and they were driving through the steep intricate heart of the town. The rows of crowded shops and commercial buildings in the sweltering downtown section soon gave way to the houses of pink and cream and pale green she had seen from the ship early that morning. Viewed close up they appeared to be climbing along with the car up the sharply angled streets, moving at the same labored pace. This was even true of the people they passed. Everyone walked as if being driven by a strong headwind, their bodies slanted forward. The entire town and its people seemed bound on an endless hegira up the terraced hill over which it was scattered.

"I was liking a girl from Carriacou once." The man spoke in the same easy-going, offhand manner in which he laughed, gestured, drove the car and kept time with one of his long sculptured hands to the twanging music. "Name of Sylvie. Now that was one girl lived only for the excursion, oui! Months before the time she would be busy making more dresses and buying more presents to take to her family over there. All her talk was 'bout the excursion. And she was always after me to go, saying it would do me good. But not me, oui!" A streak of stubbornness surfaced. "Why waste my time going to visit someplace that's even smaller than here. That's so small scarcely anybody has ever heard of it.

"You ever heard of it?" Avey Johnson felt the eyes she could not see regarding her in the rearview mirror.

She shook her head. She still had not recovered from the long wait out in the sun and the panic she had felt at not being able to make herself understood. But she was also feeling ashamed now of the way she had reacted to the out-islanders. Why had she suspected their simple friendliness? How could she have turned their smiles into lures? And then when the man had taken her elbow—simply mistaking her for someone he knew—she had completely lost her self-possession, just as she had yesterday when the old man on the Lido had grabbed her skirt. Her behavior just now. The irrationality of yesterday. She no longer recognized herself . . .

"You see," the driver was saying, "a place nobody ever heard of. That they don' even bother putting on the map it's so small. Not me, oui. I wasn't setting foot there. Still she kept after me. Every year 'round this time there would be a big noise between us about the excursion. We fell out over it finally. Oui, she got fed up with me and found herself a next boyfriend. An out-islander like herself. They goes on the excursion together . . ."

He shrugged off his loss, his shoulders rising and falling with the fluidity and loose bony grace which characterized all his movements. They were gifts he treated lightly.

Then, wistfully: "I did like her a lot though. Sylvie." He spoke the name in the intimate way he might have those times when they had been in bed together. "She had nice

77

ways. And she was a girl, oui, believed in working. In doing for herself. She wasn't one these women who sits down waiting on a man to give them everything. No, Sylvie was a serious person.

"All the out-islanders is like that. Serious people. Hard-working. They come to live here and before you know it they're doing better than those like myself that's born in the place. Is a fact. In no time they're pulling down a good job, building themself a house—nothing big and outlandish: they don' go in for a lot of show; buying themself a car—again is always a sensible car: you never see them overdoing things; starting up a business. They has a business mind, you know, same as white people. And they looks out for one another just like white people. No crab antics with them . . ." The elongated fingers described a clawing motion in the air. "You know what that is?"

She nodded ruefully. "Crabs in a barrel."

"Oh, so you has it among the black people in America too!" He laughed, shook his head sadly. "Well, the out-islanders is different to that. They's a people sticks together and helps out the one another. Which is why they gets ahead. If you was to stay on the island any time you'd hear a lot of talk against them. That they're proud. That they're playing white. But not me! I hasn't a word against them. The out-islanders has my respect. Is only"—he was baffled again—"this excursion business I don' understand."

While talking he had veered sharply away from the town, leaving it to continue its arduous climb up the hill, and had turned onto a narrow country road. The road, which was taking them back in the direction of the sea, ran along a bluff that was walled in on both sides by bush, trees and tall stands of green and golden bamboo. An occasional break in the foliage to their right revealed the bright flash of the sea below. To their left in the near-distance rose others of the coastal hills and behind them the mountains.

Up front, the shiny black screen of the man's sunglasses faithfully reproduced the little sun-bleached wooden houses with steeply pitched roofs scattered along the roadside. People, children, chickens, an occasional pig and docile cow flashed by like color slides on a speeded-up projector as he sent the car rattling forward to the sound of his voice still going on about the out-islanders, the strains of "Ramblin' Rose" from the tape deck and the jerky dance the tiny pair of cowboy boots hanging from the mirror were performing.

In back, Avey Johnson clung to the strap beside her window and was torn between asking him to slow down and letting him continue as is so that the reckless drive and the music would be over more quickly.

He was saying for the third time that it was "only this excursion business I don' understand," when the almost solid green wall to their right abruptly broke off, and the coastline which they had glimpsed only in snatches became visible along its entire length. They were on the other side of a high ridge which hid the town, the harbor and the *Bianca Pride* lying offshore. Unfolded below them, at the foot of the bluff along which they were traveling, was an immense bay with a flawless white sand beach that went on for miles in either direction until its wings were lost in the haze.

The beach was like a vast stage that curved inward, with the sky its proscenium arch and the sun a single huge spot that illuminated it from end to end.

Its beauty brought Avey Johnson sitting forward in her seat.

"Grand Anse, oui." The man dismissed it with a casual

wave; he laughed at her awed look in the mirror. "Is where I used to play as a boy."

Another wave of his hand—this one enthusiastic, proud—directed her gaze back to the section of the beach they had just passed, which had been hidden by the dense foliage along the road. There, stretching from the southern wing of the bay to perhaps halfway up the coast was a long column of Miami Beach-style hotels, all of them built so closely together, they gave the impression over the distance of being telescoped one into the other.

"What did I tell you? Plenty hotels, oui!" His blind man's smile in the mirror was equally proud. "That's all we got 'bout here now."

Avey Johnson took one look at the tall exaggerated shapes of concrete and glass behind her, and the garish blue water in the long line of swimming pools, and was filled with dismay. True, she was relieved on one hand: there would be no problem with the food or water at any of the places below. Yet she quickly turned away, and looked only at the northern half of the beach up ahead where no buildings were to be seen.

The hotel the man had chosen for her turned out to be not only the most recently built of all those there, so that it stood at the head of the marching column, it was also (at least to Avey Johnson's eyes) the most extreme-looking: a towering structure of stark white concrete and glass done in a "ski slope" design, with hundreds of balconies set at a dizzying slant up its sheer face.

As the man sent the taxi hurtling down the road leading from the bluff, the hotel rose to meet them like some transplanted Matterhorn out of the flat littoral of sand and sea, its twenty stories ("Twenty floors, oui! You can count them," he cried) dwarfing the hills behind it and reducing the tall royal palms that lined its driveway to mere seedlings.

For no reason she had caught herself near to tears that time she and Jerome Johnson had gone on a weekend tour to the Laurentians with several members from his lodge and their wives. (Thomasina Moore and her husband had been in the group.) Taking her first look out their hotel room window at the endless range of craggy, snow-covered mountains surrounding them and the Arctic sky above, she had felt the tears well up for a moment, and had had to keep her back turned to Jerome Johnson.

The mood had passed as mysteriously as it had come, and she had gone on to enjoy their brief stay. Nevertheless, for months afterwards, she would find herself thinking—again for no apparent reason—of the practice among the Eskimos long ago of banishing their old people out on the ice to die. She would see—the image vivid for a second in her mind—the bent figure of an old woman, her face hidden in the deep ruff of fur around her hood, left huddled on some snowy waste, while the sleds filled with the members of her tribe raced away toward warmer ground. For months the perplexing vision had come and gone.

"Is the best, oui," the driver was saying in bewilderment. He had pulled up outside the hotel and had come around to open the door for her, only to find her drawn back in her seat with the look of dismay on her face. "The Miramar Royale! I brought you to the best." Then, leaning into the car, his voice a whisper: "Only white people mostly stays here."

Once inside the lobby with its look of ersatz luxury, she immediately had the desk clerk call and make the plane reservation for her before checking in. Returning outside, she arranged with the taxi driver, waiting beside his car to be paid, to come back the following day to drive her to the airport. He was to come for her at least two hours before the scheduled time. Only when this had been taken care of did she sign the register and follow the bellman with her suitcases to the elevator.

Upstairs in her room she stood over near the door the man had just closed behind him, looking around her for the first time. She hadn't really done so since entering the hotel. She had walked in and then out of the lobby and back across it again without so much as glancing at her surroundings. The desk clerk had been nothing more than an English-sounding voice and a hand with blondish hair that had dialed the airline for her and minutes later handed her the pen to sign her name.

Now she warily took in the sleek veneered furniture which, along with the draperies, mirrors, lamps and abstract prints on the walls, filled the large room—filled it, yet at the same time, as with the deluxe cabin back on the ship, somehow left it feeling empty. A sliding glass door in a wall of glass directly opposite opened onto the balcony, whose enclosed railing cut off a view of the beach eight stories below. From where she stood nothing was visible beyond it but the distant sea, so that she felt as if she were back on the *Bianca Pride*'s upper decks, searching futilely for a quiet corner to herself. Or, if she dared to look over the balcony, she might find herself gazing down on the sports deck and its mayhem.

And suddenly there it was again: the mysterious welling up in her stomach and under her heart which had plagued her off and on ever since the parfait. Holding herself as if there were actually something there, some mass of undigested food that might come heaving up at any moment, she swiftly crossed the room, slid open the glass door and sank down on the side of a recliner out on the balcony.

She felt like someone in a bad dream who discovers that the street along which they are fleeing is not straight as they had believed, but circular, and that it has been leading them all the while back to the place they were seeking to escape.

Sitting there, her pocketbook on her lap and still wearing her hat and gloves, she felt betrayed. Whatever rebel spirit it was that had put her up to abandoning the cruise had skipped out on her, leaving her to face the sudden flood of doubts and misgivings alone.

As though to throw up a dam against them she tried focusing her thoughts on tomorrow evening when she would finally be home; tried picturing how the dining room would look through the archway as she entered the house and turned on the light in the hall. But although she strained in her mind to see the room and the familiar objects there—the sterling silver tea and coffee service on the buffet, her special crystal and china in the breakfront, the chandelier above the great oval table—their reassuring forms refused to emerge.

Instead she kept seeing with mystifying clarity the objects on display in the museum in the town of St. Pierre at the foot of Mt. Pelée, which she had visited three days ago in Martinique. There, in room after room, she had examined the twisted, scarcely recognizable remains of the gold and silver candlesticks and snuff boxes, jewelry, crucifixes and the like that had been the prized possessions of the well-to-do of St. Pierre before the volcano had erupted at the turn of the century, burying the town in a sea of molten lava and ash.

She might enter the dining room tomorrow night to find everything there reduced to so many grotesque lumps of metal and glass by a fire like the one she had seen raging aboard the liner for an instant that morning from the launch.

Under her hat brim, Avey Johnson's eyes again had the wide frightened look of someone given to visions that were beyond her comprehension; and in the midst of the tropical heat she found she was shivering.

II

SLEEPER'S WAKE

1

"What the devil's gotten into you, woman?"

He stood breathing his annoyance down on her from the foot of the recliner, his figure in the dark three-piece business suit blocking out the afternoon sun and causing a premature dusk to fall on the balcony.

Avey Johnson could not see his face—she had no wish to; it was enough to imagine the deep scowl there—but the white lambskin apron and the white gloves he had been buried in as a Master Mason stood out sharply in the false dusk. He seemed taller than she remembered him and more severe.

"Do you know what you're playing around with?"

He meant the money: the fifteen hundred dollars she had just forfeited by walking off the ship; the air fare she would have to turn around and spend tomorrow; the cost of the hotel room tonight. From the anxiety in his voice, she could tell he

87

was including other, more important things. "Do you know what you're playing around with?" said in that tone also meant the house in North White Plains and the large corner lot on which it stood, and the insurance policies, annuities, trusts and bank accounts that had been left her, as well as the small sheaf of government bonds and other securities which were now also hers, and most of all the part interest guaranteed her for life in the modest accounting firm on Fulton Street in Brooklyn which bore his name. The whole of his transubstantiated body and blood. All of it he seemed to feel had been thrown into jeopardy by her reckless act.

"You must want to wind up back where we started."

He meant Halsey Street. Whenever there had been a discussion between them about money, whenever they had argued, in fact, he had never failed, no matter what the argument was about, to bring up the subject of Halsey Street, holding it like the Sword of Damocles over everything they had accomplished.

He never referred to it by name. It was always "back where we started" or "back you know where," refusing to let the name so much as cross his lips—although his refusal only served ironically to bring the street and the fifth floor walkup where they had lived for twenty years more painfully to mind.

Like someone unable to recover from a childhood trauma—hunger, injury, abuse, a parent suddenly and inexplicably gone—Jerome Johnson never got over Halsey Street. When she had long purged her thoughts and feelings of the place, and had come to regard the years there as having been lived by someone other than herself, it continued to haunt him, and to figure in some way in nearly everything he did.

It was Halsey Street, for example, which prompted him—over her objections—to build an additional pantry in the house in North White Plains, which he kept stocked with enough canned goods to last out a war. That street in Brooklyn accounted for the raft of insurance policies he took out to cover everything—fire, theft, life, loss of limb—that might happen to them or the house. It was also Halsey Street, and specifically the block they had lived on, with its noisy trolley and the knot of old tenements down the street from their apartment house, which kept him going at the same unrelenting pace long after his business was firmly established, both mortgages on the house had been paid up and Marion, their youngest, was out of college, teaching, on her own.

And it was Halsey Street finally which caused him the night before his last stroke to cry out, appalled, in his sleep as he lay in the bed next to hers, "Do you know who you sound like, who you even look like . . . ?" He was repeating for the last time the question which had plagued his sleep for years, which he had first asked her all the way back on a Tuesday evening in the winter of '47. That was the night when it appeared that the ruin and defeat steadily overtaking the block had reached their walkup and was about to lay claim to them also.

She had been eight months pregnant with Marion at the time. Far too soon for it to have happened again. Annawilda wasn't even two yet, and Sis, who had been born the year after Jay came out of the army, would only be five her next birthday. Too soon. Moreover, she had only just started back to work a few months ago. As she had done before with Sis, the moment Annawilda was weaned she began leaving the two of them with the middle-aged West Indian widow down the block who minded children by the day and had returned to her job as a Grade II clerk with the State.

She tried everything in the beginning: the scalding hot baths, castor oil, the strong cups of fennel root tea she had learned about from her mother. She bought the unmarked packet of small brown pills in the drugstore and swallowed them all at one time. She douched one day until it seemed her entire insides had been flushed down the bathtub drain. And as she lay there exhausted with no sign of the hoped-for blood, she actually considered for a moment going back on the promise she had made to herself at the death of her friend, Grace, with whom she had graduated from high school. (Grace had found somebody somewhere and had had it done, and her death from a massive hemorrhage afterwards had made Avey promise herself "never that.") Another day, while Jay was at work and the children asleep, she raced up and down the five flights of stairs between their apartment on the top floor and the vestibule. For close to a half-hour she practically took and hurled her body down the steep steps and then up again, down and up repeatedly until she finally collapsed on the landing outside their door. All to no avail.

Jay's face when she told him had mirrored everything she felt. After a long despairing silence he had started to say something, to ask a question which she easily read in his eyes, and then he had quickly checked himself, also remembering Grace, who had been part of the crowd they went around with when they first married and still lived in Harlem. The question remained unasked, but as the months went by and she started to show, his eyes began to shy helplessly away from her stomach. She also avoided the sight of it in the mirror. By her sixth month she was so large she was forced to give up her job again.

Jay by then had started putting in longer hours at the small department store in downtown Brooklyn where he worked in the shipping room, as the assistant to the man in charge. Long after the store had closed he would still not be home. A backlog of orders had kept him. A truckload of merchandise had arrived just at closing time and he had stayed to check it in. They were doing inventory. The boss had asked him to work late again. There had been a large shipment to prepare for the next morning.

There was no reason to doubt him. The shipping room often remained in operation after the store itself had closed. And he had worked overtime before. Yet, as his lateness grew to be a regular thing and his look when he was home became more evasive and closed, as she was reduced to spending her evenings after the children were asleep wandering about the cramped apartment, staring at the place in front of the kitchen sink where the linoleum had worn through to the floorboards or at the clothes in the bedroom closet she could no longer fit into, something shattered in her mind. It seemed the china bowl which held her sanity and trust fell from its shelf in her mind and broke, and another reason for his lateness began to take shape in her thoughts with the same slow and inevitable accretion of detail as the child in her womb.

She began seeing them: the white salesgirls at the store (it would be years before they started hiring colored), the younger ones with their flat stomachs and unswollen breasts and their hair swept up on a rat into a pompadour or combed so it hung over one side of the face à la Veronica Lake. They were behind every counter in the stores downtown. Girls from Flatbush and Bensonhurst and Bay Ridge, who had to paint the lipstick above the natural line of their lips to give them the fullness they lacked, whose loose, flat-cheeked behinds suggested Jell-O that had not yet set.

No, it was probably someone closer to her age, in her midtwenties or older even, a woman whose husband might have been killed in the war. Someone like that would be more likely to appeal to him.

Pacing the small rooms each evening, her mind a pile of angry shards, she began blaming them. They had long been intrigued by him. There was the reputation he had acquired around the store of being hard-working, efficient, dependable. His was the kind of highly organized mind and photographic memory which permitted him to keep track of practically every piece of merchandise that came and went on the trucks for the day. It was Jay, the salesgirls secretly knew, as did everyone else in the store, who actually ran shipping and receiving and not the Irishman in charge, although he had to be careful not to make it appear so.

"Two jobs for the salary of one," he would say at home, trying sometimes to laugh it off. "They really got themselves a good thing in me."

At work he would be so absorbed in what he was doing he would scarcely notice the salesgirls when they came into the shipping room on one pretext or another. The bolder ones would stop to chat, insisting that he take heed of them, and he would be friendly enough, exchanging the usual light banter with them, gracing them with his smile, but his mind they could tell would all the while be on the sheaf of orders and invoices in his hand.

He wasn't at all the way a colored guy was supposed to be! (She could almost hear them thinking it.) Where were his jokes and his loud talk? Where his thrilling, deep-throated nigger laugh to send the terror and delight rippling like arpeggios over their flesh? Why didn't he play the clown, act the fool, do a buck-and-wing in appreciation of their interest? Or at least roll his eyes until only the whites showed like Mantan Moreland in the movies?

"And what's wit' the mustache a'ready?"—saying it to themselves in the hopeless Brooklynese they spoke. That, more than anything else about him she was certain, puzzled, irritated and at the same time held them in thrall. Now there was nothing unusual about a colored man having a mustache. But Jay had not been satisfied to copy the somewhat modest style of the day. Instead, he had gone to the sepia-colored photograph of his father in the family album they had started compiling, and as a kind of tribute perhaps had taken as his model the full, broad-winged mustache the older man had sported around World War I.

Jay didn't wear his quite as full. The shape was the same, with the thickness that more than filled the space above his lip tapering off into a pair of wings that curled down at the tips to embrace the corners of his mouth. And there was the same distinctive, slightly rakish look to it.

To care for the mustache he kept on a shelf in the medicine cabinet a small tortoiseshell rake, a diminutive pair of surgical scissors, a tiny brush and a vial of light, delicately scented oil, a drop of which he would apply when finished to give it a faint gloss. Most of his time in the bathroom each morning was spent fussing with it. And once a month he took the subway back to his old neighborhood in Harlem to have it properly trimmed and groomed by his favorite barber.

The mustache was his one show of vanity, his sole indulgence. It was also, Avey sensed, a shield as well, because planted in a thick bush above his mouth, it subtly drew attention away from the intelligence of his gaze and the assertive, even somewhat arrogant arch to his nostrils, thus protecting him. And it also served to screen his private self: the man he was away from the job.

If the salesgirls only knew what he was like at home! (Or

had been like before this latest blow.) The change that came over him from the moment he stepped in the door! His first act after greeting her was to turn up the volume on the phonograph which would already be playing their favorite records. Then, as if it was something apart from him, the sore spent body of a friend perhaps, he would lower his tall frame into the armchair, lean his head back, close his eyes, and let Coleman Hawkins, The Count, Lester Young (old Prez himself), The Duke—along with the singers he loved: Mr. B., Lady Day, Lil Green, Ella—work their magic, their special mojo on him. Until gradually, under their ministrations, the fatigue and strain of the long day spent doing the two jobs—his and his boss's—would ease from his face, and his body as he sat up in the chair and stretched would look as if it belonged to him again.

Some days called for the blues. Those evenings coming in he didn't even stop to take off his coat or hat before going to the closet in their bedroom, where at the back of the top shelf he kept the old blues records in an album that was almost falling apart. The records, all collector's items, had been left him by his father, who had been a scout for Okeh Records in the twenties. The names on the yellowed labels read Ida Cox, Ma Rainey, Big Bill Broonzy, Mamie Smith . . .

In his hands the worn-out album with its many leaves became a sacred object, and each record inside an icon. So as not to risk harming them he never stacked them together on the machine, but played them individually, using the short spindle. A careful ritual went into dusting each one off, then gently lowering it onto the turntable, sliding the lever to "on" and finally, delicately, setting the needle in place.

And he never, no matter how exhausted he was, sat down when listening to the blues records. As the voices rose one

after the other out of the primitive recordings to fill the apartment, he would remain standing, head bowed, in front of the
phonograph.

"You can't keep a good man down," Mamie Smith sang on
the oldest and most priceless of the 78s. He always saved this
one for the last. By the time it ended and he carefully replaced
it in the album with the others, his head would have come up
and the tension could almost be seen slipping from him like
the coat or jacket he would still have on falling from his
shoulders to the floor. He would be ready then, once the
album was back on its shelf in the bedroom closet, to sit and
listen to the other records.

The Jay who emerged from the music of an evening, the self
that would never be seen down at the store, was open, witty,
playful, even outrageous at times: he might suddenly stage an
impromptu dance just for the two of them in the living room,
declaring it to be Rockland Palace or the Renny. And affec-
tionate: his arms folding around her from behind when she
least expected them, the needful way he spoke her name even
when they quarreled—"Avey . . . Avey, would you just shut
up a minute!" And passionate: a lover who knew how to talk
to a woman in bed.

If the salesgirls only knew his passion at times! But they
weren't stupid. They had sensed something of the other Jay
behind that carefully protected public self. The little veiled
knowing smile he treated them to when they stopped to chat,
the mustache with its dramatic air, the arch to his nostrils—
these things alerted them. They had spied the lover in him,
and in their fantasies would draw his lips under the shapely
bush of hair down to theirs and wrap their pallid flesh in the
rich sealskin brown of his body.

They had long made up their minds to have him! And

95

finally one day, the day perhaps when she first started to show and his eyes began avoiding her stomach, he had turned from his work when the one favored came over (the somewhat older woman, surely), and the look he had given her, his smile, had spoken quietly of what he could be like at other times, in a more private place.

The first time she accused him he stared at her for an incredulous moment and then burst out laughing. "I've got enough women for the moment, thank you," he said. "There's you first of all, and you're easily a dozen women in one. Then the two ladies inside"—he waved toward the bedroom at the back of the apartment where the children were asleep. "And what's probably another young lady on her way . . ." The wave took in her swollen middle, although his eyes didn't follow it there. "That's more than enough women for one poor colored man—at least," he added with a wink, "for the time being."

That was the first and last time he joked about it. On subsequent evenings when, incensed by his lateness, she brought it up again, he tried reasoning with her; tried calming her. Would he be so foolish as to risk losing the job over one of those silly white girls down at the store? Or worse, risk finding himself down at the bottom of the East River tied to a ton of concrete when her father or older brother found out? Brooklyn might be the North but it wasn't all that different from Kansas (he had been born and raised there) when it came to such matters and there were more ways to lynch a colored man other than from a tree. Besides, with all the worries he had the furthest thing from his mind was the thought of some other woman.

Or where, he argued at other times, did she think he was getting the money to pay all the bills on his own now that they were missing her salary, if he wasn't actually putting in the extra hours? Did he suddenly have to start bringing home his pay envelope unopened as proof? Didn't she realize he needed all the overtime he could get if they were to keep afloat? "I mean, be reasonable, Avey, it's rough on me too."

Part of her saw the logic of this. That part also knew, perhaps better than he did, that it wasn't really a question of some woman, real or imagined. Even if she did exist, she was merely the stand-in for the real villain whom they couldn't talk about, who stood cooly waiting for them amid the spreading blight of Halsey Street below. And there didn't seem to be any escaping him. It was as if the five flights of stairs from their apartment to the street had become the giant sliding pond inside Steeplechase Park at Coney Island which she remembered from her childhood, and that she and Jay had already begun the inevitable long slide down.

All this she understood, but her understanding did nothing to contain her rage. She continued over the weeks to accuse him, helpless to stop herself as her ballooning stomach and the oncoming winter and the increasingly treacherous climb down the stairs kept her confined all day with the children to the four small rooms on the top floor.

Finally, an exasperated Jay ceased trying to reason with her, and took to answering her outbursts when he came in with a stubborn silence and the usual averted gaze.

Until that fateful Tuesday night during her eighth month.

It had snowed all day, the first heavy snowfall of the winter. A strong wind had accompanied the snow, piling it in great drifts up the high stoops of the brownstone houses on the block and plastering it over the ravaged fronts of the tenements. By the time evening came Halsey Street looked as though a huge dust cover had been flung over it to hide the evidence of its decay.

The snow also muffled the clang of the trolley which continued to run despite the storm and the rattle of the chains on the tires of the occasional passing car. The silence outdoors only served to magnify the sounds inside the apartment as Avey, the children in bed, took up her angry vigil on a chair at the living room window.

The ticking of the clock, whose every stroke added to his lateness, seemed louder. The knocking in the pipes as the meager heat struggled to reach the top floor was more maddening than ever. (The radiators had been only lukewarm since morning, so that in addition to the kerosene burner they used to supplement the heat, she had had to keep the oven of the gas stove lighted all day.) Loudest of all in the silence the snow had brought was the coughing of Sis and Annawilda in the back bedroom. It was a sound heard all winter. One night, she feared, one of them would quietly choke to death on the phlegm trapped in her throat while she and Jay slept.

The child inside her would fall heir to the same winter-long cold. All the cod liver oil, orange juice, Scott's Emulsion and the like she fed it, all the sweaters she piled on its small body even at night, would not prevent the rattling cough and the clogged asthmatic breathing once winter settled into the porous brick of the aging building like "the misery" into the bones of the old.

In the room they went to after work the radiator threw off the heat in visible waves, creating a summer of warm shimmering light and air for them behind the drawn shades. It was so warm in the room there was never a need for a blanket. They would even fling off the top sheet, and laugh as it snapped and billowed like a sail above their nakedness before falling to the floor.

Suddenly she was struggling to her feet, and the restless pacing that was a nightly ritual began. Even though her ankles had been swollen for some weeks now, she still spent the better part of each evening wandering from one room to the other.

She usually followed a set path. From the living room overlooking Halsey Street her lumbering steps would take her through the short passageway that led past the kitchen and bathroom crowded together in the middle of the apartment to the door of the children's room, which she always left half open. After listening in despair to their breathing she would return to the front of the house, and drift into the narrow hallway bedroom off the living room where she and Jay slept. (They had given the children the larger room to the back, away from the noise of the trolley.)

Some nights she was scarcely conscious of being on her feet or of the endless trudging back and forth, until she would feel the child inside her begin to twist and tumble against the wall of her belly, as if made nervous by her seething thoughts. Or she would be brought to herself by a sudden racket under her feet, as the old man downstairs, who complained constantly about the noise the children made over his head, would start banging with a broom handle—or perhaps it was the cane he used—on his ceiling.

That Tuesday night, more agitated than usual, she suddenly broke off the pacing once she reached the hallway bedroom, and first yanking on the ceiling light and then pulling open the door to the closet, she planted herself in front of the full-length mirror on the inside of the door, and for the first time in months actually looked at herself.

The beige chenille robe she had had to wear all day over her clothes to keep warm could no longer be buttoned beyond the third one down. And there was an orange stain on the collar where Annawilda, tiring of the mashed carrots she was feeding her for lunch, had sprayed her with a mouthful. (Forgetting herself, she had slapped her sharply on the leg, and then had had to walk her in her arms for a half-hour before she quieted down.) On her water-logged feet was a pair of Jay's old slippers, the only things she could fit into now. And had she remembered to comb her hair that morning? She stole a furtive glance upward. It didn't appear so.

Who—*who*—was this untidy swollen woman with the murderous look? What man wouldn't avert his gaze or try to shut out the sight of her in someone else's flesh? Even the clothes hanging next to her in the closet, which she could see at an angle in the mirror, appeared to have turned aside from her image. The dark green pleated skirt she glimpsed at the end of the rack had been bought during the one brief year she had gone to college—the first year they were married, while Jay was in the army—taking classes in general studies at Long Island University in the evenings after work. She had thought of herself as a coed and had bought the skirt, and kept it although it was over six years old. The brown tailored suit there she had worn the day she had attended her first union meeting as an organizer of the clerical workers in her section of the Motor Vehicle Bureau. Tuesday, she suddenly remembered with an enraged pang, was the day the meetings were usually held. And the teal blue dress hanging beside it she had worn to work along with her high-heeled shoes and her hair done in a flawless pageboy no more than four months ago . . .

In the warm pool of light from the lamp beside the bed, the woman's stomach was flat, smooth, a snow-white plain, with the navel like a tiny signpost pointing to the silken forest below. Jay could not get over the flatness. Stroking it, he would tell her—his mouth against her ear, her lips—what it did to him, how it moved him. Talking as his hand slowly and with the lightest touch moved down. Until, under his caress and the quiet power of his voice, the woman would cry out and pull him down between her arched, widespread legs.

Her own legs in the next three or four weeks would find themselves in the same position: raised, bent, open wide. But it would not be that lovely flowering gesture of arousal and invitation. Nor would her cries be those of ecstasy. Moreover, on the other side of the sheet they would have flung over her knees, her feet would be strapped into the stirrups at the bottom of the table. And although she would beg them not to do it, her hands would be tied as usual to the long bars on either side.

There was the sound of glass on the verge of falling and shattering as she slammed the closet door and left the room. Out in the living room, her mind inflamed, she resumed her heavy-footed prowling.

What if she had a difficult time with this one, as had been true with Sis. Then, her arms already bound at her sides, she had been left to lie for hours screaming up into the antiseptic lights of the labor room. From time to time the nurse had appeared to feel the high mound of her stomach and to chide her about the noise. And the doctor the few times he came simply repeated after examining her that she wasn't ready yet. It had taken ten hours in all.

And how would she make it down those stairs? The thought brought her to a standstill on the cold floorboards. The last time, with Annawilda, it had taken three people—Jay, the doctor and the ambulance driver—to maneuver her unwieldy body down the five flights. It had been like lowering a stricken

climber, his bulky clothes frozen solid on him, down a snow-
covered mountain.

This time she might not even make it down to the street
and the waiting ambulance. This time when her water broke,
Jay might be at work or—and she trembled with rage at the
thought—lying somewhere with the woman's legs locked
around him. She would have to send Sis to ask a neighbor to
go to the candy store up on Broadway and call the ambulance.
But by the time all this was done and the ambulance arrived it
might be too late. The head might present itself even as they
were bringing her down the stairs. She would find herself
giving birth on one of the dim landings, with her screams and
curses echoing from the top floor to the street, terrifying the
children.

2

That Tuesday night she met him in a fury at the door.

As he had done so often over the past four or five months, Jay simply stood and heard her out in silence for a time, the windblown snow on his hat and overcoat and flecked on his mustache, and on his haggard face, in his evasive eyes the look of someone who carried a weight on his spirit that was as heavy in its way as the child in her womb.

She bet it was nice and warm where he'd just come from. Their little hideaway. That wasn't some dump where you had to keep the stove on all day so's not to freeze to death. No, the love nest had heat all the time. Why didn't he just stay there? Why bother coming home at all? Shouting it at him. Brooklyn. She hated it! Why couldn't he have found a job in the City? She was somebody who was used to the City. Everybody she knew was there. She couldn't even get to see or talk to her mother. She should never have moved with him to this godforsaken place. Should never have let him stick her up on some freezing top floor having a baby every time she looked around. Should never have married him . . .

Normally he would have turned from her by then and gone to hang up his damp coat in the bathroom or to sit in a chair, his head bowed, till she was done. And he did start to move away, but as if the knife edge in her voice tonight had finally succeeded in cutting away whatever it was that had kept his own anger in check over the months, he stopped and, suddenly hurling the newspaper in his hand to the floor, began shouting also.

No sooner did his voice erupt than a small figure appeared at the head of the passageway. On all the other evenings when only her mother was to be heard in the living room, Sis had not stirred. But the sound of Jay answering back at last, and with the same if not greater fury in his voice, had brought her at a run from the back bedroom.

Wearing a sweater over her pajamas and woolen socks, she hung for a moment in the opening, fear written on the face which everyone said had taken the best from them both. Then, cautiously, she started across the living room, and coming to a halt just outside their raging circle, she quietly asked them to stop. Like a mediator seeking to introduce a note of reasonableness and calm, Sis pleaded with them to be still, not realizing that she couldn't be heard in the hailstorm of recriminations filling the room. The two quarreling weren't even aware of her presence. Abandoning the quiet tone after a time, she tried ordering them: "Stop shouting, do you hear me! Stop it!"—growing angry herself now. Until finally, in tears, she started hitting them. Rushing wildly back and forth

between them—a referee who had become part of the fight—
she pummeled first one and then the other with her fists.

Sis dealt her ineffectual little blows, and from her crib in
the bedroom, a terrified Annawilda sent up the ear-splitting
shriek, which she could sustain for what seemed hours without
taking a breath. Even the unborn child was in an agitated
state. Dimly, in the hysteria overtaking her, Avey felt it
pounding away with its little watery limbs on the wall of her
stomach like an outraged neighbor in a next-door apartment
protesting the noise.

". . . cooped up all day looking at the beat-up linoleum in
that closet of a kitchen . . ." She was scarcely conscious anymore of what she was saying.

"Okay," he cried, "you go take my job at the store then! Go
on. Go on down there and see how you like working for some
red-faced Irishman who sits on his can all day laughing to
himself at the colored boy he's got doing everything . . ." His
anger was such his nostrils were arched high and quivering
and the muscles along his jawline were as hard and prominent
as bone under his dark skin. He was fed up with her com-
plaints and criticism and suspicions. She didn't appreciate
when someone was trying their best. It was her attitude more
than anything else that was making them so miserable. A year
of college and she thought she was somebody. A prima donna
from Seventh Avenue in Harlem. He should have left her
right there. Should have turned and run the other way when
he saw her coming.

Finally, with their voices stranded on a peak from which
they would never, it seemed, find the way down, an inflamed
and trembling Avey stepped to within inches of him. One
hand was raised to strike him. The other hand had grabbed

the distraught Sis and was holding her fiercely to her side. The huge belly thrust forward defiantly, and she was screaming in his face, *"Goddamn you, nigger, I'll take my babies and go!"*

It took some time in the silence that fell for Jay to find his voice again, and when he did it was scarcely audible. "Do you know who you sound like," he whispered, choked, appalled, "who you even look like?"

There was no need for him to elaborate. She knew who he meant. They had both watched any number of times the woman he was referring to as she opened the drama that took place nearly every Saturday morning on the sidewalk below their bedroom window.

Sometime between midnight and dawn, when Halsey Street stood empty and the trolley had all but ceased to run, the woman, who was not much older than herself, would be seen leaving the cluster of three or four tenements which had already given way to the ruin slowly overtaking the rest of the block.

Out of the wide-open front door with its broken lock, past the overflowing garbage cans at the gate, she would come, a housedress thrown over her nightgown in the summer, a rag of a coat on in winter, the headtie she slept in still on, railing loudly to herself, waking the street, the dialogue already under way. Up past the one- and two-family brownstones and their still presentable-looking walkup she would charge, headed for Broadway and the string of beer gardens which peeped out from the darkness under the El like the eyes of the Gold Dust twins on the boxes of soap powder.

By the time she found him, the rotgut in the false-bottom glass would have already eaten into his Friday's pay. And his buddies whom he had set up repeatedly at the bar would have drunk their share of it. The same for the fly young thing perched on the stool next to his, with her powder and store-bought hair and paste diamond rings. She too would have had hers by then.

". . . Spending your money on some stinking 'ho . . . !" *whose brains are red jelly stuck between 'lizabeth Taylor's toes . . .*

("Oh-oh, here come your folks again, Jay." "My *folks?* Who told you I was colored, woman? I'm just passing to see what it feels like." Vaudeville-like jokes which they sprinkled like juju powders around the bed to protect them. Jokes with the power of the Five Finger Grass Avey's great-aunt Cuney used to hang above the door of the house in Tatem to keep trouble away.)

Down the five stories from their bedroom the woman's voice—loud, aggrieved, unsparing—did violence to the stillness as she herded the man, stumbling along in surly compliance just ahead of her, back down Halsey Street. He was a tall, solidly built man perhaps a few years Jay's senior. Occasionally, in the light of the streetlamps, his shoulders could be seen to flicker under the whiplash of her voice. Sometimes when her abuse became too much he would start around menacingly in his tracks: "Look, don't mess with me this morning . . ."

But she never left off telling him about himself—his no-'count, shiftless ways, his selfishness, his neglect of his own. ". . . Spending damn near your whole paycheck on some bar-fly and a bunch of good-timing niggers and your children's feet at the door . . ." She sent her grievances echoing up and down the deserted street, and strumming along the power line to the trolley, telegraphing them from one end of Brooklyn to the other. She acquainted the sleeping houses with her sorrow.

Her rage those dark mornings spoke not only for herself but for the thousands like her for blocks around, lying sleepless in the cold-water flats and one-room kitchenettes, the railroad apartments you could run a rat through and the firetraps above the stores on busy Fulton Street and Broadway; waiting, all of them, for some fool to come home with his sodden breath and half his pay envelope gone. Lying there enraged and vengeful, planning to put the chain on the door, change the lock first thing in the morning, have his clothes waiting out in the hall for him when he came lurching in at dawn. Or she'd be gone, her and the kids. She'd just take her babies and go! The place stripped of all sign of them when he got there. Vowing as she lay there straining to hear his unfocused step on the stairs and the key scratching blindly around the eye of the lock, that there would be no making up this time, no forgiving. This was one time he wasn't going to get around her with his pleas and apologies and talk, with his hands seeking out her breasts in the darkness. Not this morning! "Nigger, you so much as put a finger on me this morning and you'll draw back a nub!" Praying (Lord, please!) that he wouldn't turn on the light and simply stand there looking at her with his shamefaced self, his pain, until her love—or whatever it was she still felt for him—came down.

Some Saturdays the woman even made the five-story leap to the hallway bedroom to stand over Avey—or so she felt at times. Lying there next to Jay, listening to the voices from below, she would sense the woman's enraged presence on her side of the bed; would feel her accusing eyes in the darkness. Yeah, they saw, the eyes said, the way she always quickened her step when passing the house. They had seen her many a time from the upstairs window hurrying by with her nose in the air and her gaze trained straight ahead. She thought she

108

was better. She didn't want anything to do with her kind. She couldn't wait till she could move from around them.

Standing over her, the woman also envied her for having found a Jay—steady, dependable, hard-working Jay—who didn't throw his money away in bars. With a man like that she had a chance to make it from Halsey Street. Where did they make his kind? How had she landed him? She wasn't anything all that much to speak of with her dark self and that rare lip of hers. Her hair didn't even cover her neck and it was far from what you'd call good. Lashing out at her for her luck.

Then, abruptly, her manner would change, her anger would vanish and, bending close to Avey, tears in her eyes, she would quietly beg her not to turn her back on them, not to forget those like herself stranded out there with the men who just wouldn't do right.

". . . What kinda man is you anyway, spending all your money on . . ."

"Goddamit, din' I tell ya don' mess with me this mornin'!"

He swung around, a hard palm raised, but the woman long anticipating his move leaned easily out of its way. And when he righted himself, after being thrown off balance by the missed blow, she gave him a light contemptuous shove forward, setting him on course again but also, at the same time, dismissing his threat. Because she knew his would be a different tune once she had him home, in bed, with her back turned to him like the Great Wall of China. He'd be sounding a whole lot different then: "Now, baby, why you wanna act like that? Gotcha back all turn to me and everything. I was only having a little taste with the fellas, that's all. A man works all week taking Charlie's shit he gots to relax hisself a little come the weekend. You know what it's like out there . . . Whore? What whore? You not gon' believe this,

baby, but I don't even know that girl. She just somebody be
'round the bar. Come on, sugar. How'm I suppose to sleep
with your sweet butt lyin' up here next to me? Lemme just res'
a hand on it. You know you my weakness. Baby . . ."

> *Love in the garbage-strewn dawn,*
> *Above the jimmied mailboxes*
> *And the gaping front door; its aphrodisiac*
> *The smell of cat piss*
> > *on the cellar landing.*

"Goddamn you, nigger, I'll take my babies and go!"
Her cry that Tuesday made the scene they witnessed almost
every weekend so vivid, it seemed that they had changed
places with the two down in the street; had even become
them. She was suddenly the half-crazed woman, her children
left alone in the apartment, scouring the bars and beer gardens
in her nightgown, and Jay was the derelict husband taking the
wild swings at her under the streetlamps, the delinquent husband whom she would inevitably search the bars in vain for
one night and never see again.
As if that inevitable night had already caught up with
them, she thought she saw Jay take a slight step backwards.
Without his actually moving, he appeared to be slowly backing toward the door to the hall which stood just a few feet
behind him. Moving away from her and the tearful Sis, whom
she still held pinned to her side, away from the huge melon of
a stomach. And although he continued to stare appalled at
her, his eyes gave the impression as he crept backwards of
being tightly closed against the sight of his slippers on her feet
and the chenille robe with the stain on the collar. His hands,
the gloves still on them, appeared to be clapped over his ears
to shut out Annawilda's prolonged shriek from the bedroom.

Any second and he would be at the door. A swift turn and he would have snatched it open. Before either she or Sis could think to run after him or find the voice to call him back, he would be racing down the stairs, taking them three and four at a time in his haste to be gone. The loud slam of the front door would reach them up the five flights. And the last they would see of him ever as they rushed to the window would be his dark figure in the overcoat fleeing up Halsey Street through the high snow.

As he stood there straining to make his escape, another force equally strong held him in place and even seemed to be trying to nudge him toward them. His anguished face, his eyes under the hat with the melted snow on the crown and brim reflected the struggle. He was like an embattled swimmer caught in the eye of two currents moving powerfully in opposite directions. That Tuesday night it was impossible to tell which one would ultimately claim him.

It appeared finally that the street had won. All of a sudden, in the interminable silence, there could be heard the faint scraping of his shoe on the floor, and one foot could actually now be seen moving back. One foot and then the other and he would have taken the first (and she was convinced) irreversible step toward the door.

Before the step could be completed, he stopped short with a kind of violence, the other current asserting its hold on him.

He drew himself up, tensing every muscle of his body to the point where it was clearly painful and he was trembling. Having steeled both his body and his will, he stepped forward, Jay stepped forward, and the sound of his tears as he held her and Sis, the strangeness of it in the small rooms, brought Annawilda's shrill cry to a startled halt for a moment.

111

3

Shortly afterwards he took a regular job in the evenings as a watchman and elevator opera-tor in an office building in downtown Brooklyn that remained open late. Proof that he was actually working this time came in the unopened pay envelope he handed over to her each week along with his salary from the department store—some-thing he had never done before.

From then until they moved from Brooklyn some twelve years later he was never without two jobs. At various periods it was three. During the months for example before Avey returned to work after having Marion, he spent his Mondays off from the store and every holiday that came along, as well as his ten-day vacation, working as a door-to-door salesman in their section of Brooklyn. He sold everything from bedspreads to dictionaries to hair products, but mainly the Filter Queen vacuum cleaner that was in vogue at the time. The heavy sample case containing the tank and the various accessories became part of the furniture in their cramped bedroom at the front of the apartment.

Moreover, as if he still had time and energy that were going begging, he began a correspondence course in accounting and business management soon after that near-fatal Tuesday, paying for it with his GI benefits. These were things he had wanted to study ever since high school. He took to reading books on career building, personality improvement, selling techniques, business English and the like. The long trolley ride to and from downtown Brooklyn each day, the time he had to himself on his evening job, and all day Sunday at home were spent immersed in the study manuals for the course or in one of the books.

At night, in bed, Avey could sometimes scarcely pry away the book or manual he had fallen asleep gripping in his hand. And these were the first things he reached for—still half asleep—on the night table beside the bed in the mornings. Some mornings, getting up at five or six to nurse Marion, she would find him already up in the living room, studying.

The course took him close to four years to complete. He then spent nearly another two years looking for an apprentice or beginner's job in accounting. Every Monday, wearing the dark suit he had been married in, his mustache carefully trimmed, and the Sunday paper under his arm with the want ads that looked most promising circled in ink, he would set out—neat, personable, well-spoken—for the firms and offices in downtown Brooklyn and Manhattan. And Monday nights late, after having gone to his evening job, he would return to tell Avey of his day.

He had gone to one after the other of the places he had circled only to discover that the job had been filled just minutes before he got there, or to learn that they were looking for someone with at least five years' experience. Or to be told that the ad in the paper was incorrect; it should have read only CPAs need apply. Or to be assured that they would keep his application on file . . .

The apprenticeship program would not be suitable for him. He was too old.

He would have no problem if he were licensed.

They would be in touch if anything came up.

It became a standard set of litanies over the months. After a time, coming home those Monday nights, he kept the day's rebuffs to himself, and simply let his shoulders, collapsed under the jacket or coat, speak for him. They would look to Avey as if he had been carrying around the heavy sample case containing the vacuum cleaner all day while looking for the job, lugging it up and down a thousand flights of stairs, and in and out of a hundred offices.

He was told repeatedly during the futile search that what he really needed was a college degree. With it he would stand a much better chance, and it should not take very long for him to obtain it since he would be given credit for the work he had already done on the correspondence course.

After the two years, when he finally abandoned the search for the job, he also stopped working in the evenings. And as he had done that Tuesday in the living room, harnessing both his body and his will, he enrolled at age thirty-two at Long Island University, where Avey had gone for the one year when he was in the army.

What followed was another long siege of the job at the department store during the day, and in the evenings a steady round of classes, fall, winter and spring. And summer as well, because he took advantage of the accelerated courses offered then to build his credits. Moreover, in that way he had of somehow finding time where none existed, he resumed his door-to-door selling (he had been forced to abandon it while looking for the job) on his Mondays off, on Saturday evenings, on Sundays even at times. "It's neck and neck sometimes with me and the Jehovah Witness folks to see who gets to the doorbell first," he said with a flash of his old humor.

Jay. He went about those years like a runner in the heat of a long and punishing marathon, his every muscle tensed and straining, his body being pushed to its limits; and on his face a clenched and dogged look that was to become almost his sole expression over the years.

He ran as though he had put on blinders to shut out anything around him that might prove distracting, and thus cause him, if only momentarily, to break his stride. Even things that had once been important to him, that he needed, such as the music, the old blues records that had restored him at the end of the day, found themselves abandoned on the sidelines, out of his line of vision.

In the summer, by way of a vacation, they used to take the bus down to Tatem (changing to the Jim Crow seats in the rear once they reached Washington) and stay in the old house her great-aunt Cuney had left her. On their first visit, the year they were married, she had walked him over to the Landing, and standing beside the river which the Ibos had crossed on foot on their way back home, she had told him the story.

"What do you think?" she had asked him at the end, half expecting him to dismiss the whole apocryphal tale with a joke.

Instead, his gaze on the dark still floor of water, he had said quietly, "I'm with your aunt Cuney and the old woman you were named for. I believe it, Avey. Every word."

115

During their early years on Halsey Street he would look forward to the trip to Tatem each summer even more than she did. He used to say the "down-home" life of the place reminded him of Leona, Kansas, where he had been born and raised before coming to New York by way of Chicago at the age of twelve.

The yearly trip south became a thing of the past following that Tuesday in the living room. So did the trips they used to regularly make over to Harlem to see their old friends, and the occasional dance they would treat themselves to. All such was soon supplanted by the study manuals, the self-improvement books, the heavy sample case containing the vacuum cleaner. And the man Jay used to become at home, who was given to his wry jokes and banter, whose arms used to surprise her as they circled her from behind, gradually went into eclipse during the years following that near-fatal day.

Avey scarcely noticed the changes, she was kept so much on the run. Or more truthfully, she noticed them but did not dare to stop and reflect; there was no time for that kind of thing, she told herself; there was just too much else she had to do. Shortly after Marion was weaned and could toddle around on her own, she returned to her job at the Motor Vehicle Department. Mornings after Jay left for work once again found her headed down Halsey Street to the large, well-kept brownstone house belonging to the West Indian widow, Mrs. Bannister. Marion in her arms. A fractious Annawilda, demanding to be carried also, by the hand. And Sis, who was going to school by then, on her other side lugging the heavy bag containing the day's supply of bottles and diapers and baby food, along with her book satchel.

After leaving off the younger two, with Annawilda performing as usual because she wanted to go to school also, she would walk Sis over to P.S. 10 a short block away. And every morning, her finger punctuating and reinforcing the words, she would repeat the list of instructions: she was to cross the street only on the green light: "Not a foot off the sidewalk till it's green, you hear me!" and she was to go straight to Mrs. Bannister's house at lunchtime—no stopping to play, no speaking to anyone—and straight back there again at three o'clock, and . . .

"and I'm to have all my homework done—the parts I can do by myself anyway—by the time you come to pick us up at six. Right?" Sis interrupted her with a weary sigh one morning.

Avey looked down into the small face raised to hers and had to laugh. "I know. I'm getting to sound like a broken record. But just do exactly what I say anyway"—the finger like a schoolteacher's pointer. Then, in a softer vein, she reached down and straightened the wide collar of the middy blouse, tightened the ribbons on the braids and, holding out her hand for Sis to take, she led her over to where the second-graders were lining up in the yard.

The first hour or two at work was always spent recovering from the morning routine and the long, slow, rattling trip into Manhattan on the BMT El. While her hands sped over the typewriter keys, busy with the endless reports on license applications, suspensions, revocations and the like, she would sit there quietly recuperating. She was glad that what she did was just a job, something that paid her a salary while leaving her to her own thoughts most of the day. Anything else would have been too much.

That morning she thought of Sis in the schoolyard. Her little weary sigh. The expression on her upturned face. Sis's look had silently admonished her for thinking she would ever

do otherwise than she had been instructed. Solemn. She was a
solemn child. And she had grown more so since that Tuesday
night. It was as if, seeing the childish way they had behaved,
she had become the adult and assumed responsibility for them
all. Sometimes as early as five-thirty in the morning she was to
be found sitting in her bathrobe beside Jay in the living room,
keeping him company while he studied. And later, in addition to readying herself for school, she bathed and dressed
Annawilda (which was no mean feat), and afterwards packed
the bag with the bottles and other things. Some tasks, like the
dishes and helping to clean the house, were assigned her;
others she simply did. Sis. How would she manage without
her?

There would be no training that other one though! Her
fingers paused on the typewriter; she shook her head, frowning, yet also half-smiling. Annawilda with her demands and
her temper! But with her genius also. She had learned her
alphabet and numbers in no time along with Sis, and she
could easily recognize most of the words in Sis's Dick and Jane
reader from last year. But her shriek of a cry when she couldn't
have her way! Jay's voice was the only thing sometimes that
could get her to mind.

Marion? Thank goodness, she was another Sis in that she
seemed to sense the state of things from the moment she was
born and cooperated by being as little trouble as possible.
Quiet, even-tempered, well-behaved, she was the one Mrs.
Bannister liked taking care of most. Yet for all her quietness,
Avey sometimes had the impression when she held her, kissed
her, dressed her in the mornings, of her waiting almost impatiently for the baby talk to form itself into intelligible words.
Once this happened she might have more to say than Annawilda even. And the huge eyes that were Jay's would look in

118

their faces in such a way at times it seemed she had come to judge them all.

Avey laughed to herself as though to exorcise the thought, and her mind shifting, she began dreaming as usual of the day when they would be able to move from Halsey Street into a larger apartment on another block, a clean, quiet, tree-lined block with no trolley. Someplace like that might even, finally, reconcile her to living in Brooklyn! Or better yet, they might be able to rent the basement and parlor floor of a brownstone. Now that she was working again that might be possible in a few years. Mrs. Bannister's kitchen came to mind. It was practically the size of their entire apartment. With a brownstone there would be a backyard for the children in the summer, a decent bedroom for her and Jay, a third bedroom perhaps for Sis to have all to herself, a large dining room . . .

The thought of rooms, of large, warm, sunny rooms, sustained her through the long hours at the typewriter and the tedious work, through the hectic mornings and evenings and weekends, through the hardship.

In four years' time Jay completed the degree. Shortly after he easily passed the CPA examination and obtained his certification. Armed with the two he began the search for a job that would provide him with the two years' experience he needed to qualify for a license. It was to prove as fruitless as before. But this time he gave it only a year. One morning, on a Monday off from the store, instead of taking the train to Manhattan he spent the day dropping in on the small businesses and stores in their section of Brooklyn and, showing the owners his credentials, he offered to be their accountant.

Tirelessly, from that Monday on, he canvassed the beauty

parlors, barbershops and bars along Fulton Street and the main avenues, the ladies'-wear, dry goods and small jewelry stores, the larger candy and stationery stores, those selling phonograph records, liquor, groceries, the filling stations and car repair shops. And everywhere his offer was the same: he would manage their books, do their taxes, perform whatever service of a financial nature they needed for less than they were paying at present. And he would show them how to run their businesses more profitably.

Surprisingly, in spite of the merits of his offer, he was refused more often than not. Some of those he approached were suspicious of him. They didn't know quite how to take him. There he was, black as they were, with a degree and the certification in his hand, offering to do their modest books. Also, the almost frightening determination to be sensed in him made some of them uneasy.

But he persisted, steeling himself in the way that had become characteristic of him by now each time he set out. He kept at it until slowly, over the months, he began acquiring something of a clientele, mostly the smaller shops in the neighborhood. To these would be added over a time some of the larger stores and businesses, a number of doctors and dentists, and the accounts of fraternal organizations such as the Elks and the Masons, which he also thought it in his interest to join.

He had long ago given up the sales job, and there soon came the day when he was finally able, after close to twenty years, to quit the job at the department store. By the time this happened, they had already moved from Halsey Street to a larger apartment, Sis was in high school and Annawilda, who had been skipped more than one grade, was about to start.

The year 1957, twelve years after that snowy Tuesday

night, found Jay with a solid and growing clientele, his name in small print on the window of a lawyer's office where he rented desk space, and with plans in mind to expand into insurance and real estate. Halsey Street and the job where for years he had done the work of two people for the one salary were behind him. His own office on Fulton Street with his name in large gold letters on the window and the house in North White Plains lay ahead.

4

It was an act of betrayal. But although she tried she couldn't help herself. The closing for the house in North White Plains had taken place, the actual move was only weeks away, when suddenly she found herself thinking not so much of the new life awaiting them but of the early years back on Halsey Street, of the small rituals and private pleasures that had lasted through the birth of Sis. And in the face of Jay's marathon effort and her own crowded wearying days, such thoughts seemed a betrayal. A sin against the long, twelve-year struggle. She felt like a secret tippler who, when everyone in the house was asleep, sneaked down to the liquor cabinet where the memories of that earlier period were a wine she could not resist. During those final weeks in Brooklyn they were a habit she indulged on the sly.

The thoughts usually waylaid her in bed at night, during the half-hour or so when she would lie there waiting for her overtaxed body to relax enough for her to fall asleep.

Sometimes the most frivolous things from those vanished years on Halsey Street came to mind. One night, she caught herself reliving the ridiculous dances Jay used to stage just for the two of them in the living room whenever the mood struck him.

"What's your pleasure this evening, Miss Williams?"—calling her by her maiden name. "Will it be the Savoy, Rockland Palace or the Renny again?"

"Oh, I don't know," she would say, entering the fantasy with him. "Why don't we go on over to the Audubon for a change. I hear there's a dance there tonight. I'm kinda tired of those other places. And afterwards if we're hungry we can go back crosstown for chicken and waffles at Wells."

"Your wish, ma'am, is my command."

In minutes he would have the records stacked high on the turntable spindle and the three-way lamp in the room turned to low. Back at her side he would offer her his arm, and with his other hand clearing a way for them through the imaginary crowd in the make-believe ballroom he would lead her out to the center of the floor.

One by one the records would drop: "Flying Home," "Take the A-Train," "Stompin' at the Savoy," "Cottontail"—they would have to off-time to that one it was so fast. She was the better dancer, and sometimes partway through a number, he would spin her off to dance by herself, and standing aside watch her footwork and the twisting and snaking of her body with an amazed smile. Once, teasing her: "I hope you don't mind my saying it, Miss Williams, but when the white folks came up with the theory about all us darkies having rhythm, they must have had you in mind. Girl, you can out-jangle Bojangles and out-snake Snake Hips."

Those fanciful nights-out-on-the-town always ended with

123

Avery Parrish's recording of "After Hours." This they played over and over again. Jay's arms around her waist, hers circling his neck, their bodies fused and swaying, they would slow-drag in the dimly lit room to the sound of Parrish's unabashedly sensuous, crystalline musings on the piano.

"You know something, old lady, you still feel like new"— whispering it in her ear.

There also had been the small rituals that had made Sundays a special day back then, truly their day. Some nights, lying awake beside an exhausted Jay whose every muscle remained painfully tensed even as he slept (she could feel them), her thoughts would turn to that one priceless day off for them both.

Getting up early, Jay used to slip his clothes on over his pajamas and leave her in bed to walk over to Broadway to buy the papers, the coffee ring they always treated themselves to for Sunday breakfast and a hard roll for Sis when she came along and was teething.

That was the day when the phonograph in the living room remained silent. But like spirits ascending, black voices rose all morning from the secondhand Philco next to it. The Southerneers, The Fisk Jubilee Choir, Wings Over Jordan (which was her favorite of the groups), The Five Blind Boys of Atlanta, Georgia . . .

Whenever the Five Blind Boys sang "Dry Bones," Jay would join their complex harmonizing, forcing his modest baritone down to a bass: "'. . . knee bone connected to the leg bone/ leg bone connected to the ankle bone . . . Them bones, them bones, them-a dry bones,'" he sang in a deep field-holler of a voice. "'Oh, hear the word of the *L-O-R-D*. . . !'"

Sis loved it.

Later on, when Jay recited from memory fragments of poems he had learned as a boy, her eyes would all but take over her small face. He had been taught the poets in the small segregated school in Leona, Kansas, which he had attended as a boy. The schools up north didn't teach colored children anything about the race, about themselves, he used to complain.

"'. . . I bathed in the Euphrates when dawns were young . . .'" he loved to recite, standing in his pajamas in the middle of the living room, while Avey, Sis in her lap, sat listening and eating coffee cake in the armchair.

"'I built my hut by the Congo and it lulled me/to sleep. I looked upon the Nile and raised the pyramids/above it . . .'"—with a raised hand he indicated their great height, their grandeur. Then quietly: "'. . . I've known rivers:/Ancient, dusky rivers./ My soul has grown deep like the rivers.'"

He would go on then to offer them the other half-dozen or so poems he remembered from his boyhood.

"'Little brown baby wif spa'klin'/eyes . . . !'" He would burst out in dialect and, coming over, scoop Sis up in his arms. "'Come to yo' pappy an' set on his knee/. . ./Who's pappy's darlin' . . .'" he'd ask her, "'. . . an'/who's pappy's chile . . . ?'" Then: "'. . . Wisht you could allus know/ease an' cleah skies;/Wisht you could stay jes' a chile on my breas'—/Little brown baby wif spa'klin' eyes!'"

Another of his favorites—one which Sis was also to recite some years later in a Sunday school program—was about the creation of the world. Striding up and down the living room he would perform the portions he remembered with all the appropriate gestures:

"'. . . He batted His eyes, and the lightnings flashed;
He clapped His hands, and the thunders rolled;

125

And the waters above the earth came down,
The cooling waters came down . . .
And God said, "That's good . . . !" "

"The end," he would say finally. "That's it for today." And
an enthralled Sis, who, it seemed, had forgotten even to
breathe during the entire recital, would then take a deep and
wondering breath.

        ". . . oh children think about the
        good times . . ."

Best of all had been the times when it was just the two of
them, off to themselves in the narrow hallway bedroom, their
limbs in a sweet tangle on the bed.

Lying awake nights her thoughts, her aching body, would
secretly drink the heady wine of that memory.

Her pleasure had always been greatest those times when he
had talked to her. Amid the touching and play at the beginning Jay sometimes talked, telling her, his mouth with the
neat bush of hair against her ear, her cheek, and the feather-
touch of his hand on her skin, what he thought of her skin,
how the rich smooth feel of it had got all up inside him the
first time they had met and he had taken her arm to lead her
to the dance floor. Telling her also what he thought of her
breasts as his hands and lips moved slowly over them—what
they did to him—and her thighs, whose length and shapeliness excited him, he said, even when she was dressed and he
couldn't see them. This when his hand, taking its time, had
passed down the length of her body to caress them. And her
behind was Gulla gold! Treasure that belonged to him alone.
He wanted to kill the bastards who ran their thoughts over it

as she walked down the street. He spoke then, his voice a whisper, of her trim, gently bringing his hand there to touch her in the way she had taught him; her lovely, still incredibly tight trim. It stayed on his mind. "How does Mr. B. put it in the song again? '. . . killed my mammy, and ran my pappy stone-blind . . .'? It's that powerful, Avey, that strong." He teased her about what and what he was going to do when she finally permitted him in, how he was going to carry on, tear up, go out of his mind. Jay! Talking that talk until he turned her into a wanton with her nightgown bunched up around her neck like an airy boa she had donned as a fetish to feed his pleasure, or abandoned altogether on the floor beside the bed.

There was his scandalous talk, and then, when she finally drew him into her, his abrupt, awestruck silence. His stillness. He would lie within her like a man who has suddenly found himself inside a temple of some kind, and hangs back, overcome by the magnificence of the place, and sensing around him the invisible forms of the deities who reside there: Erzulie with her jewels and gossamer veils, Yemoja to whom the rivers and seas are sacred; Oya, first wife of the thunder god and herself in charge of winds and rains . . . Jay might have felt himself surrounded by a pantheon of the most ancient deities who had made their temple the tunneled darkness of his wife's flesh. And he held back, trembling a little, not knowing quite how to conduct himself in their presence.

It was her turn then. Bringing her mouth to his ear and her limbs securely around him—in command now—she led him forward. Until under her touch and the words she whispered to him—telling him what it felt like having him inside her, how he filled and completed her—his hesitancy fell away, and he was suddenly speaking again. But with his body this time. A more powerful voice. Another kind of poetry.

127

The end always took her by surprise. There would be the thick runaway beating of her heart (*"Just the beat, just the beat of my poor heart in the dark"*: Lil Green on the record they loved), the heat and her dissolving limbs. And then, without warning, a nerve somewhere in her body which had never before made itself felt would give a slight twitch, and growing stronger take over the work of the pulse at her wrists and temples and throat, and begin beating. But in a more forceful way. And in a swift chain reaction—all of it taking less than a second—the upheaval would spread to a host of other nerves and muscles, causing them to erupt also. Until pulsing together they brought to life the other heart at the base of her body.

And the miracle which was strictly a private matter, that had only to do with her, then took place. She slipped free of it all: the bed, the narrow hallway bedroom, the house, Halsey Street, her job, Jay, the children, and the child who might come of this embrace. She gave the slip to her ordinary, everyday self. And for a long pulsing moment she was pure self, being, the embodiment of pleasure, the child again riding the breakers at Coney Island in her father's arms, crowing in delight and terror. The wave she was riding crested, then dropped. But not abruptly. It was a long, slow, joyous fall which finally, when it had exhausted itself, left her beached in a sprawl of limbs on the bed, laughing wildly amid tears.

The sweetness of it!

One morning she awoke to find Jay—propped on his elbow on the pillow next to hers—gazing down at her with a smile that was both playful and amazed.

"I hope you know you carried on somethin' disgraceful last night, Miz Johnson, ma'am. *Almost had to turn on the lights and call the Law.*" He was misquoting a line from a Billy Daniels record.

She pushed him away in mock indignation, even as she fought back her laughter. "There you go getting your women mixed up again, Jay Johnson. I don't know a thing about that hussy you had in here with you last night."

Those private times in the bedroom! They had seemed inviolable. Yet, as with everything else, they gradually fell victim to the strains, to the sense of the downward slide which had brought on that Tuesday night in the living room, and to the punishing years that followed. Jay's touch increasingly became that of a man whose thoughts were elsewhere, and whose body, even while merged with hers, felt impatient to leave and join them.

Moreover, in place of the outrageous talk which she loved and needed, there was eventually only his anxious question at the beginning: "Did you remember to put in that thing . . . ?" And at the end his wrenching cry, "Take it from me, Avey! Just take it from me!"

Love like a burden he wanted rid of. Like a leg-iron which slowed him in the course he had set for himself.

Sometimes, lying there with her body left abandoned far short of the crested wave, she wanted to shove him over to his side of the bed or to hit him with her fist as he fell into a dead sleep still clinging to her. But then she would think of his shoulders collapsed from the weight of the heavy sample cases when he came in from the futile search on a Monday and of the harried, bloodshot eyes that met hers whenever he glanced up briefly from the manual or textbook he was studying, and then not only would she hold him as tightly, she would want to take to the streets with an avenging sword.

A hint of the angry, deep-throated cry she might have uttered as she rushed forth slashing and slaying like some Dahomey woman warrior of old could suddenly be heard on the balcony of the hotel room. But it was only a hint; the full, terrible sound was quickly suppressed. What little escaped was enough though to alarm the figure in the Masonic apron and gloves who had come to stand disapprovingly at the foot of the recliner earlier, his presence blocking out the sunlight and turning the day into a false night. He hastily withdrew, as if fearful that once her wrath broke it would be so vast and wide-sweeping it might reach out to include him also. In vanishing, he left behind the genuine dusk that had fallen by now, along with Avey Johnson sitting there, still struggling to press back the cry which was strange and frightening to her as well, given what she had become.

Not long after the move to North White Plains, Jay shaved off his mustache. A small thing, Avey quickly told herself as he emerged from the bathroom that morning with it gone; nothing to get upset about. Why then did the sight of that suddenly naked space above his lips fill her with such dismay, and even fear?

"Damn thing was getting to be a nuisance," was all he said by way of explanation. Then, irritably, as she continued to stare at him with the troubled, apprehensive look: "What're you looking like that for? It's just a little hair, for God's sake. You'll soon get used to me without it."

After a while it was as if he had always been clean-shaven. Nevertheless, at a deeper level, she remained unreconciled to the change, and as distressed and uneasy as she had been the first day. With the mustache no longer there it seemed that the last trace of everything that was distinctive and special about him had vanished also. Why she felt this she could not say.

Then, too—and this was what made her obscurely fearful—that thick bush above his mouth had served, she had always sensed, as a kind of protection, diverting attention from his intelligent gaze and the assertive, even arrogant flare to his nose. With it shaved off he had lost a necessary shield. He was as exposed and vulnerable suddenly as a prizefighter who had foolishly let drop his guard.

There was something even more disquieting which she slowly became aware of over the years. On occasion, glancing at him, she would surprise what almost looked like the vague, pale outline of another face superimposed on his, as in a double exposure. It was the most fleeting of impressions, something imagined rather than seen, and she always promptly dismissed it.

Nonetheless, there it was every so often, this strange pallid face, whose expression was even more severe and driven than Jay's, looming up for a subliminal moment over his familiar features.

Worse, during the same period, he began speaking in a way at times she found hard to recognize. The voice was clearly his, but the tone and, more important, the things he said were so unlike him they might have come from someone (perhaps the stranger she thought she spied now and again) who had slipped in when he wasn't looking and taken up residency behind his dark skin; someone who from the remarks he made viewed the world and his fellow man according to a harsh and joyless ethic:

"That's the trouble with half these Negroes you see out here. Always looking for the white man to give them something instead of getting out and doing for themselves . . ."

Saying this to people like Thomasina Moore and her husband, who were part of their new circle of friends.

Or: "Just look at 'em! Not a thing on their minds but cutting up and having a good time."

And again: "If it was left to me I'd close down every dancehall in Harlem and burn every drum! That's the only way these Negroes out here'll begin making any progress!"

Jay took to saying things like that. Or rather, it was Jerome Johnson who spoke. While continuing to call him Jay to his face, she gradually found herself referring to him as Jerome Johnson in her thoughts. She couldn't account for the change in any conscious way. Perhaps it was that other face she sometimes thought she detected hovering pale and shadowy over his. Or the unsparing, puritanical tone that had developed in his voice. Or the things he had taken to saying. Whatever it was, it eventually became impossible for her, even when she tried forcing herself, to *think* the name Jay. His full name, with its distant formal sound, became rooted in her mind during their last ten years together in the house in North White Plains. By the time of his death she could scarcely remember when he had been anyone other than Jerome Johnson in the privacy of her thoughts.

"Do you know who you sound like?" he had cried, starting up out of his sleep the night of his final stroke. *"Who you even look like?"* Still haunted up to the moment of his death by the memory of Halsey Street.

The day of his funeral when she was led forward, just her alone, to view the body for the last time, she had stood with her head bowed over the open top half of the coffin, giving the impression that she was gazing down at the face lying amid the wealth of shirred, cream-colored satin. But behind her widow's veil her eyes had been carefully averted. In the three days that the body had been on view she had not once fully looked at the face, afraid of what she might find there.

That final day she had simply stood, her gaze off to one side, waiting for the funeral director stationed next to her to lead her away after the proper interval. Then, just as she felt his slight pressure on her arm, signaling her that it was time, she had gathered together her courage and glanced down. And there it had been, as she had feared, staring up at her from Jerome Johnson's sealed face: that other face with the tight joyless look which she had surprised from time to time over the years. Jerome Johnson was dead, but it was still alive; in the midst of his immutable silence, the sound of its mirthless, triumphant laughter could be heard ringing through the high nave of the church.

Suddenly she had started forward, the upper half of her body lunging out until she was within inches of the laughing, thin-lipped mouth. At the same instant, her gloved hand, hidden in the folds of the dress at her side, had closed into a fist, and as it started up the first note of a colossal cry could be heard forming in her throat. The man beside her, thinking she was giving way at last to her grief, had quickly restrained her. Then, holding her firmly around the shoulders, consoling her in his professional undertone, he had led her trembling and wild-eyed behind the thick veil back to her seat.

Afterwards everyone had congratulated her on how well she had held up in the face of her great loss.

5

The lights from the surrounding balconies caught the sheen of the tears against her blackness. The tropical night resonated with the sound of her grief. For the first time in the four years since Jerome Johnson's death, she was mourning him, finally shedding the tears that had eluded her even on the day of his funeral.

Bent over almost double on the side of the recliner, Avey Johnson mourned—not his death so much, but his life.

His life: that massive unstinting giving of himself which had gone on for more than forty years.

His life: that the struggle had been so unrelenting. "When you come this color, it's uphill all the way," he would say, striking the back of one dark hand with the other—hard, punishing little blows that took his anger out on himself. Or, with even greater vehemence, out on his own: "The trouble with half these Negroes out here is that they spend all their time blaming the white man for everything. He won't give 'em a job. Won't let 'em in his schools. Won't have 'em in his neighborhood. Just won't give 'em a break. He's the one keeping 'em down. When the problem really is most of 'em don't want to hear the word 'work.' If they'd just cut out all the good-timing and get down to some hard work, put their minds to something, they'd get somewhere." Holding them solely responsible. When she reminded him of the countless times he had been refused despite all his efforts, his reply would be swift. Naive. He had been young and naive. He hadn't understood back then that it was *their* companies, *their* firms, *their* offices, *their country*, and therefore, theirs the power to give or deny, to say yes or no. Naive. But he had learned his lesson. He had come to understand one thing: That we had to have our own! "That's what most of these Negroes out here still haven't gotten through their heads. Instead of marching and protesting and running around burning down everything in the hope of a handout, we need to work and build our own, to have our own. Our own! Our own!" Shouting it at her. Lashing out periodically at her, himself, his own and at that world which had repeatedly denied him, until finally the confusion, contradiction and rage of it all sent the blood flooding his brain one night as he slept in the bed next to hers.

His life: that it had ended with a stranger's cold face laughing in Mephistophelian glee behind his in the coffin . . .

And Avey Johnson mourned Jay, sobbing wildly now, the tears raining down on her gloved hands gripping the pocketbook on her lap. This was a much larger grief, a far greater loss, and as if in recognition of this the plaintive voice of the sea in the darkness eight stories below rose up to mourn with her.

Jay's death had taken place long before Jerome Johnson's.

There had been nothing to mark his passing. No well-dressed corpse, no satin-lined coffin, no funeral wreaths and flowers. Jay had simply ceased to be. He had vanished without making his leaving known.

When had it happened? She remembered that Tuesday in the winter of '45. Just moments before he had steeled himself and stepped forward, gathering her to him, she had sensed him, hadn't she, slowly backing away from her and Sis, easing toward the door to the hall behind him, a man eager to be gone.

Perhaps he had left after all. While she had stood in the arms of the tearful man who had stepped forward, Jay might have slipped quietly out of the room, down the five flights of stairs and up Halsey Street out of their lives, leaving Jerome Johnson to do what he perhaps felt he had neither the strength nor the heart for . . .

And in leaving he had taken with him the little private rituals and pleasures, the playfulness and wit of those early years, the host of feelings and passions that had defined them in a special way back then, and the music which had been their nourishment. All these had departed with him that Tuesday night. Her tears flowing, Avey Johnson mourned them.

They were things which would have counted for little in the world's eye. To an outsider, some of them would even appear ridiculous, childish, *cullud*. Two grown people holding a pretend dance in their living room! And spending their Sunday mornings listening to gospels and reciting fragments of old poems while eating coffee cake! A ride on a Jim Crow bus each summer to visit the site of an unrecorded, uncanonized miracle!

Such things would matter little to the world. They had

nonetheless been of the utmost importance. Dimly, through the fog of her grief, Avey Johnson understood this. Not important in themselves so much as in the larger meaning they held and in the qualities which imbued them. Avey Johnson could not have spelled out just what these qualities were, although in a way that went beyond words, that spoke from the blood, she knew. Something vivid and affirming and charged with feeling had been present in the small rituals that had once shaped their lives. They had possessed qualities as transcendent as the voices on the radio each Sunday, and as joyous as their embrace could be at times in that narrow bedroom.

And they had expressed them—these simple things—in the most fundamental way! They had been as much a part of them as Jay's wing-flared nose and his seal-brown color, and her high-riding Bantu behind (Gulla gold he used to call it, his hand coming to rest there) and the deep earth tones of her skin.

Moreover (and again she only sensed this in the dimmest way), something in those small rites, an ethos they held in common, had reached back beyond her life and beyond Jay's to join them to the vast unknown lineage that had made their being possible. And this link, these connections, heard in the music and in the praisesongs of a Sunday: ". . . I bathed in the Euphrates when dawns were/young . . . ," had both protected them and put them in possession of a kind of power . . .

All this had passed from their lives without their hardly noticing. There had been no time. Their exhaustion at the end of each day had been too great. Running with the blinders on they had allowed that richness, protection and power to slip out of the living room, down the stairs and out of the house, where it had vanished, along with Jay, in the snowy wastes of Halsey Street.

"Too much!" Her sudden outcry caused the darkness on the balcony to fly up for a moment like a flock of startled birds.

"Too much!" Loud, wrenching, issuing from her very center, it was a cry designed to make up for the silence of years.

Too much! She found herself thinking suddenly of the Christmas she had spent with Sis and her family in Los Angeles the year after Jerome Johnson's death. That Christmas morning her youngest grandson, who was just turning three at the time, had sat crying amid the scores of presents he had received, all because he had not been given a toy xylophone he had fallen in love with when out shopping with her and his mother the day before. He had been promised it to keep him quiet and the matter had been forgotten. But he had remembered, and he had sat crying inconsolably next to the Christmas tree that morning and kicking from around him the shiny new tricycle and train set, the Corgi cars and the walking space man and all the rest. She had been appalled at his behavior, and had secretly accused Sis of having spoiled him. Now, three years later, on an island thousands of miles away, she found herself wanting to applaud his outburst. She understood suddenly what it must be like for a child to find itself surrounded by a wealth of Christmas toys but finding no pleasure in them because the one it wanted most wasn't there. This might be nothing more than a toy xylophone, as in her grandson's case, or one of those paper pinwheels from the five-and-dime store she had loved as a little girl, whose colored vanes would whirr into singing life when she held it up to the wind. Something that simple, yet containing all the magic in the world.

Too much! They had behaved, she and Jay, as if there had been nothing about themselves worth honoring!

Too much! Couldn't they have done differently? Hadn't there perhaps been another way? Questions which scarcely had any shape to them flooded her mind, and she struggled to give them form. Would it have been possible to have done both? That is, to have wrested, as they had done over all those years, the means needed to rescue them from Halsey Street and to see the children through, while preserving, safeguarding, treasuring those things that had come down to them over the generations, which had defined them in a particular way. The most vivid, the most valuable part of themselves! They could have done both, it suddenly seemed to her, bowed over in tears there on the hotel balcony. She and Jay could have managed both. What would it have taken? What would it have called for? The answers were as formless as the questions inundating her mind. They swept through her in the same bewildering flood of disconnected words and images. All of it the bursting forth of a river that had long been dammed up. Awareness. It would have called for an awareness of the worth of what they possessed. Vigilance. The vigilance needed to safeguard it. To hold it like a jewel high out of the envious reach of those who would either destroy it or claim it as their own. And strength. It would have taken strength on their part, and the will and even cunning necessary to withstand the glitter and the excess. To take only what was needed and to run. And distance. Above all, a certain distance of the mind and heart had been absolutely essential. "*. . . Her body she always usta say might be in Tatem, but her mind, her mind was long gone with the Ibos . . .*"

Too much! What kind of bargain had they struck? How

much had they foolishly handed over in exchange for the things they had gained?—an exchange they could have avoided altogether had they been on their guard!

Too much! ". . . the trouble with *these* Negroes out here . . ."; ". . . that's the only way *these* Negroes around here will ever begin to make any progress . . ." Speaking of his own in the harsh voice that treated them as a race apart. She used to wince in the beginning hearing him, and she had even objected on occasion. But had she been any better? Hadn't she lived through most of the sixties and the early seventies as if Watts and Selma and the tanks and Stoner guns in the streets of Detroit somehow did not pertain to her, denying her rage, and carefully effacing any dream that might have come to her during the night by the time she awoke the next morning. Years!—she had spent nearly a decade avoiding the headlines and pictures on the front pages of the newspapers and the nightly television newscasts. There was the time Marion had telephoned her collect from the Poor People's March in Washington, and she had almost refused to accept the call she had been so annoyed. Why? Because in the second or two between the time the operator asked if she would accept the charges and her reply, she seemed to hear in the background the great hungry roar of the thousands encamped in the mud near the Lincoln Memorial, the sound reaching out to draw her into its angry vortex, to make her part of their petition. And not only that. She had also seen, in a sudden vivid flash, the poor half-crazed woman from Halsey Street, who would sometimes, it seemed, herding the man home from the bars of a Saturday morning, make the five-story leap to their bedroom. And there, standing over her in the bed would berate her in one breath for the superior airs she gave herself ("I see you lookin' the other way when you pass by . . ."), and in the next breath, plead with her to be remembered. Marion's call had brought the woman vividly to mind. What had happened to her and her children? Where were they today? Unsettling thoughts that had made her so annoyed with Marion and her Poor People's March she had wanted to refuse her call.

"What's she doing down there anyway?" Jerome Johnson had wanted to know afterwards. (He and Marion hardly spoke to each other.) "When did she ever have to go without three square meals a day?"

Too much! They were getting to look, even to sound alike, their friends had started teasing them. As often happens when two people have been married a long time, she and Jerome Johnson, their friends insisted, had grown to resemble each other—the same little mannerisms, the same facial expression almost, the rather formal way they held themselves. They could almost pass for twins!

Too much! "Jerome Johnson," she had taken to calling him in the privacy of her thoughts, no longer able to think of him as "Jay." But hadn't she, in the same formal way, also started referring to herself as Avey Johnson? Hadn't she found it increasingly difficult as the years passed to think of herself as "Avey" or even "Avatara"? The woman to whom those names belonged had gone away, had been banished along with her feelings and passions to some far-off place—not unlike the old Eskimo woman in the strange recurring vision that had troubled her for a time after that trip to the Laurentians, who had been cast out to await her death alone in the snow. The names "Avey" and "Avatara" were those of someone who was no longer present, and she had become Avey Johnson even in her thoughts, a woman whose face, reflected in a window or mirror, she sometimes failed to recognize.

Too much! At her funeral, when Sis and Annawilda and

Marion were led forward to view her body for the last time, they might sense, they might even glimpse, gazing down at her, the pale outline of another face superimposed on hers like a second skin, a thin-lipped stranger's face, alive and mocking. And to their further puzzlement, to their horror, they might hear, echoing above them in the church, the sound of someone laughing in cold glee . . .

Suddenly, with a cry that again startled the darkness holding the wake with her on the balcony, Avey Johnson was lunging out. It was the same abrupt and threatening movement that had sent her surging forward over Jerome Johnson's bier that day in the church. This time, though, there was no one to restrain her, so that the moment she sprang forward still seated on the edge of the recliner, her gloved fist came up, and she struck the wall of air just in front of her. Over and over, in a rage of tears, she assaulted the dark and empty air, trying with each blow to get at the derisive face she saw projected there. Her own face was tear-streaked and distorted in the light reaching it from the surrounding balconies, and she could be heard uttering the same murderous, growl-like sound as on the Lido yesterday, when she had snatched her skirt and fled from the skeletal old man in the bikini.

Repeatedly she sent her fist smashing out. Her hat slid to a crazy angle over her ear from the force of her blows. The constant lunging out soon sent the pocketbook on her lap crashing to the floor, where its contents came spilling out as the catch sprung open. Eventually, the violence of her blows brought her sliding off the edge of the chair and down to the floor on her knees. And still she continued to pound away at the face she alone could see, bathed in furious tears, growling, repeating her angry litany: *"Too much!"*

Finally, all the strength went out of her, and still on her

knees, she slumped forward until her forehead was almost touching the floor. She remained like this—prostrate before the darkness, a backslider on the threshing floor, at the mourner's bench. *"Come/Won't you come . . . ?"* her great-aunt had pleaded silently with her in the dream. *"Come/Will you come . . . ?"*

What lights there had been were all but extinguished by the time Avey Johnson finally struggled to her feet. Slowly, her pocketbook forgotten, she groped her way across the darkened balcony toward the sliding glass door to the room, suddenly a feeble old woman with a painful lower back and stiff noisy joints, muttering incoherently to herself: "Too much . . . !" Time might have played a trick on her while she was on the balcony, and brought her to the senile end of her days in the space of a few hours. The years telescoping, she might have lived out the rest of her life in a single evening.

Inside, she didn't bother to search for the light switch. She had no wish to encounter herself in one of the mirrors there. It was bad enough to feel in her bones the old woman she had become hobbling off to her grave. Nor did she bother to undress once she felt her way across the unfamiliar room to the bed.

When was the last time she had slept in her clothes? It came to her almost immediately, her life passing in swift review, her mind leapfrogging back over the years.

It had been a New Year's Eve not long after they had moved to Halsey Street, just months before Jay went in the army. They had gone with friends to a dance at the Renny; and afterwards, nearing dawn, their group had stopped off at Dickie Wells for the ritual chicken and waffles. Given the hour, their friends had urged them to sleep over. Or they could have gone and stayed with her mother, who still lived in the apartment on Seventh Avenue where Avey had been born.

But she and Jay had wanted to usher in the new year in their own bed, so that sunrise had found them taking the long train ride to Brooklyn. By the time they reached Halsey Street and climbed the five flights of stairs, it had been all they could do just to pull off their coats, toss aside their gloves and shoes and turn on the kerosene burner they kept in the room before falling exhausted across the bed.

That afternoon when they awakened she had started to undress, only to have Jay stop her. He had done it himself, slowly removing each piece of her clothing and laying it on a nearby chair, his hands and lips caressing each new place he bared before continuing; talking his talk. Leaving her briefly he slipped across the room to swing open the closet door with the full-length mirror on the inside and to turn up the burner; then, hurrying back, he resumed the undressing.

He removed everything that day except her party hat, a conical affair held on by a thin elastic band under her chin, and with the year, 1941, printed in iridescent numbers across the front; a magical Merlin's hat which she had worn at a rakish angle all evening.

It was not to remain there long. In their playfulness at the beginning, they heard the elastic band give a snap, and laughing watched the hat tumble from the bed and roll across the floor until it came to rest with the peak pointing to the reflection of their tangled bodies in the mirror . . .

Avey Johnson shucked the gloves off her hands with such violence the fingers turned inside out. The hat slanted to one side on her head found itself being hurled into the nether darkness of a corner. The plush carpeting failed to completely muffle the thud of the shoes she flung down one after the other. With the last of her strength she reached under her dress and, fumbling, unhooked the long-line girdle. (Her hair-shirt Marion insisted on calling it.) That was all she could manage before collapsing onto the bed.

"*Too much! Too much! Too much!*" Raging as she slept.

III

LAVÉ TÊTE

Papa Legba, ouvri barrière pou' mwê.
  —*Vodun Introit, Haiti*

Oh, Bars of my . . . body, open, open!
  —*Randall Jarrell*

1

In the final turn of her sleep she smelled it. An odor faint but familiar. Somewhere a baby needed changing. It hadn't soiled itself or even wet the diaper, but it was summer—New York summer with its sodden heat—and it had been left lying in the same cotton kimono for too long. The cloth had absorbed the perspiration with its slight odor of curdled milk, as well as the staleness of the Johnson's Baby Powder caked in the creases of baby fat, and had begun to smell. It needed to be stripped, given a sponge off, then patted dry, oiled and freshly powdered. And afterwards clothed only in a diaper. A diaper alone would do in this heat. The crib sheet needed to be changed.

Gently, so as not to awaken him, she removed Jay's arm from around her. He had been up late the night before poring over the manuals and would rise at dawn to study again, as was his habit, before leaving for work. Still almost as soundly asleep as he was, she sat up on the side of the bed, felt for her slippers on the floor and reached blindly in the darkness for her robe hanging on the bedpost. For a moment, after drawing the light seersucker material around her, she sat with her face bowed in her hands, waiting for her head to clear. Behind her she heard Jay roll over in his sleep to bury his face in her pillow. She would lie in his place when she returned.

On her feet finally, she held out a hand to guide her and reluctantly began the long trek (it only seemed long at night) from their small bedroom above the noisy trolley to the children's room at the back of the apartment.

Which of them was it this time? Annawilda probably. She was a child who perspired even in winter. Damp, roly-poly Annawilda, who in her greediness would continue to nurse— her small mouth fastened like a leech on the breast—until she broke out in a sweat and began to spit up. Avey sighed: Annawilda was a trial.

She easily made it halfway through the adjoining living room, feeling her way along the wall where the phonograph stood. She was just about to skirt the machine and head toward the passageway leading to the back bedroom when she was brought to a jarring halt, as someone suddenly turned on all the lights in the room, including even the overly bright ceiling light that was seldom used, and she came awake with a start.

The lights were nothing less than the seven-o'clock sun which had just climbed to the level of the balcony. Poised atop the railing, it appeared to be staring round-eyed with shock at the sight of Avey Johnson lying fully dressed on the still-made bed. The baby smell was nothing more than the staleness of her own flesh in the slept-in clothes. Coming in last night, she had neglected to close the sliding glass door,

and the tropical heat, entering with her, had easily over-
powered the air conditioner and turned the room into a sweat-
box while she slept.

There, directly across from the bed, stood the gaping door.
Beyond it, lying outside under the shocked eye of the sun, was
the pocketbook she had forgotten, with its contents—wallet,
passport, cosmetics bag, sunglasses and the rest—spilled out
around it on the floor.

With her head on the soaked pillow turned toward the
balcony, Avey Johnson stared across at the pocketbook, the
sleep lines still on her face, and a curiously blank expression in
her eyes. She might not have remembered how it had gotten
there, or even recognized that it belonged to her. The same
was true when her gaze drifted back into the room and encountered her hat in the corner and her gloves and shoes
strewn angrily on the floor beside the bed. Nothing crossed
her drawn, spent face or stirred in her eyes. It was as if a saving
numbness had filtered down over her mind while she slept to
spare her the aftershock of the ordeal she had undergone last
evening. Or that her mind, like her pocketbook outside, had
been emptied of the contents of the past thirty years during
the night, so that she had awakened with it like a slate that
had been wiped clean, a *tabula rasa* upon which a whole new
history could be written.

She bestirred herself finally and, first sitting up on the edge
of the bed and then rising unsteadily to her feet, began taking
off the stale, rumpled clothes. Each piece proved a struggle.
She was as slow and clumsy as a two-year-old just learning
how to undress itself as she wrestled with the jacket and dress
to the ensemble and peeled the underclothes and stockings
from her still-perspiring flesh. The sodden girdle came last and
after stripping it away she stood for a moment gazing vacantly

151

down at her breasts. At the stretch lines like claw marks. At the scar where the small benign tumor had been removed when she was in her forties. At the bruised-looking nipples. Annawilda. A thought stirred in the emptiness: It had actually seemed that she was on her way to the back bedroom in the dream just now. Back on Halsey Street. And hadn't she struck her great-aunt Cuney on the breasts that were as fallen as hers had become in the other dream, her fist coming down repeatedly . . . ?

She brought her arms up to cover herself. A robe and a clean set of clothes. Slowly, uncertain on her feet, she started toward the suitcases near the closet where the bellman had placed them yesterday. And then a long shower. And afterwards . . . She could think ahead no further.

Two hours later found her standing down on the beach in front of the hotel, looking up at the building as if she had never seen it before. She was wearing flat-heeled shoes and a pink linen shirtdress which she had chosen haphazardly from the first bag she opened and put on without even bothering to iron out the creases. Her hair was half combed. She was without even a little face powder. Her watch, which she never failed to put on after showering in the mornings, had been left on the vanity in the bathroom.

She had wandered outdoors from the dining room where, in the same awkward manner she had gone about everything since waking up, she had eaten breakfast. It was the first meal she had had since the dinner she had picked over after leaving the sanctuary of the library two days ago.

On her way out to the beach afterwards she had passed through the lobby, and the desk clerk, who had been on duty yesterday, had called her name. He was forced to repeat it several times. When she did finally pause and turn his way, the man's shock at her appearance was obvious: Could this be the same well-dressed black woman with the half-dozen suitcases who had arrived the day before?

"Just thought I'd remind you that your flight's this afternoon at four."

She had nodded absently and continued toward the door.

Now, with the same absent air, she bypassed the lounge chairs out in front of the hotel where a few guests could be seen reclining and began walking up the beach. Aside from her shoes, she was ill-prepared to go on a walk. Her head was uncovered and she had not even brought along her sunglasses to protect her from the glare. They were in the pocketbook which she had retrieved, along with its contents, from the balcony and then tossed carelessly on the bed. She had walked out leaving it there, with only the "Do Not Disturb" sign on the doorknob as a safeguard.

On setting out she had turned without being conscious of it toward that section of the beach where there were no hotels as yet, and the magnificent shoreline which called to mind a huge stage stood intact. It was completely deserted as far up as the eye could reach.

To her right, down from where she was walking on the tree-shaded upper level of the beach, lay the wide, flawless apron of sand. Not a footprint was to be seen. At the bottom of the slight incline the low-breaking waves foamed up and withdrew with scarcely a sound. The bay, as far as the horizon, was a glittering amethystine blue under the nine-o'clock sun.

To her left, just beside her, stretched an endless wall of coconut palms, with here and there tall stands of bamboo giving off their incredible light and an occasional almond tree. Just above the treeline hung the bluff along which she had traveled in the taxi yesterday. Above this rose the hills,

153

and with no hotels to dwarf them on this length of beach, they stood in command of the landscape. Highest of all was the sunlit bandshell of the sky.

Avey Johnson drifted aimlessly along, indifferent to her surroundings, unaware of the distance she was covering, simply moving through the soundless air and the transcendent morning light. Behind her the long column of hotels that had overrun the southern half of the beach steadily receded. By the time she had gone close to a mile they had not only shrunk dramatically, they had become, for all their solid concrete, stone and glass, as insubstantial as mirages created by the tremulous light and air and the distant haze. Finally they disappeared behind a sudden outthrust in the line of trees.

All to be seen were two or three crude shelters of thatch set at wide intervals over the expanse of beach. Built down near the water as a shade perhaps for the local people when they came to swim or as an on-the-spot market for fishermen, the shelters consisted simply of a circle of poles supporting a roof of palm thatch that resembled a coolie hat.

Each one Avey Johnson passed was deserted.

She had not seen the hotels vanish behind her, but as if she had sensed their disappearance, a change came over her. Slowly she felt the caul over her mind lifting and she began looking around her.

With a child's curiosity and awe Avey Johnson surveyed the familiar elements which made up the still-life of the beach— sand, sea, trees and overarching sky—as if she were seeing their like for the first time. As accustomed as she had grown to the sight of palm trees from the yearly cruise, she was suddenly stopping every few minutes to gaze up at the fronds clashing and parrying in the wind. The saucer-shaped leaves of the almond trees—a lacquered green on top and dark gold beneath—came in for a lengthy inspection. The Christmas red of a flamboyant emblazoned on a hill above the bluff held her rapt and questioning gaze.

Abandoning the shade of the trees, she descended the sloping bed of sand and for almost an hour continued her desultory stroll alongside the surf. She was unaware of the blazing sun, so absorbed did she become in the small marine life and non-life to be found near the water. The sandcrabs scuttling in and out of their holes, the shells and coral scattered about, the occasional sandpiper goosestepping quickly out of the way as a wave broke, all came in for a close examination, repeatedly evoking the look of wonder and awe as she steadily, without realizing it, drifted farther and farther up the beach.

For long minutes she remained bent over a dead, rainbow-colored fish the ebbing tide had left behind. Unmindful of the stench, the bottle-green flies and the mid-morning sun bearing down on her, she hung over the fish as if it weren't dead (how could it be with those colors and that clear direct gaze?) but simply lying there quietly waiting for the tide to rise and send the waves washing over it again. It would rouse itself then, chase the flies swarming over it with a slap of its tail and swim away.

As she raised up from over the fish, she suddenly felt dizzy, and dark spots whirled up like cinders before her eyes. She was aware then not only of the sun beating down on her bare head, but of the hot sand under her feet, the perspiration pouring off her, and her fatigue.

Quickly she turned to start back up to the shelter of the trees, only to discover as she looked in their direction that they were no longer there. During her long walk near the foot of the beach, the coconut palms had given way to a series of low sandhills that could be seen reaching back almost as far as the half mile and more she had covered in that time.

She looked around her in alarm. The hotel? It too had vanished. How far had she come? What time was it? Her flight that afternoon? Where was some shade? She could easily pass out in this heat . . .

She remembered then the makeshift shelters she had passed earlier. She had scarcely noticed them before. Now, a hand shading her eyes, she anxiously searched down the coast for the last one she had passed. She made it out finally through the glare-filled light: a small, dark, mushroom shape that appeared to be as far away as the last of the trees.

Suddenly, no longer aware in her panic of what she was doing, she swung toward the line of sandhills once more, took a step in their direction and stopped. The next moment, quickly turning to her left, she made as if to head back over the long stretch she had come, and faltered. With the same confused movement she spun around again, this time toward that part of the shore which lay ahead; and there, about two hundred yards away, near a jumbled wall of rocks that brought the beach to an end, stood another of the round, thatch-roofed shelters.

For a moment she held back, distrusting her eyes: it might be nothing more than an illusion created by the moving curtain of heat and the dizziness that had come over her. The next moment, with a surge of relief she was hurrying toward it, keeping to the line of surf where the sand was less hot underfoot.

The shelter, she discovered when she was perhaps halfway there, was a larger, more substantial affair than the others she had passed. This one was walled in under its wide, flattened cone of a roof. It was a building rather than just a hastily thrown-up refuge from the sun. Perhaps someone even lived there. She might be able to sit for a while and be offered a glass of water. The thought spurred her ahead.

Just beyond the building, the outcropping of rock which ended the beach trailed out into the water for some distance to form a natural jetty. From there came the playful ring of children's voices. Glancing in the direction of the sound, Avey Johnson made out a group of little boys who were diving repeatedly off the rocks into the deep water at the end. The faint breeze brought their shouts and whooping cries as they flung themselves, black arms and legs spread-eagle against the sky for a moment, into the sea. They must have come from the small fishing village up the coast, whose sun-bleached roofs of tin and strung nets could be glimpsed above the rock wall.

They were the first people she had encountered, theirs the first human voices she had heard since leaving the hotel.

By the time she neared the odd-shaped building, her head was spinning and she was staggering from exhaustion and the heat. She feared she would never manage the few yards she still had to go. There was a sign on the front of the building, but in the state she was in she failed to notice it. All she was conscious of as she finally dragged herself to the entrance was that the door stood slightly ajar, and that through the opening there came a cool dark current of air like a hand extended in welcome. And without her having anything to do with it, it seemed, before she could even knock or find the voice to ask if anyone was there, the hand reached out and drew her in.

2

She found herself in a bar, or what she had learned was called a rum shop in the islands. Dimly visible in the sunlight that entered with her as she pushed open the door and stood hesitantly peering in were three or four roughhewn wooden tables and chairs set out on a dirt floor and the glint of a few bottles on a shelf halfway across the room. There appeared to be no one around.

One of the tables and its rickety chairs stood within just feet of the doorway, and with her legs about to give way under her, Avey Johnson stumbled over to it and sank down. Bringing her elbows to rest on the table, she buried her throbbing forehead in her hands and closed her eyes.

For a long while, as if she were still out in the sun, her head continued to spin and the blood kept up the pounding at her temples. But gradually, in the midst of the vertigo, she became aware of the cool dark current of air that had met her at the door. She felt it come to rest, like a soothing hand on her head, and it remained there, gently drawing away the heat and slowing down both her pulse and the whirling ring of harsh light behind her closed eyes. Finally, under its calming touch, the dizziness subsided enough for her to raise up and look around her.

Aside from the few tables and chairs there was not much else to be seen in the place. Midway across the room stood a scarred, worm-eaten counter, a gas lamp on top of it at one end and at the other a small cluster of jiggers and water glasses turned down on a tray. Where was the person who ran the place so that she might ask for a glass of water? A number of shelves behind the counter were bare except for a half-dozen small bottles of white rum. Behind the shelves a partition of palm leaves leaning upright against some sort of a support blocked off the other half of the room.

After this there was only the circular wall, which appeared to be made simply of mud plastered over a framework of woven sticks. The mud, long dry, had crumbled away in a number of places, creating small openings through which the sunlight entered freely.

The rum shop was seedy, run-down, stripped almost bare, yet somehow pleasant. The dirt floor under Avey Johnson's feet felt as hard and smooth as terrazzo, and as cool. The chinks in the earthen wall allowed thin rays of the sun to penetrate but barred its heat and glare. The sunlight, mixing with the shadows filtering down from the thatch roof, gave the place the hushed tone of a temple or church. Through the open door could be heard the faint shouts of the children diving off the jetty: a lyric sound in the silence.

"Hello, is there anyone around . . . ?" Her parched throat could scarcely manage the words.

She was about to call out again when a voice, sharp, thin, hoarse with age, came from behind the partition. "The place is closed, oui."

Moments later a stoop-shouldered old man with one leg shorter than the other limped from behind the screen of leaves, advanced as far as the counter and stood there peering irritably across at her. He was dressed in a tieless long-sleeved white shirt frayed at the collar and cuffs and a pair of shapeless black pants without a belt that were more a rusty brown than black. He was holding the jacket to the pants in his hands along with a needle and thread. He had apparently been quietly mending behind the partition while she had been sitting there.

"Is closed!" he repeated, and made to shoo her away with the jacket.

The thought of being driven back out into the sun after having only just escaped it caused Avey Johnson's head to start throbbing again. At the same time the man's rudeness provoked a child-like stubbornness in her, so that she found herself reaching down to grip the sides of her chair, ready to resist him, as he suddenly tossed the jacket onto the counter and started rapidly toward her on his uneven legs.

"You ain' hear me say the place is closed?" From where he was standing now, directly across the table, he appeared to be no more than five feet two or three inches tall.

"Yes, but is it all right if I just sit here for a few minutes anyway?" Her voice was as testy as his. "I won't trouble you for anything . . ." (The glass of water? She wouldn't even ask him for that.) "It's just that I walked all the way from my hotel at the other end of the beach and need to rest out of the sun for a while before starting back. I won't be long."

There was no indication that the man had heard her or, for

that matter, that he had even seen her—really seen her—as yet. Because although his dimmed gaze was bent on her face and he was looking at her, it clearly hadn't registered with him that she was a stranger.

"I'll just be a few minutes."

He said nothing, only stood there. He was close to ninety perhaps, his eyes as shadowed as the light in the rum shop and the lines etched over his face like the scarification marks of a thousand tribes. His slight, winnowed frame scarcely seemed able to support the clothes he had on. Yet he had crossed the room just now with a forced vigor that denied both his age and infirmity. And his hands, large, tough-skinned, sinewy, looked powerful enough to pick up Avey Johnson still clinging to the chair and deposit her outside.

He was one of those old people who give the impression of having undergone a lifetime trial by fire which they somehow managed to turn to their own good in the end; using the fire to burn away everything in them that could possibly decay, everything mortal. So that what remains finally are only their cast-iron hearts, the few muscles and bones tempered to the consistency of steel needed to move them about, the black skin annealed long ago by the sun's blaze and thus impervious to all other fires; and hidden deep within, out of harm's way, the indestructible will: old people who have the essentials to go on forever.

"Sit, then!" He spoke at last. "But the minute I finish putting on my clothes, anybody that's still here gon' be marched to the door and the door locked on them."

He swung around, and the disjointed up-and-down walk that was almost comical bore him quickly back across the room. Disagreeable old man! As if she were a schoolgirl again and he a teacher she disliked, Avey Johnson almost felt like

161

making a face at his retreating figure. Let him go on back behind the partition and stay there until she was rested enough to leave!

But as the man reached the counter with the turned-down glasses and the lamp he suddenly stopped and stood thoughtfully in the fretwork of sunlight and shadows that gave the place its special ambience, his head bowed and his weight resting on his left leg, the shorter of the two.

After remaining there for a time he slowly turned and made his way back to the table.

"Any other day you could sit as long as you wanted, oui," he said. His voice had softened, his look was less harsh, but his eyes still had not yet taken in who she was. "But everybody knows that come this time of the year the place is closed. The excursion, oui!" he cried at her vacant look. "I's closed for the excursion."

"Come time for the excursion they close down everything and they gone!" The taxi driver's voice came to her faintly over the gulf that had opened in her mind since last night.

"There was this crowd . . . on the wharf yesterday . . ." (had it been only yesterday? it seemed an entire lifetime ago!). "They were going on an excursion to . . ." Her speech was slow, halting; she had to search for the words in the emptiness.

"Is the same!" the man interrupted her impatiently. "Some went yesterday. The rest going today."

". . . to someplace, some island . . . I forget the name."

"Carriacou!" he declared, and drew himself up sharply on his longer leg; he looked tall enough suddenly to reach up and touch the roof of thatch. "The name of the island is Carriacou!"

"Yes, that sounds like what he said . . ." Out-islanders. He had called them out-islanders. "And you're from there . . . ?"

"How you mean?" he cried indignantly. "Where else I could be from with the name Joseph? You din' see the sign outside the door when you came in: 'Rock Haven Bar. Lebert Joseph, Proprietor?' Well, that's me. I's a Joseph, oui!"—it was said with the same pride that had lifted him high onto his right leg just now. "From Ti Morne, Carriacou. The oldest one still living from that part of the island, if you please. Near everybody in Ti Morne is family to me. They all got to call me father or uncle or grandfather, granduncle or great-grand-father or cousin or something. I's also family—close family— to the Josephs at Plaisance and Bushnell and Friar Village, Carriacou. As well as those living in Maribel and up Green Hill. And I's a far-distant relation to the ones at Spring Hole and Meridien over to the other side of the island. As for that crowd of Josephs living out at Walker's Bay, they all got to call me . . ."

Avey Johnson stared dumbfounded at the man. Only min-utes ago he had scarcely had a civil word to say to her; he had been all set to throw her out of the place. Now, in a sudden turnabout, he was telling her his family history, going on like some Old Testament prophet chronicling the lineage of his tribe. Why didn't he go on back to his living quarters behind the screen of leaves! His cracked, hoarse old man's voice only added to her thirst. And the rush of words she could barely follow made her feel all the more dazed and confused.

". . . And another thing: Near all the Josephs you meet here in Grenada is family to me too. All is Carriacou people. Just because we live over this side don' mean we's from this place, you know. Even when we's born here we remain Car-

163

riacou people. And I don' mean just the Josephs now but every Carriacouan you see 'bout here. And come time for the excursion we gone! Everybody together. We don' miss a year. Take me. I been on this beach running this shop for more years than you can count, but I has yet to miss an excursion. Even when I had to get up from a sickbed to go, I was there."

He paused finally and stood waiting for her to speak. She didn't know what to say. But if she remained silent he might become annoyed and order her to leave again, so that, snatching at the first thing that came to mind, she asked him if there was a special reason for the excursion.

"How you mean if there's a special reason?" he spoke incredulously, his eyes—the whites a stained tobacco brown against his blackness—stretched wide. "It have many 'special' reasons!"—all of which she should have known, his tone implied. "Family for one. A man lives in this place all year he must go look for his family. His old father and mother if they's still in life, and the rest of his people. Sometime he has a wife or a woman who has children for him back in Carriacou. He must go look for them. He's sure to have a piece of ground there he has to see to. Or he might be building a house for when he goes home for good, or a schooner—thinking to get into the trade—and he must tend to that. It have many 'special' reasons," repeating it irritably as if she were someone from the fishing village next door who had come barging in on the wrong day to ask him questions she ought to have known the answers to.

Then, in another abrupt change of mood, he said conversationally, "And a man goes to relax hisself. To bathe in Carriacou water and visit 'bout with friends. And to fete—dance, drink rum, run 'bout after women"—this with a roguish smile that revealed the few broken teeth he had left. "A little sport, oui. The excursion ain' all business.

"But it have another reason." He spoke after a long pause and the smile had vanished. "Is the Old Parents, oui," he said solemnly. "The Long-time People. Each year this time they does look for us to come and give them their remembrance.

"I tell you, you best remember them!" he cried, fixing Avey Johnson with a gaze that was slowly turning inward. "If not they'll get vex and cause you nothing but trouble. They can turn your life around in a minute, you know. All of a sudden everything start gon' wrong and you don' know the reason. You can't figger it out all you try. Is the Old Parents, oui. They's vex with you over something. Oh, they can be disagreeable, you see them there. Is their age, oui, and the lot of suffering they had to put up with in their day. We has to understand and try our best to please them . . .

"That's why," he continued humbly, "the first thing I do the minute I reach home is to roast an ear of corn just pick out from the ground and put it on a plate for them. And next to the plate I puts a lighted candle. Everybody does the same. Next thing I sprinkles a little rum outside the house. They likes that. And every year God send I holds a Big Drum for them.

"And who's the first one down on his knees then singing the 'Beg Pardon'? Who?" he cried, and immediately answered himself by shifting his weight to his shorter leg so that he appeared to drop all of a sudden to his knees. And as suddenly he began singing in a quavering, high-pitched voice, his eyes transfixed, "'Pa'doné mwê/Si mwê merité/Pini mwê . . .'" His arms opened wide in a gesture of supplication: "'Si mwê merité/Pa'doné mwê . . .'"

She felt the dizziness coming on again. The man's garrulousness, the bizarre turn his talk had taken (what was this voodoo about lighted candles, old parents, big drums and the rest?) and now his shrill, unintelligible song, all had the same effect as the sun beating down on her head. She longed for the silence that had filled the room before his appearance and the feel of the cool dark air on her head.

" '*Pa'doné mwê!*' " The song ended. His abbreviated arms with the powerful hands at the ends fell slowly to his side. He shifted back to his good leg, appeared to rise. "Down on my knees, oui, at the Big Drum, begging their pardon for whatever wrongs I might have done them unbeknownst during the year," he said, his gaze slowly returning from wherever it had gone. "Humph, you best beg them, if not they'll get vex and spoil up your life in a minute. They's not so nice, you see them there. And when it comes time at the Big Drum to dance their nation for them, I tries my best, never mind I'm scarce able with these hill-and-ditchy legs I got. The Old Parents! The Long-time People!" There was both fondness and dread in his voice. "We must give them their remembrance."

Then with the pride again—and this time it almost brought his bent shoulders straight: "I's a Chamba! From my father's side of the family. They was all Chambas. My mother now was a Manding and when they dance her nation I does a turn or two out in the ring so she won't feel I'm slighting her. But I must salute the Chambas first."

Suddenly he was leaning across the table, his unsettling eyes just inches from Avey Johnson's. "And what you is?"

His face was a dizzying blur. His smell a mix of old flesh, seldom worn clothes and his yeasty breath. She pulled back sharply and for a moment, overwhelmed, had to close her eyes.

"What's your nation?" he asked her, his manner curious, interested, even friendly all of a sudden. "Arada . . . ? Is you an Arada?" He waited. "Cromanti maybe . . . ?" And he again waited. "Yarraba then . . . ? Moko . . . ?"

On and on he recited the list of names, pausing after each one to give her time to answer.

"Temne . . . ? Is you a Temne maybe? Banda . . . ?"

What was the man going on about? What were these names? Each one made her head ache all the more. She thought she heard in them the faint rattle of the necklace of cowrie shells and amber Marion always wore. Africa? Did they have something to do with Africa? Senile. The man was se- nile. The minds of the old . . .

She darted a frightened glance toward the door: she might be safer out in the sun.

"Manding . . . ? Is you a Manding like my mother, maybe? The Long-foot people we calls them . . .

"Wait!"—a smile began to work its way through the maze of lines around his mouth—"don' tell me you's a Chamba like myself . . . ?"

He waited, the smile slowly emerging, his arms in the frayed shirt poised to open in a fraternal embrace.

Avey Johnson was shaking her head back and forth as if trying to clear it of the sound of his voice. "I . . . I don't know what you're talking about . . . what you're asking me . . ."

"I's asking if you's a Temne, Moko, Arada or what!" He had lost patience with her again.

"I'm a visitor, a tourist, just someone here for the day," she said lamely. "I was on the cruise ship that came in yesterday. I . . . I left it intending to fly home right away, but I missed the plane yesterday and had to stay over . . . I'm leaving this afternoon."

Then, as the man maintained his irritated silence: "I'm afraid you've mistaken me for someone from around here, or from one of the other islands . . . who might know what you're talking about. I'm from the States. New York . . ." And she repeated it, "New York."

He gave a sharp, disparaging wave of the hand. Nevertheless, the magical name had its effect: his eyes came into focus. For the first time since he had planted himself across the table from her, the man was actually looking at her, actually registering the fact that she was a stranger and not just one of the local folk who had wandered in on the wrong day.

Frowning, wary suddenly, he examined in quick succession her face, her chemically straightened hair, the expensive linen shirtdress, the cobalt brilliance of the rings on her left hand. His eyes lingered for a long time on the rings, becoming strangely fearful, and then they closed.

There was a chair next to him at the table, and blindly pulling it out, he sank down and lowered his head.

"I has grands and great-grands born in that place I has never seen!" It was a bitter outburst. "Josephs who has never gone on the excursion! Who has never been to a Big Drum! Who don' know nothing 'bout the nation dance!"

He fell silent, but the angry bereavement in his voice hung on in the room, troubling the air and darkening the almost sacred light that filled the place.

Avey Johnson gazed at the slumped figure across from her and was at a loss as to how to take the sudden sadness that had come over him. The man swung constantly from one mood to another. He might any second now raise up and start laughing or singing or declaiming. And why had he looked at her like that just now? She had wanted to hide her left hand under the table . . .

168

In the silence the faint shouts of the children playing out on the rocks could be heard again at the open door. She had forgotten them. They sounded undaunted by the sun. Could she perhaps risk venturing out in it? She might just be able to make it down to where the trees began . . .

"I think I'll be leaving now."

The man gave no sign of having heard her. Doubled over at the edge of the table, he continued to grieve and silently rage over the loss of the grandchildren and great-grandchildren he had never seen.

She tried again. "I really must leave. Try to get back to the hotel. My plane's this afternoon at four . . ."

Easing her chair back on the dirt floor, she slowly rose to her feet. "I appreciate your letting me sit here. I never would have made it if I had had to start back down the beach right away. Not with that sun and the way I was feeling. I'll be all right now, though. Thanks so much . . ."

He failed to stir, and she stood there waiting, unable to leave without some sign from him. Now that she was standing, he looked even more bowed and saddened, more bereft. The hands that had looked capable of depositing her bodily outdoors lay slack on the table. The white shirt he had on suddenly appeared sizes too big for his shrunken frame.

Avey Johnson waited a while longer, and then, reaching for the chair, sat back down.

"I don't remember the last time I walked so much," she began after a time in the dazed, uncertain voice, her eyes abstracted. "I just kept going and going. I wasn't even aware of the sun until I was almost down at this end of the beach. And by then it was unbearable. And there I was without a hat. What would have possessed me to come out without a hat? And when I looked around the trees had all disappeared.

Not a bit of shade anywhere. I felt as if I was going to pass out. That's why when I saw the door here open I just barged in . . .

"You see I haven't been feeling myself the past few days. I don't know what it is. Everything was going along fine, I was enjoying the cruise as usual, and then for no reason, two, three days ago, I began feeling strange. Not sick or anything, just 'off,' not myself. And then all kinds of odd things started happening. It became so upsetting I finally decided there wasn't any point continuing the trip, that I might as well leave and go home. That's why when the ship came in yesterday I got off . . .

"It was this dream I had!" The small part that was still her old self heard her declare, and was astonished. Could this be Avey Johnson talking so freely? It was the place: the special light that filled it and the silence, as well as the bowed figure across the table who didn't appear to be listening. They were drawing the words from her, forcing them out one by one.

Slowly, in the searching voice, she went on to tell of the dream. She described each stage of its unfolding, from the moment her great-aunt Cuney appeared on the road to the Landing with her raised hand beckoning her forward to the bruising fight between them at the end.

". . . There we were fighting, of all things. And it seemed so real, the fight, that when I woke up the next morning I was actually hurting, physically hurting. And my wrist was sore from her holding it. In fact all the next day I could still feel her hand there. Isn't that the oddest thing . . . ? I'm not one to put much store by dreams, but I almost wished I had had my mother's old dream book to figure that one out.

"And that wasn't all . . ." She began again after a long pause. For the first time she spoke of the peculiar sensation

170

that had developed in her stomach following the dinner with the parfait, and of the frightening tricks her eyes had played on her the morning she had spent searching the decks for a quiet corner to herself.

". . . I was like someone hallucinating," she said—the shuffleboard games had turned into a brawl; there had been the skeleton in the red-and-white bikini on the Lido— ". . . seeing things that couldn't possibly be there."

Caught up in the sudden need to talk, she failed to notice the change that had taken place in the old man. From the moment she started recounting the dream his head had come up, his eyes had opened and he had begun quietly studying her from beneath his lowered brow. His gaze never left her face. Intense, probing, it was like a jeweler's loupe he might have fitted into his eye to get at her inner workings. There was no thought or image, no hidden turn of her mind he did not have access to. Those events of the past three days which she withheld or overlooked, the feelings she sought to mask, the meanings that were beyond her—he saw and understood them all from the look he bent on her.

". . . So I simply got up in the middle of the night and started packing," she was saying. "Just threw things into the suitcases like a crazy woman. And in the morning told the two friends I was traveling with I was leaving. One of them was furious with me. But there was nothing I could do about it. I couldn't explain what had come over me. All I knew was that I wanted to go home . . . I was sure I'd get a flight out yesterday, but—did I mention it before?—I missed it, I was too late . . ."

She paused, took a deep breath, steeled herself. "And then last night out on the balcony of my room . . ." Her voice faltered. She waited a moment and tried again, only to have the same thing happen. She sat there struggling to speak, but was unable to find the voice or the words to continue. She kept seeing Jerome Johnson's disapproving figure blocking out the afternoon sunlight from the foot of the recliner when it all began; she sensed the yawning hole down which her life of the past thirty years had vanished by the time it was over. Yet she could not, although she needed to, bring herself to speak of either.

Finally, behind the tears welling up, her eyes went blank, and the saving numbness she had awakened to that morning, which had lifted partly during her walk along the beach, closed over her mind again.

It didn't matter that she could not go on. Because the man already knew of the Gethsemane she had undergone last night, knew about it in the same detailed and anguished way as Avey Johnson, although she had not spoken a word. His penetrating look said as much. It marked him as someone who possessed ways of seeing that went beyond mere sight and ways of knowing that outstripped ordinary intelligence *(Li gain con-naissance)* and thus had no need for words.

Slowly he rose to his feet, a diminutive figure in a worn shirt and faded black pants, with a look like a laser beam. He used it now to examine her again, this time seeing her half-combed hair, the damp wrinkled dress and the self crouched like a bewildered child behind the vacant, tear-filled eyes. He saw how far she had come since leaving the ship and the distance she had yet to go, and he said in a voice that was all understanding, all compassion, "Wait here for me, oui. I gon' bring you a little something. You's not to leave yet."

3

Moving with the briskness that again denied his age and lameness, the man quickly crossed the room and dropped out of sight behind the counter. The jacket he had been mending lay where he had tossed it, near the tray of glasses. For a time he could be heard rummaging around and dragging what sounded like heavy objects over the floor. When he raised up he was holding a machete, and with the long blade gleaming in the dimness, he began hacking away at something hidden from sight below.

The hacking was followed by the sound of liquid being poured, as well as other small mysterious noises, and then he was hurrying back to the table bearing what looked like a glass of cloudy water in his oversized hands.

Without a word but with the knowing and compassion in his eyes, he held the glass out to Avey Johnson across the table.

"Coconut water?" she asked, pausing after the first swallow. Her eyes were dry now, the tears having receded, but she still felt the numbness inside.

He nodded. "Fresh out of the shell."

"And . . . ?" She was frowning slightly.

"And a drop of rum, oui," he said. "But not from those bottles you see there," he dismissed with a wave the half-dozen bottles of white rum on the shelves across the room. "I put a little Jack Iron from Carriacou in yours. Is the best. I don' give that to everybody."

Rum and coconut water, a standard in the islands. She had had much stronger versions of it in other places. Nevertheless she almost instantly felt that first swallow of the drink soothe her parched throat and begin to circle her stomach like a ring of cool wet fire. Eagerly she raised the glass to her lips again.

The man resumed his seat then. He watched in silence while she drank, giving a little cryptic nod each time she took a sip, and smiling faintly to himself. She was holding the glass cupped between her hands, as if fearful of spilling a drop.

She was blind to both the man's smile and her hands clutching the glass. She was aware only of the effect the drink, for all its mildness, was having on her. In no more than seconds it had spread from her stomach out into the rest of her body, moving through her like the stream of cool dark air that had greeted her when she first entered the rum shop. Spilling into the dry river bed of her veins. Before she had finished half the glass, it had reached out to her dulled nerves, rousing and at the same time soothing them; and it was even causing the pall over her mind to lift again.

"You's not the only one, oui," he began in his abrupt fashion the moment she had drained the glass. She thanked him and set it down, but kept her hands around it. "It have quite a few like you. People who can't call their nation. For one reason or another they just don' know. Is a hard thing. I don' even like to think about it. But you comes across them all the time here in Grenada. You ask people in this place what nation they is and they look at you like you's a madman. No, you's not the only one . . ."

He had gone back to his queer, obsessive talk. The words reached Avey Johnson through the lifting numbness. But this time, with the mellowness of the rum moving through her, they did not make her as uneasy as before. She still did not know what he was talking about; his voice rang without meaning in the hollowness that had opened inside her since last night. Yet she did not find herself glancing toward the door this time, thinking to escape. In fact, she found she was suddenly reluctant to leave either the place or the man in spite of his endless bewildering talk.

"That's why," he was saying, "when you see me down on my knees at the Big Drum singing the Beg Pardon, I don' be singing just for me one. Oh, no! Is for *tout moun'*," he cried, his short arms in the tieless dress shirt opening as though to embrace the world. "I has all like you in mind. 'Cause you all so that don' know your nation can't take part when the Beg Pardon or the nation dances is going on. Oh, no! *Pas possible!*" he declared emphatically. "The Old Parents would be vex. You all has to wait till the creole dances start up later in the fete. Then you can join in. Every and anybody can dance then . . ."

There was a pause. Then, watching her closely with the fey, stained eyes, he said in a voice shadowed by doubt yet hopeful, "Now I know you know somethin' 'bout the old-time creole dances. At leas' you've heard their names some-place . . ." It was both a question and a statement. "The

Belair . . . ? The Cariso . . . ? The Chiffone . . . ? The Old
Kalenda? Everybody knows that one. The Granbelair . . . ?"

Once again he was reeling off a list of names Avey Johnson
had never heard before. It was clear he had already forgotten
where she said she was from. And as he had done earlier he
was being careful to pause after each name to give her a
chance to respond.

All she did was to shake her head each time and clutch the
empty glass. With it between her hands nothing the man said
or did seemed strange.

"The Bongo? Have you heard of that one maybe? Is the one
I like best, oui. The song to it tells what happened to a
Carriacou man and his wife during the slave time. The smallest child home knows the story. They took and sold the husband—the chains on him, oui—to Trinidad and later the
same day they put the wife on a schooner to Haiti to sell her
separate. Their two children the people that owned them kept
behind in Carriacou. Is a true thing, happen during the slave
time. Both of them cry so that day we say it's their tears
whenever there's a big rain. The Bongo man and his wife
crying we say. And when they came with the irons to take
away the wife she begged a friend of hers name Lidé to grieve
for her and to console the children. It says it clear-clear in the
song . . ."

Slowly, painfully, as if he were suddenly feeling his age, he
pulled himself up from the chair, and throwing back the bald
crown of his head, began singing:

" '*Pléwé mwê, Lidé, Pléwé Maiwaz, oh . . .*' "

For several long minutes his shaky falsetto directed the song
toward the vaulted roof of thatch and sent it in a piercing call
out the door. Without understanding the words, Avey John-

son felt the tragic weight that underscored them pressing her down in the chair, holding her more firmly inside the bar.

From the anguish in the man's voice, in his face, in his far-seeing gaze, it didn't seem that the story was just something he had heard, but an event he had been witness to. He might have been present, might have seen with his own eyes the husband bound in chains for Trinidad, the wife—iron on her ankles and wrists and in a collar around her neck—sold off to Haiti, and the children, Zabette and Ti Walter (he even knew the names), left orphaned behind.

"'. . . kôsolé Zabette ba mwê,'" he sang, transformed in voice and person into the grief-stricken mother. "'. . . kôsolé Ti Walter . . .'"

When the song finally ended, the silence in the rum shop, like that in the high nave of a church, held on to its echo as if to preserve it for others to hear. Outside, the children had abandoned their noisy play and had come up on the beach. They could be seen through the door sitting quietly in a row down near the water. They were resting, chatting, looking out to sea.

"Was a hard thing, oui," he said, taking his seat. "A hard, hard thing.

"And what about the Hallecord?"—this, in the next breath: he had resumed his interrogation. "Is a dance that has a pretty song to it.

"The Dama then . . . ? The Juba . . . ?"

She was about to shake her head again when she stopped herself. "Juba? Did you say Juba?"

"Oui," he cried. "Juba! You knows it?"

"Yes . . . no . . . I mean I remember hearing or reading about it somewhere . . ."

177

The man's relief at this was so great it weakened him and he had to sit down. "So you know, you remember Juba!" And from the way he said it, omitting the word "the" and with the heightened note in his voice, it was as if he meant more than just the dance. He might have been also referring to the place that bore the name: Juba, the legendary city at the foot of the White Nile. And it was clear from his tone that he wasn't thinking of the forgotten backwater it had become, a place where lepers and goats freely roamed the sun-baked streets, but the city as he remembered it from memories that had come down to him in the blood: as Juba, the once-proud, imperial seat at the heart of the equatoria.

"So you know, you remember Juba," he repeated, giving it the wide meaning. "Come, show me how they dances it where you's from."

She went back to shaking her head. "No one dances it anymore. It's only something you might hear or read about."

"*We* still dances it!" he cried, and the next second, jumping up from the table, he was charging on the mismatched legs over to where the sunlight pouring in the doorway created a rectangular stage on the dirt floor. He stopped in the middle of the brightness, shook off his indignation, and drew himself up on his longer leg.

"In Carriacou is mainly the women dances the Juba," he explained. "They does it in pairs, facing each other and holding the long skirt to their dresses up off the ground"—with one hand he delicately lifted an imaginary hem off the floor. "Is a dance that puts you in mind of a cockfight"—he stuck his other hand akimbo.

Before beginning the dance, he raised his threadbare voice again, his song this time a startling, high-pitched outburst full of a showy aggressiveness. Singing, he launched into a series

178

of bristling steps back and forth which did call to mind a combative fowl. Each move forward was accompanied by menacing thrusts of his shoulders and the elbow at his hip. With his other hand he whipped the make-believe skirt insultingly back and forth in his opponent's face. His own face was being held at an angle that suggested a beak poised to strike. All this he affected while darting forward. When forced to retreat, on the other hand, he did so in a pantomime of ruffled feathers and outraged squawks.

At first, the dance had clearly been too much for him and he had had to force his lame, aged body through the strenuous movements. But gradually, as he kept on, the strain and stiffness became less apparent. His stooped shoulders appeared to come into line. The foreshortened left leg seemed to grow with each step until it was the same length as his right. He once again looked tall enough to reach up and easily touch the thatch overhead. One by one his defects and the wear and tear of his eighty- or perhaps even ninety-odd years fell away and he was dancing after a time with the strength and agility of someone half his age.

"*We di la wen Juba . . .*" he sang, and his voice also sounded more youthful. Moreover, it had taken on a noticeably feminine tone. The same was true of his gestures. The hand snapping the invisible skirt back and forth, the thrusting shoulders, the elbow flicking out—all were the movements of a woman.

"A skirt! I needs a real skirt!" he suddenly cried with the petulance of a temperamental movie star, stopping briefly to look down in disgust at his trousers. "Is the skirt in the Juba gives it beauty."

Avey Johnson heard herself laugh, and it didn't seem as if she had anything to do with it, but that the man had reached a hand inside her and pulled the weak, short-lived laugh from somewhere out of the numbness there, determined to draw her into his playful mood. Ever since he had jumped up and rushed over to the door and started dancing, she had sat there baffled, not knowing what to make of him, wondering again about his sanity. And now he had made her laugh in spite of the emptiness.

"Come," he was gaily beckoning to her, "I needs a partner. The Juba calls for a pair."

He invited her to join him on the sunlit stage, and then did not give her a chance to refuse him. Because no sooner than he uttered the last word, he broke off the dance and, darting back over to the table, he brought his wrinkled mask of a face close to hers and said, "You must come, oui. On the excursion." He was suddenly serious. "You must come today-self so you can see the Juba done proper." His voice was his own again.

Avey Johnson stared dumbly at him as if he had spoken to her in Patois and she had not understood a word. Then, springing back from the face crowding hers, she was scrabbling in her lap for a pocketbook that wasn't there, pushing back her chair and struggling to her feet against the weight of the strange reluctance to leave that had come over her.

"I really have to be starting back . . . It must be getting late." She held up her left wrist, and when she failed to find her watch, cried in sudden panic, "What time is it? How long have I been sitting here?" She swung wildly toward the door, and for a moment, confronted by the blinding sunlight, she felt as if she were looking into the open door of a blast furnace.

"Is only a little past the noon hour," the man said calmly; and added, "You must come. Is only for a day or two, oui.

Three at the most. The excursion don' last longer than that. You'll be back here in no time."

"But I couldn't possibly do something like that! I'm leaving today. Didn't I say that before? I plan on being home tonight, in my own house . . ."

She faltered at the word "house," seeing projected suddenly on the blank screen of her mind the vision that had assailed her on the balcony yesterday afternoon, just minutes before Jerome Johnson appeared: home again, she entered the dining room only to find that it had turned into the museum at the foot of Mount Pelée in the wake of the eruption that had taken place during her absence, and which had reduced every-thing there to so many grotesque lumps of molten silver and glass.

And suddenly, at the thought of the dining room and the house in North White Plains, there it was again: the peculiar clogged and bloated feeling in her stomach and under her heart which could not be accounted for. It quickly spread across her entire midsection and caused her head to start aching again. She sat back down.

"You must come for the two days, oui." The man spoke after a long silence. He had also seated himself again. "You'll like the place. Carriacou is small but sweet. It has some the best sea-bathing in the . . ."

"Didn't you hear me, I'm taking a plane this afternoon at four." She had been sitting with her head bowed and eyes closed, trying to banish the sight of the devastated room and to calm her stomach. But now she looked up irritably.

"Take it a next day," he said.

"But I just can't pick up and go someplace on a moment's notice . . ."

181

Hadn't she picked up and left the cruise overnight? Avey Johnson felt a dangerous confusion, and to escape the gaze from across the table which seemed the cause of it she hid her forehead in her hand.

"You must come. You'll be back here before you know it."

As if he had developed a little nervous tic, the man's head, in the silence that followed, began an almost imperceptible rocking from side to side. The slight movement, which he seemed unable to control, was as steady and strictly timed as the wand on a metronome or the pendulum of an old-fashioned clock. And it was to continue for as long as the two of them remained at the table.

"And how would someone like myself get there? There's no plane, is there?" She heard herself ask the question in utter disbelief as she looked up again.

"Oui, it have a plane." He spoke serenely. "But nobody takes it for the excursion. At leas' not going. Some people returns on it if they has to be back in a hurry. But everybody goes by boat. Is the custom."

"You mean those boats I saw yesterday . . . ?"—remembering the bedraggled fleet of schooners and sloops crowding the harbor.

"Oui. Is the custom."

"But those things aren't safe!"

"I has never known one I was traveling on to give trouble, and I been going on the excursion more years than you can count."

His unworried air irritated her all the more. He reminded her of Thomasina Moore that time in St. Vincent, when she had blithely sailed off on the listing sloop with others from the *Bianca Pride* to visit the black sand beaches to the north of the island. Just before departing, she had fanned down her and Clarice, declaring them to be cowards in front of everybody.

As annoyed as she was she nonetheless heard herself (or whoever it was speaking in her voice) next ask the man how long the trip took.

"Two hours. No more than that. Carriacou is just up the way. Is even less than two hours if we catch a good wind. You'll be there in no time."

"And where would someone like myself stay? Does the place have a hotel or a guest house . . . ?" She spoke angrily.

His voice in contrast was calm. "Oui, it have a small hotel and one or two guest houses. But you wun' be concern with them. A daughter of mine has a big bungalow her husband died and lef' her. It has in current, water, a inside toilet, everything. You wun' want for a thing. You'll stay with her. She'll be glad for the company. Is only her one and a servant in the house. All her children gone to live up that way long ago—" an aggrieved wave of his hand spelled out Canada, England, the States, but he refused to call the names. (". . . grands and great-grands I has never seen . . .") "Her place is just down the hill from where I stays so I'll be near to hand." Then, like a litany: "You must come." And although the man had never once touched her, she felt as if he had reached out and taken her gently but firmly now by the wrist. She almost jerked back her hand. She heard herself blurting out in an almost childish rage, "Those boats . . . I can't see how anybody would go on those boats. What if the weather turns bad . . . or the sea gets rough? You never can tell what might happen . . ."

He nodded. "Is true. You don' know what's to happen in this life. We might run into rough water. Is a channel where two currents butt up and sometimes it has a little rough water there. Nothing to speak of, though. Nobody takes it on. Mostly the sea does be smooth as silk. But rough water or smooth, you seldom ever hear of a boat giving trouble on the excursion. Tha's one thing you can put your mind to rest about."

They had reached a final silence. The man, who from his look had known all her objections before they were even born in her thoughts, sat quietly waiting, his eyes on her. Across the way, Avey Johnson was leaning wearily against the table. She felt as exhausted as if she and the old man had been fighting—actually, physically fighting, knocking over the tables and chairs in the room as they battled with each other over the dirt floor—and that for all his appearance of frailty he had proven the stronger of the two. She continued to search her mind for an excuse, for an argument strong enough to lift her from the chair and bear her out the door. But nothing more emerged. There was only the gaping hole and the darkness. In her desperation she even tried holding on to her anger, only to feel it being slowly drawn from her by the silence and tempered light in the place, and by the quiet figure opposite.

"I don't suppose another day or two would matter. My vacation won't be over for another week . . ."

He said nothing. His head, though, kept up the little pendulum-like motion.

"I shouldn't have any problem changing my reservation to another day since it's the off-season . . ."

Finally—and as she said the words she realized that the strange discomfort in her stomach was gone and her head had stopped aching: "All right. I think I'd like to see the place. But you have to promise to get me back here no later than the day after tomorrow."

"Oui," he said. "You has my word."

4

At two o'clock that afternoon, the hour Avey Johnson had been scheduled to leave for the airport, she found herself back down on the wharf instead. In front of her stretched the harbor filled with the shabby boats. Behind her, on the slopes of the hill, rose the crowded pastel town.

She wasn't altogether sure how she had gotten there, everything had moved so swiftly once she had given in. After quickly finishing dressing and closing up the rum shop, the man had led her up a winding network of steep sandy paths to the bluff and the main road overlooking the beach. There, a car that also served as a taxi had materialized outside a shop belonging to a friend his age. In minutes, with the granddaughter of the shopowner, a young woman in her twenties, at the wheel (she announced she had also once gone on the excursion), they were on their way to her hotel. When they

185

arrived the man sent their driver with her to collect the few things she needed. With the young woman's help this was quickly done. Before Avey Johnson knew it, her luggage was being carted away to the storage room, the reservation for her flight home had been changed (to the further mystification of the desk clerk) and she was back in the car beside the old man, headed for the wharf.

Just as they were leaving the rum shop he had formally introduced himself. Dressed by then in the rusty jacket to the pants, and wearing a tie and what looked like a clergyman's discarded black hat, he had stopped her at the door and with an Old World courtliness held out his hand. "Lebert Joseph's the name. I din' introduce myself proper before. And you is Mistress who . . . ?"

She had to laugh. "That's right. Here we are about to go off on a trip together and we don't even know each other's names." And taking his hand, she had told him hers—but only after having to pause for a long moment to think of it. When it did come to her and she said it aloud, it sounded strange, almost like someone else's name.

He had left her for the moment to go in search of the boat he traveled on each year. Before bounding away on the un-even legs, he had deposited her in the arcade to one of the warehouses lining the harbor road. "Stay right here, oui, out the sun and this mob of people. You's not to leave. I gon' be back just now."

She stood there, wondering at herself, filled with misgiv-ings, yet waiting as obedient as a child for him to return. On the ground beside her stood the smallest of her suitcases, containing her night things and a change of clothes, and next to it a battered valise belonging to the man. Her pocketbook was on her arm. She had remembered to put on her watch.

And she had thought to wear a hat this time. It was the same one she had flung into the corner last night.

She had wanted during the brief stop-off at the hotel to change out of the pink shirtdress. It had become stained with perspiration from her long walk up the beach and even more wrinkled than when she had put it on from the two hours spent sitting in the rum shop. But there had not been enough time.

Little had changed on the wharf since yesterday. As large a crowd of out-islanders was to be seen thronging the area between the roadway and the sea, and those up front, nearest the water, were eagerly boarding the long line of schooners and sloops tied up at the edge. The air rang with the Patois they insisted on speaking these two or three special days of the year. *"They can speak the King's English good as me and you but the minute they set foot on the wharf for the excursion is only Patois you hearing."* The bright polished surface of the sky appeared to reflect the myriad colors and patterns of their clothes and the umbrellas the women were carrying. Underscoring the festive din was the solemn note she had detected yesterday and wondered about: a sound like the summoning of a church bell only they could hear distinctly.

She was feeling more dazed and confused than ever, yet there now seemed to be a small clear space in her mind; looking out from it she found the scene on the wharf less overwhelming today, less strange. The milling, moving tide of bodies, the colors and sounds, the pageantry of the umbrellas were like frames from a home movie she remembered Marion had made her last trip to Ghana. She had filmed something she had called a durban or was it durbar? There had been a showing of the movie for the parents and children at her school, and Marion had insisted that she come. In the talk

Marion had given along with the film she had spoken of something called a New Yam, of a golden stool that descended from the sky, and of ancestors who were to be fed.

Moreover, the scene in front of her also vaguely called to mind something from her own life. Just what, she couldn't say. But the surging crowd, the rapidly filling boats, the sheen of sunlight on the water were reminiscent of something. And slowly it came to her, drifting up out of the void she sensed in her: the annual boat ride up the Hudson River to Bear Mountain!

Each summer before her father, on orders from her great-aunt, took her to spend August in Tatem, she would go with the family up the river to Bear Mountain Park on the excursion sponsored by the neighborhood social club.

As early as six in the morning would find them among the small but growing crowd already gathered on the pier at 125th Street. Behind them, hidden by the tall buildings along Riverside Drive lay Harlem and Seventh Avenue where they lived. Across the Hudson, New Jersey rose like the landfall of another country. But the green unbroken palisade over there scarcely claimed their attention. Every eye those mornings would be trained south, toward the Battery, where the S.S. *Robert Fulton* was scheduled to make its appearance at eight o'clock out of the rising mist downriver.

The *Robert Fulton* was invariably late.

"You would think that old boat could get here on time at least once, just to surprise us": her mother, wearing the bright floral print dress she had made for the occasion. With the new dress on, her hair freshly marcelled and her face powdered, she didn't look as if she had been up half the night frying chicken, making potato salad and preparing the inevitable rice for her father. Lord, deliver me from these Gullahs and their rice rice rice! she was always saying.

"What's it got to be on time for? Ain't nobody here but us darkies": her father, looking the dandy. He had exchanged the gray work clothes he wore every day as one of a crew of janitors in a large apartment building downtown for a lemon-yellow sport shirt and a pair of tan slacks with razor-sharp creases down the front. As an extra touch he had tied one of her mother's colorful head scarves like an ascot at the open collar of the shirt. (She had long since vowed never to marry a man who didn't know how to tie a scarf just that way.) The scarf was special for the boat ride. Later he would use it to cover his face as he napped stretched out on the grass at Bear Mountain during the afternoon heat.

"I said what's it got to be on time for? Ain't nobody here but us . . ."

"Negroes, you! Or Coloreds. Don't you see the children standing here? Always bringing down the race."

But behind the cut-eye she dealt him she had been subtly smiling. A smile Avey knew that was part of their private language. That night, on the run home over the black river, under the stars, they had danced to the live band inside the main cabin, her father clasping her mother in the floral dress close to him, his face which was dark like her own pressed against her mother's with its light coppery mix of red and brown—the color of her three brothers.

That night, standing watching them along with her brothers and the other children crowded near the bandstand, she had felt her body flush hot and cold in turns, and she had understood something for the first time, the knowledge coming to her like one of the stars above the boat bursting in a

189

shower of splintered light inside her: simply, that it was out of this holding and clasping, out of the cut-eyes and the private smiles that she and her brothers had come.

Boat rides up the Hudson! Sometimes, standing with her family amid the growing crowd on the pier, waiting for the *Robert Fulton* to heave into sight, she would have the same strange sensation as when she stood beside her great-aunt outside the church in Tatem, watching the elderly folk inside perform the Ring Shout. As more people arrived to throng the area beside the river and the cool morning air warmed to the greetings and talk, she would feel what seemed to be hundreds of slender threads streaming out from her navel and from the place where her heart was to enter those around her. And the threads went out not only to people she recognized from the neighborhood but to those she didn't know as well, such as the roomers just up from the South and the small group of West Indians whose odd accent called to mind Gullah talk and who it was said were as passionate about their rice as her father.

The threads streaming out from her even entered the few disreputable types who occasionally appeared in their midst from the poolrooms and bars where the posters advertising the boat ride were displayed. They were the ones who could be counted on to act the fool or worse once they had in a few drinks. Some years, on the return run down the river, there would be a sudden eruption among the dancers inside the cabin or out on one of the decks and two figures, locked together in what looked like a violent bunnyhug of a dance, would come grappling and spinning and cursing out of the scattering crowd. There might be the flash of a blade in the starlight, followed by the sight and smell of blood, and her father saying in love and disgust as he quickly herded them away, "My people, my people. They don't feel they had a good time lessen somebody gets cut."

She would even feel the threads entering them.

Then it would seem to her that she had it all wrong and the threads didn't come from her, but from them, from everyone on the pier, including the rowdies, issuing out of their navels and hearts to stream into her as she stood there holding the bag containing the paper plates and cups, napkins and tablecloth which she was in charge of. She visualized the threads as being silken, like those used in the embroidery on a summer dress, and of a hundred different colors. And although they were thin to the point of invisibility, they felt as strong entering her as the lifelines of woven hemp that trailed out into the water at Coney Island. If she cared to she could dog-paddle (she couldn't swim) out to where the Hudson was deepest and not worry. The moment she began to founder those on shore would simply pull on the silken threads and haul her in.

While the impression lasted she would cease being herself, a mere girl in a playsuit made out of the same material as her mother's dress, someone small, insignificant, outnumbered, the object of her youngest brother's endless teasing; instead, for those moments, she became part of, indeed the center of, a huge wide confraternity.

By the time the *Robert Fulton* finally made its appearance, the crowd on the pier would have grown so large it would look as if all of Harlem was there. And the numbers lent a certain importance to the occasion. They raised it above the ordinary. It didn't seem that they were just going on a day's outing up a river to a state park a few miles away, but on a voyage—a full-scale voyage—to someplace far more impressive. No one there could have said where this place was. None present could have called its name. Yet the eagerness with which they

191

swarmed up the gangplank the moment it was laid, the high drama in their voices and laughter and gestures, in the bright, brash, here-I-come, see-me-here colors they had on said they were confident of reaching there. And they weren't just going to this place, wherever it was, whatever its name, just to loll on the grass and eat fried chicken and potato salad and to nap or play bid whist during the afternoon heat. But to lay claim: *"We gon' put on our robes and shout all over God's heaven!"*

Boat rides up the Hudson were always about something that momentous and global.

For a moment, caught up in the memory, she failed to notice Lebert Joseph as he came rushing up.

He had found the schooner, he announced out of breath, after having searched up and down the wharf. It was all the way at the southern end, a good distance from where they were. And it was about to sail. "We gon' have to make haste, oui." He was already snatching up the two bags and moving off.

They were to cover almost the entire length of the wharf, the man charging ahead at an almost comical near-run, Avey Johnson struggling despite her long legs to keep up behind. For most of the way he stayed close to the line of buildings, out of the heart of the crowd. But as they neared the end of the dock area, he abruptly turned and plunged into its midst, clearing a swift path for them with his shouts, the startling black suit and hat he wore and the fact that everyone there knew him. "M'sieur Joseph!" they hailed him.

The two of them finally reached the edge of the wharf and he brought her to a halt before a two-master lying among the last boats there. And immediately her doubts and misgivings flared up again. Because although the schooner she found herself facing was larger than most of the others, it was as much of a relic, with the same scarred and battered look and exhausted air. Why had she expected anything different! Up front it boasted the crudely carved figurehead of a saint on the bow. And this was also the worse for wear, the salt spray having eaten away most of the face and the sandaled feet and the long girdled robe it had on. Only the crucifix in its hand had by some miracle remained intact. This it held out over the water as though it were a divining rod that had once led the way to a rich lode of gold.

"The *Emanuel C,*" he announced as he rushed her on board up a makeshift gangplank. He was holding her firmly by the elbow.

The main deck was scarcely larger than her living room at home. And it was packed. A small multitude of out-islanders—men, women and children—had already claimed every inch of space on the worn planking. Those who had boarded early had made seats for themselves on the covered hatch, the cleats for the ropes and the piles of cargo lying about from the schooner's regular run. A lively group of young men had encamped on top of the small deckhouse midship. The only seating as such was a long bench built into the starboard flank of the boat, where a number of old women and mothers with babies sat crowded together. To shield them from the sun an awning made from a discarded sail had been strung between the deckhouse and the rigging over their heads.

Everyone else was standing.

Lebert Joseph led her across to the oldest among the women on the bench. And the moment she saw them sitting there in their long somber dresses, their black hands folded in their laps and their filmy eyes overseeing everything on deck, she experienced a shock of recognition that for a moment made

193

her forget her desire to bolt. They were—she could have sworn it!—the presiding mothers of Mount Olivet Baptist (her own mother's church long ago)—the Mother Caldwells and Mother Powes and Mother Greens, all those whose great age and long service to the church had earned them a title even more distinguished than "sister" and a place of honor in the pews up front. From there their powerful "Amens" propelled the sermon forward each Sunday. Their arms reached out to steady those taken too violently with the spirit. And toward the end of the service when the call went out: *"Come/ Will you come . . . ?"* and the sinners and backsliders made their shamefaced calvary up to the pulpit, it was their exhortations which helped to bring them through.

The only thing those before her on the bench lacked were the fans from the local mortician with a picture of Jesus feeding the lambs on one side and the address of the funeral parlor on the other. These they should have been holding on their laps or panning slowly back and forth across their faces.

Space was quickly made for her between a stout woman in her eighties with large capable hands and a gold-rimmed smile, and her thinner neighbor of the same age or older, who wore her white hair in a crown of braids above her dimmed eyes and a shawl around her shoulders. The face she turned to Avey Johnson was simply bone and a lined yellowish sheeting of skin. Old people who have the essentials to go on forever.

Waving Lebert Joseph aside, they took charge. They relieved him of her suitcase and placed it out of the way under the bench. Her pocketbook was gently taken from her arm and laid flat on her lap. Reaching up, they removed her hat—doing it with such delicacy she scarcely felt it leave her head—and placed it on top of the pocketbook: there was no need for it with the thick canvas awning overhead. Then they indicated the railing just behind her: she was to rest her head there whenever she felt like it.

By the time the *Emanuel C* edged away from the wharf and under power of a fitful motor began threading its way through the other boats in the harbor, Avey Johnson found herself comfortably settled and the worst of her fears put to rest. She felt so reassured that when they reached the outer harbor minutes later and the first of the sails went up, she greeted it with something of the excitement she had felt as a child when the *Robert Fulton*, with a blast of its horn, would swing out into the Hudson, the boat ride finally under way.

The lesser foresail was up; and shortly afterwards with much shouting and hauling of the ropes on the part of the small crew, the large mainsail went aloft. The sight of it made the housewife in her recoil. Both sails could stand a good bleaching, a good, old-fashioned bluing. But even as she sat there feeling embarrassed on their account, a wind swept up off the sea, unfurled them and then, with a sound like a giant bellows, filled them; and from just so many yards of patched and dingy canvas, they were transformed into sails that called to mind those huge ecclesiastical banners the Catholics parade through the streets on the feast days of their saints. And for no reason, not understanding why, she caught herself thinking: it had been done in the name of the Father and of the Son.

And the sea? Glancing over her shoulder at the waves no more than six feet below, she saw that it was as Lebert Joseph had described it earlier: "a sea smooth as silk."

As unworried suddenly as Thomasina Moore setting off on the listing sloop, she watched the island with its coastal hills and distant mountains and steep little town slowly recede and drop to the level of a sandbar over the widening plain of the sea. At the same time, her gaze shifting leisurely between the two, she was observing the out-islanders as they stood chatting amid the confusion of their belongings and the many children on board. No one appeared bothered in the least by the crowding or the searing sun on their heads or their sometimes unsteady footing.

Once as the schooner gave a sudden roll and pitch a young woman in a brightly patterned sundress with a wide skirt grabbed the arm of the man beside her. Thrown off balance himself he was no help, so that for a moment they staggered about in their little patch of deck space, laughing and clinging to each other, until the boat righted itself.

Was she perhaps the taxi driver's old girlfriend? The one he said had thrown him over for a man who would accompany her on the excursion? What was her name again . . . ? Sylvie. He had spoken of her with bittersweet regret.

She leaned her head back on the railing and smiled reassuredly at Lebert Joseph, who was keeping a watchful eye on her from the crowded hatch nearby where space had been made for him to sit. She closed her own eyes. Breathed deep the salt air which, it was said, could cure anything. Allowed her mind to drift on the sound of the wind in the transformed sails and the singing voices around her. Martinique. That was where she had first heard it—the Patois. And its odd cadence, its vivid music had reached into a closed-off corner of her mind to evoke the sound of voices in Tatem. She hadn't even realized what had happened, that a connection had been made, until two nights later when her great-aunt had appeared. She had stood there large as life in the middle of her dream, and as a result there was a hole the size of a crater where her life of the past three decades had been.

Avey Johnson stirred fitfully as the bewildering events of the last few days laid siege to her again, and immediately—

her eyes still closed—she felt her elderly neighbors on the bench turn toward her. A quieting hand came to rest on her arm and they both began speaking to her in Patois—soothing, lilting words full of maternal solicitude. And just as they had relieved her of the heavy pocketbook and her hat earlier, their murmurous voices now set about divesting her of the troubling thoughts, quietly and deftly stripping her of them as if they were so many layers of winter clothing she had mistakenly put on for the excursion.

And as her mind came unburdened she began to float down through the gaping hole, floating, looking, searching for whatever memories were to be found there. While her body remained anchored between the old women who were one and the same with the presiding mothers of Mount Olivet in their pews up front, her other self floated down. And the deeper it went, the smaller everything became. The large, somewhat matronly handbag on her lap shrank to a little girl's pocketbook of white patent leather containing a penny for the collection plate and a handkerchief scented with her mother's cologne. There were suddenly new hightop shoes that buttoned along the sides on her feet, and a pair of little sheer marquisette gloves on her hands. A bow of pale blue satin that felt bigger than her head matched the Easter outfit she had on. And above the racing of the silken sea just below the railing she soon began to hear—the sound reaching her clearly over the years—the inflammatory voice from the pulpit.

5

"... And what did they find be-
loved when they came to pray that morning, the poor, grief-stricken
Mary Magdalen and the other Mary, mother of James and Joses?
Can you tell me? What was the first thing struck their eyes that
Sunday morning in the garden? You guessed it. The stone to the
sepulchre was gone. The great stone that it had taken nearly an
army to put into place had been rolled just as nice as you please off
to one side. And the soldiers the Pharisees had left to guard the
sepulchre were as dead men, we are told standing there. And as if
that wasn't enough who should the two Marys see sitting on the
rolled-away stone but one of God's angels, his countenance of
lightning, his raiment white as snow. Now you know the effect
all this must've had on those two poor simple women. They were
Mark Sixteen tells us affrighted but also, you can imagine, filled
with wonder . . .

"And when beloved the two Marys got up enough courage to

look inside the sepulchre, you know what they found, don't you? Nothing. That's right. There wasn't nothing to be seen in there but some linen burial clothes lying in a heap. The Savior though wasn't nowhere around. Jesus was gone! Soon as the angel came and rolled away the stone, He just picked Himself up and walked out of there like a natural man. Just as He said He would. You remember don't you what He told His disciples that time in Galilee. The son of God He said must be delivered into the hands of sinful men and be crucified, and the third day rise again. And didn't it turn out just like He said. Wasn't He beloved delivered into the hands of the chief priests and Pharisees—all sinful men by another sinful man (I don't even want to call his name this morning) for a paltry thirty pieces of silver. And didn't He suffer under an indifferent Pontius Pilate (man just washed his hands of the whole thing), was crucified, dead and buried. It says it right in the Creed. And didn't He like He said He would rise up beloved on the third day? You know He did. And when the soldiers the Pharisees had left there saw Him come walking out the tomb big as life they became—you know the story—as dead men. Then along came the two Marys to pray. And when they, poor things, saw what had happened they were what . . . ? What does the good Book say . . . ?

"'Affrighted and filled with won-d-a-a-h!'" And suddenly there it was: that strangled scream, stolen from some blues singer, that he was noted for. Each Sunday he carefully husbanded it, unleashing it only when he felt it was time to move the sermon to higher ground. From all over the church the amens rushed forward to embrace it. The dust motes in the spring sunlight slanting into the pews from the windows broke into a holy dance. Seated between her mother and older brother, in her hair ribbon and bow, the new patent leather pocketbook on her lap, Avey felt the church begin to tilt and rock ever so slightly around her.

"'Affrighted.' Mark used the word 'affrighted.' What he really meant beloved was 'scared half to death.' That's what they were, the two poor dumbstruck Marys. But they were also, I believe it, filled with wonder. And who wouldn't have been? For didn't they see with their own eyes God's power at work that morning? A mountain of a stone pushed aside like it was nothing but a pebble. An angel setting on it with a face that nearly blinded them in its heavenly radiance. Live soldiers turned to dead men. And the dead man risen and gone on about His business. Talk about power! Talk about miracles! The two Marys got a taste of what God can do when He puts His mind to it . . .

"I sometimes wonder though whether those two poor simple women could really appreciate the nature, the dimension of that power. It's something we need to think about this morning beloved as we reflect upon that miracle in the garden. You see, God's power isn't reserved for any one man alone, even though that man might be the only Son He'll ever have. It's at the disposal of every man, from the high-born to the low. From the saint to the sinner. We need to understand this Easter Sunday that the same power which rolled aside the stone and led Jesus from the darkness and death of the tomb into the light of the resurrection morning can also if we call upon it roll away the stones sealing up our spirits, our souls from the light of redemption.

"Oh . . . ? There ain't nothing sealing up your spirit, you say? No stone over the door to your soul? Ha!" Then: Aha, ha, ha, ha, ha!" It was God's own cosmic laugh with which he assailed them.

"Well, I hate to be the one to break the bad news to you beloved, but some of you are sitting up here this morning dressed back in your fancy new hats and your brand new Easter outfits with your souls walled up in a darkness deeper than midnight. Giant stones have done buried your spirit, your heart, your minds, shutting you off from the precious light of salvation.

"Lemme tell you about 'em. There's the stone of selfishness for one. The stone of hypocrisy for another: Folks that come to church on a Sunday and then go out and do some of every kind of wickedness beginning Monday right on down to next Sunday. You know 'em. And there're the stones of lying, cheating and stealing. Of jealousy, envy and hate. Of self-righteousness and puffed-up pride. All kinds of stones. Of bad-mouthing, back-biting, small-mindedness and malice. There's one that's got carved on it 'Indifference to the suffering of others.' Another has the name of your best friend's wife or husband writ large across it even though the Bible tells us 'thou shalt not covet thy neighbor's wife'—meaning husbands too. There's the shameful stone of false values, of gimme gimme gimme and more more more . . ."—and his outsized hands (he was a large ruddy mulatto man with great rawboned wrists and hands and a pair of restless feet that kept him stalking the pulpit)—his hands made like a croupier's stick raking in the money and chips on a gaming table.

"Stones!" He hurled the word like a fiery meteor out over their heads. His restless tread, shaking the pulpit's weakened floorboards, reverberated through the nave, and Avey felt the rocking of the building increase around her.

Then, in a quieter tone he said, coming to a halt at the lectern with its huge Bible, "But there's a way beloved to remove those great boulders from the temple of your life. Lemme tell you about it. It's simple. Simplest thing in the world. You just got to do like Jesus in His final hour on the cross. Remember how He cried out at the end, 'Oh God, my God, why hast thou forsaken me?'—called on the Lord to deliver Him from the pain. And God heeded. Three days later He threw open the sepulchre and set His Son free from death for all time. Jesus called and God acted. It was as simple as that. And that's all you have to do beloved. When you find yourself buried behind a dark stone of sin just call on the Lord. Ask Him to loose His mighty power in your behalf and roll away that old stone so that the bright light of your soul—your soul-light—can shine forth . . .

"'This little light of m-i-n-e . . .'"

It was a hoarse, ecstatic song, torn raw and bleeding from his abraded throat.

"What're you gonna do with it?"

And the answer came in a great outpouring: "'Let it shine.'"

"Shine in all its glory! But you got to do like Jesus first. You got to raise up your voice and call on the Lord. Just call Him. What must you do beloved?"

And once again the tumultuous response: "Call Him."

"Call Him in the midnight hour."

"Call Him."

"Call Him in the stillness of dawn."

"Call Him."

"Ask Him to roll away the stone of unrighteousness."

"Ask Him."

"The stone of sin."

"Ask Him."

"Just ask Him beloved."

"Ask Him."

"Call on the Lord."

"Call Him."

Back and forth it went: the call, the thrilling response. Until after a time it seemed Reverend Morrissey ceased being merely God's messenger, a mortal charged with bringing the Word, and was God Himself. And he wasn't the gentle, magnanimous God the Father of the New Testament who so loved the world that He gave His only Son as a ransom, but rather the wrathful Jehovah of the Israelites, given to His endless angers. And this choleric old God, hurling the exhortations like cosmic stones over their heads and

*lashing them with His strangled cries, had laid hold of the church
and was rocking it with increasing fury between his enormous
hands.*

*She could feel her breakfast and the chocolate Easter egg she had
eaten after Sunday school sloshing around like a great sour wave
inside her. The building reeled again and the wave threatened to rise
from her stomach into her throat. Should she squeeze past those in
the pew and make a dash for it up the aisle? Or turn and alert her
mother or older brother who would run with her to the bathroom
downstairs? She thought of doing both and then did neither, because
she knew she would not make it up the aisle. All would be lost if she
so much as turned her head. The least movement and everything
she had eaten that morning would come spewing out of her, and her
youngest brother would have something to tease her about for years
to come.*

*And so she sat there in an agony, her eyes shut tight, her hands
in the sheer gloves gripping her pocketbook, trying to stem the rising
tide of nausea on her own. Let the Easter sermon end, she prayed.
Let the song for the offering begin. Let Reverend Morrissey loose
the church.*

*But the voice from the pulpit that had become God's voice
hurtled on. And with each exhortation the hands grasping the building tightened their hold. Until finally they began rocking it with a
violence her heaving stomach could no longer withstand, and her
eyes opening, a hand flying to her mouth, she was looking wildly
around her for help.*

6

The women next to Avey Johnson on the bench took one look at her stricken eyes, at the hand clapped over her mouth, and were instantly on their feet. As if she weighed no more than the child she had been in her dream they quickly stood her up—after first snatching away the hat and pocketbook from her lap—turned her around between them and quickly put her to kneel on the bench with her head over the railing. All this they managed to do just seconds before the swollen waves that could be seen charging the schooner from all directions over a wide area of the sea sent it reeling and pitching again, and her entire insides erupted.

She vomited in long loud agonizing gushes. As each seizure began her head reared back and her body became stiff and upright on the bench. She would remain like this for a second or two, her contorted face giving the impression she was cursing the sky, which was the same clear impeccable blue as before despite the turbulence of the sea. Then, as her stomach heaved up she would drop forward and the old women holding her would have to tighten their grip as the force of the vomiting sent her straining out over the railing, dangerously close to the water.

The paroxysms repeated themselves with almost no time in between for her to breathe. Hanging limp and barely conscious over the side of the boat after each one, she would try clearing her head, try catching her breath. But before she could do either the nausea would seize her again, bringing her body stiffly upright and her head wrenching back. There would be the strange moment with her face lifted to the sky beyond the canvas awning. And then she would be hawking, crying, collapsing as her stomach convulsed and the half-digested food came gushing from her with such violence she might have fallen overboard were it not for the old women.

They held her. Hedging her around with their bodies—one stout and solid, the other lean, almost fleshless but with a wiry strength—they tried cushioning her as much as possible from the repeated shocks of the turbulence. (They themselves were surprisingly unaffected by it, which was also true for everyone else on board, including the children.) Their lips close to her ears they spoke to her, soothing, low-pitched words which not only sought to comfort and reassure her, but which from their tone even seemed to approve of what was happening.

"Bon," they murmured as the gouts of churned-up, liquefied food erupted repeatedly, staining for a moment the white spume on the waves below. "Bon," they whispered at the loud hawking she was helpless to control and at the slime hanging in long tendrils from her mouth. "Bon," at the stench.

When, after what seemed the longest time, the large meal

205

she had eaten that morning was exhausted, there followed an endless stream of fluids the color and consistency of a watery lime gelatin. *"Bon."* The tears being forced from her eyes by the violence of each contraction mixed with the mucus streaming from her nose and the acids and bile off her raging stomach, and the church mothers, holding fast to her, murmured, *"Bon. Li bon, oui."*

And their words were being echoed by others there as well. A distressed Lebert Joseph had rushed over the moment Avey Johnson had started up out of the dream with her hand to her mouth and now stood hovering anxiously behind them at the railing. He kept frantically repeating something about a channel and currents and a little rough water: ". . . Is only the channel I tol' you about, oui. The channel with the two currents! We gon' be soon past it . . ." (In her fleeting moments of clarity she made out his voice, and her anger with him would bring on another seizure.) Yet whenever she heaved up, he would break off to say along with the old women and the other out-islanders gathered nearby: *"Bon, li bon."*

Finally there was nothing either solid or liquid left for her to bring up and the vomiting gave way to a dry empty retching that was as painful and that went on almost as long. Signaling each other after a time, the old women gently drew her away from the railing and, turning her around, slowly eased her— still retching uncontrollably—back down on the bench between them. They continued to hold her and to shore her up with their bodies. They kept up the whisper in her ear.

But she no longer heard them. Sunk in her misery she even failed to hear Lebert Joseph who, standing directly in front of her, was telling her in a loud voice that the rough water was finished, they were through the channel. In her dimming consciousness she was only aware of the continuing upheaval inside her which had grown worse with the empty retching. Not only were the contractions more wrenching now that there was nothing left, they had reached below her stomach to the place where up to this morning in the rum shop she had felt the strange oppressive fullness. As if there was actually something there, some mass of overly rich, undigestible food that had lodged itself like an alien organ beneath her heart and needed to be expelled, all of her body's fury was suddenly concentrated there.

So that the long siege began again, but with even greater intensity this time. And it kept on, the massive contractions doubling her over between the women on the bench and rendering her insensible to the fact the channel was behind them and the schooner was once again riding a silken sea.

Until, for no reason, after what in her agony seemed to be hours, the contractions changed direction. Instead of passing up through her emptied stomach into her throat, they reversed themselves and began—she could feel them!—moving down into the well of her body. All of a sudden, before she could even grasp what was taking place, the powerful spasms were reaching deep into her. She tried clearing her head of the dimness. She started to ask herself some unformed question. But it was already too late. Because with the sudden shift in direction, the bloated mass that couldn't be—whatever was left of it—was being propelled down also. Down past her navel. Down through the maze of her intestines. Down into her bowel.

Until, to her utter disbelief, there it was: the familiar irresistible pressure, followed by the clenched muscles easing, relinquishing their hold under the pressure; and then, quickly, the helpless, almost pleasurable giving way.

The horror which swept her was darker and more powerful than any wave the sea could have thrown up. And in her overturned and darkened mind she was seven or eight years old again and had gone somewhere—the zoo, Coney Island, on a trip with her class—and had eaten too much, too much candy and popcorn, too many hot dogs and sodas; and the next day, her bowels in revolt, she had stood writhing outside the locked bathroom door, screaming at her youngest brother who could be heard laughing inside to open the door, pleading with him to stop teasing and open it, that she had to go bad. Screaming at him, pleading, even after it was too late.

With Lebert Joseph quickly clearing a path for them, the two old women half-led, half-carried her—barely conscious and with her hands over her face—through the crowd over to the small deckhouse midship. They had read her look the moment she leaped up with the silent scream, and had acted. While the stout one restrained her and hid her with her bulk, her friend with the crown of braids quickly pulled the shawl she had on from around her shoulders and in a deft motion that was like a sleight-of-hand had it tied around her waist. Then turning to Lebert Joseph they had motioned for him to clear a way through the crowd.

The bunk inside the cramped deckhouse consisted of a shelf of planks built out from the wall with a dirty pallet mattress on top. Aside from this one piece of furniture the rest was darkness, a fetid heat and the airlessness of a hold.

While an anxious Lebert Joseph waited at the door, the women put her to lie down. Placed her pocketbook and hat beside her. Made certain the shawl was in place. Then: "*Bon, li bon.*" Saying it as if even this final ignominy was a good thing in their eyes.

It was nearing dusk and the *Emanuel C* was almost to port when the pall over Avey Johnson's mind lifted momentarily and she became dimly conscious. She was alone in the deckhouse. That much she was certain of. Yet she had the impression as her mind flickered on briefly of other bodies lying crowded in with her in the hot, airless dark. A multitude it felt like lay packed around her in the filth and stench of themselves, just as she was. Their moans, rising and falling with each rise and plunge of the schooner, enlarged upon the one filling her head. Their suffering—the depth of it, the weight of it in the cramped space—made hers of no consequence.

IV

THE BEG PARDON

"Ultimately the only response is to hold the event in mind; to remember it."
— *Susan Sontag*

1

On an old-fashioned buffet in the main room of the house lay the sacred elements: a lighted candle in a holder and, next to it on a plate, a roasted ear of corn fresh from the harvest. An embroidered runner—a starched, immaculate white—had been placed under them for the occasion, and the high polish given the buffet made it gleam in the sunlight filling the room.

Outside the house, which belonged to Lebert Joseph's daughter, the ground at the four corners had been liberally sprinkled with rum from a bottle of Jack Iron. The steps to the veranda in front had also received the traditional "wetting," as had the ones around to the back which led to the outdoor kitchen and the maid's room next to it.

All the necessaries had been done. The Old Parents, the Long-time People would be pleased. Before attending the Big Drum to be held in their honor later on—to give them as

213

Lebert Joseph put it "their remembrance"—they would slip unnoticed into the house and warm their chill bones over the candle flame and sample a few grains of the corn, commenting among themselves on the quality of this year's crop. But that would have to wait. They were too busy at the moment with the Jack Iron sprinkled on the steps and at the corners of the large bungalow, busy tossing it down (before the sun dried it) through the pores of their skin, which was the same as the earth's dark cover.

The candle burned in the sunny room to the front of the house, and in a shuttered bedroom to the back, a small pink-shaded lamp that was reminiscent of Thomasina Moore's night-light on board the *Bianca Pride,* also burned on a dresser across from the bed where she lay.

The lamp had kept vigil all night. It had been turned on the moment she had been brought in the evening before and then left on, as though to monitor her heartbeat and breathing, all during the long hours she had spent tossing and moaning on the bed. Even when she finally slipped into an exhausted sleep toward dawn, no one had thought to turn it off. And it was still burning despite the fact that it was almost noon, with the sun clamoring to be admitted at the shuttered windows, and that Avey Johnson's eyes had been open for some time.

She lay gazing humbly around her. For the longest while when she first woke up she had lain there as if still asleep with her eyes open. Framed by the pillow her face had retained the inanimate cast of sleep. Her body under the sheet covering her had remained motionless. Flat, numb, emptied-out, it had been the same as her mind when she awoke yesterday morning, unable to recognize anything and with the sense of a yawning hole where her life had once been.

Even her eyes, when open, had maintained a kind of fixity

for a time, as if staring at some horror that had turned her to stone. With a sharp, quickly muffled cry her hands had come up to cover her face again, and the convulsions of humiliation and shame that swept her—the same ones that had racked her sleep for most of the night—made it appear that the painful retching had begun all over again.

But she had recovered somewhat by now and was gazing around her with a look almost of humility.

The room in the rosewater glow of the lamp was large, high-ceilinged and plain, with a bare wooden floor, bare walls and curtainless windows that suggested it was seldom used. There was even the slight mustiness of closed unused rooms in the air. And it was sparsely furnished. There was the carved old-fashioned bed in which she lay, the dresser with the lamp on top across from the bed near the door, and one or two other heavy old-style pieces which reminded her of the discarded furniture her father used to bring home from time to time, given him by the tenants in the apartment building downtown where he worked.

She made out a tall wooden wardrobe over in a shadowy corner, with mirrored double doors and a high cornice—a massive affair—that was similar to one in her parents' bedroom long ago. When her father had brought it home in a rented truck her mother had scrubbed and aired it out repeatedly before putting anything of theirs inside. How they had had to make do!

She was still thinking of the hand-me-down wardrobe—the pleasant things about it: the faint comforting smell, for example, of her mother's cologne among the dresses there—when the door over near the dresser suddenly opened, admitting a small, quick-stepping woman; and for a second, as yesterday's horror came flooding back, her hands started up to cover her face again.

The woman who entered did not immediately come over to the bed. Instead, after pausing at the dresser to turn off the lamp, she briskly proceeded across to the two windows on the far side of the room and, moving quickly from one to the other, partly opened the wooden jalousies covering them. Then, with the sun entering the room in long slanting bars of light, she turned and was striding toward the bed.

Tel père tel fille. She was unmistakably the old man's daughter. There, faithfully reproduced, was his brisk, purposeful walk, although in her case there was no up-and-down limp to make it appear forced and even comical. Her movements, her abrupt gestures as she turned off the lamp and opened the jalousies bore his stamp. And although she appeared to be only in her fifties, younger than Avey Johnson, her taut little body had already achieved his pared-down, annealed, quintessential look. She might have sprung whole from his head, a head-birth without benefit or need of a mother; an idea made flesh.

Her name? Rosalie Parvay. A name in keeping with the touches of gold at her ears and wrists, with the Madras headtie arranged to form two little peaks like antennae above her forehead and the wedding band she had shifted to her middle finger to denote that she too was a widow.

"Ah, a mind tol' me you had to be wake by now." She stood smiling her father's fey little smile from beside the bed. "You din' settle down for a time there last night, but you finally had you a good long sleep."

"But I kept you up all night, I'm afraid." She spoke with her eyes averted. "You were back and forth the whole night. Forgive me." Because seeing the glint of the earrings and the jaunty headtie she suddenly remembered the slight figure of a woman who had repeatedly come to stand like a votary beside the bed all during her restive half-sleep. She hadn't known who it was standing there. In her confused state, the figure had been any number of different people over the course of the night: her mother holding in her hands a bottle of medicine and a spoon, the nurse in the hospital where she had had her children leaning over her spent body to announce that it was healthy and a girl: "a beautiful baby girl, Mother, and with so much hair!"; the figure had even grown to twice its height at one point to become her great-aunt beckoning to her in the dream.

"Come, oui," Rosalie Parvay was saying, "is time now to have your skin bathe. And this time I gon' give you a proper wash-down."

Avey Johnson abruptly turned away her head on the pillow, because she now also remembered the hands that had taken charge last night when the two old women from the boat, Lebert Joseph assisting them, had brought her in too weak and disgraced to even stand on her own. The hands, small and deft and with a slightly rough feel to the palms, had immediately stripped her of everything she had on, hastily washed her off and then slipping on her the nightgown from her suitcase had put her to bed. A baby that had soiled itself! And shame once again brought her body heaving up with a strangled sob.

Immediately she felt the small hands from last night come to rest on her arm, on top of the sheet covering it. And they remained there, their light touch calling to mind the current of cool air that had come to rest on her head when she had staggered into the rum shop yesterday. A laying on of hands.

217

Until finally, under their gentle pressure, she risked opening her eyes.

And the gaze which met hers from under the Madras head-tie was the same as Lebert Joseph's when she found herself telling him—driven by the strange compulsion to talk—about the mystifying events of the past few days: far-seeing, knowing, compassionate. The man had not only made her in his image physically: the small sinewy frame, the walk, the gestures, he had also passed on to her his special powers of seeing and knowing. *Li gain connaissance.*

Her gaze bent on Avey Johnson, Rosalie Parvay spoke, and her voice was as gentle as her touch. "Is a thing, oui," she said, "could of happen to anybody their first time on the excursion. After all you wasn't used to that old channel like people in Carriacou. You din' know nothing about it. It don' bother us 'cause we get to know it from small. But when those waves in there start to butt up that's a thing could upset anybody." Then—and this was to be the final word on the subject from her tone: "You's not to take on about it anymore."

With that, saying she would be back "just now," she turned and left the room, and for Avey Johnson it was like watching Lebert Joseph hurrying across to the counter yesterday to make her the drink.

When she returned minutes later she was accompanied by a tall, big-boned young woman of perhaps twenty with an impassive face under a maid's cap. The latter was carrying a large washtub of galvanized zinc filled with water between her hands and two or three towels in a neat stack on her head.

They entered the bedroom in a procession of two, Rosalie Parvay in front with Avey Johnson's clothes from yesterday, all freshly washed and ironed, draped over her arm; and the closed-faced maid looming tall behind her with the heavy washtub, which she carried as effortlessly as if it were a small basin.

Avey Johnson tried protesting being given the bath. There was no need, she could do it herself, she no longer felt weak—speaking out of her obsessive privacy and the helpless aversion to being touched she had come to feel over the years. "I've put you to enough trouble already," she said.

By way of a response, Rosalie Parvay simply reached over a hand from where she stood at the bedside and gently closed her eyes. "Is no trouble, oui"—saying it in a way that suggested she knew (knew as intimately as if she had lived them!) all the things that had happened over those years that would make her object to something as simple as being given a bath. Then putting the clothes she was holding on a chair, she turned and spoke in Patois to the maid standing beside the tub of water which she had placed on the floor, and the young woman immediately handed her a damp washcloth and a cake of soap.

She went about the bath with great discretion. While Avey Johnson kept her eyes closed she first meticulously washed her face and neck, soaping, rinsing, drying them, her touch light and impersonal. Only when this was done did she remove the nightgown—and she managed to slip it off without scarcely disturbing the sheet covering her. From then on she took care to turn back the sheet only enough to expose the limb or place she was washing at the moment. And whenever Avey Johnson flinched or stiffened involuntarily, she would stop, give the towel or washcloth to the maid to hold, and bring her hands to rest quietly on her for a minute or two before continuing.

Slowly, in a manner designed to put Avey Johnson at ease,

she washed a hand, an arm, a shoulder, a breast, bathing only one side of her at a time which made it easier to keep her covered. When, after some time, she reached the emptied-out plain of her stomach and her pelvis below she did not turn or fold back the sheet, but simply held it up slightly with one hand so that it formed a low canopy as she thoroughly washed her there.

Her long legs came next, and then Rosalie Parvay, followed by the maid bearing the washtub, was moving around to the other side of the bed.

For a long while there was silence in the room. As if the bath was an office they performed every day for some stranger passing through, Rosalie Parvay and the maid smoothly ex-changed the washcloth, towels and soap between them without uttering a word. The younger woman, her face closed and expressionless under her white cap, did not budge from beside the washtub. Nor did she speak the whole time she was in the room.

Rosalie Parvay also remained silent. With her sharply planed, thin-lipped face she quietly and with great tact went about the bath, her earring glinting against her blackness whenever she turned to signal the maid, the peaks on her headtie probing the air like antennae. Until finally, as she was washing the other shoulder, her lips began to move, and the silence was broken by what sounded like a plainsong or a chant—a long string of half-spoken, half-sung words in Pa-tois. It was a curious, scarcely audible singsong, addressed neither to the maid nor to Avey Johnson. And it was to go on for the rest of the bath, without once changing inflection or tone.

Gradually, under Rosalie Parvay's discreet touch and the welcome feel of the soap and water on her skin, Avey Johnson had found herself growing less opposed to being bathed. Now, there was the hushed singsong voice in the room, and this also helped ease her tension. So that by the time, halfway through the bath, when Rosalie Parvay briefly interrupted herself to ask her to turn over to have her back washed, she had come to accept and even to enjoy somewhat the feel of the small expert hands on her body.

She gave herself over then to the musing voice and to such simple matters as the mild fragrance of the soap on the air and the lovely sound, like a sudden light spatter of rain, as the maid wrung out the washcloth from time to time over the water in the galvanized tub.

Hadn't there been a tub like it out in back of the house in Tatem? It suddenly came to her that there had been—another memory drifting up out of the void. One the same size even, and with the same three or four grooves by way of decoration running around the top that she had glimpsed on the washtub here before Rosalie Parvay had closed her eyes. And the same dull gray in color. It had been her bathtub during those August visits. While her great-aunt rigorously administered the weekly scrubbing, she would sit drawn up in the tub, picking the patches of sunlight from the live oak tree overhead off her knees and blowing them like soap bubbles or thistledown into the air.

The memory took over, and for long minutes she was the child in the washtub again.

Limes. The faint cool smell of limes on the air brought her back to the room, and her eyes opening, looking—questioning—over her shoulder, she discovered Rosalie Parvay, the bath finished at last, gently rubbing her back with a lime-scented oil from a bottle the maid was holding.

The instant her eyes opened, the small hand immediately

went up to silence any protest she might have. "Is only a little light oil, oui, to see to it your skin don' get dry. I gon' be finish just now."

With that said the hand dropped, and on its way down, it touched Avey Johnson's eyes, closing them for the second time, and taking up her speechlike song again, Rosalie Parvay finished oiling her back before asking her to turn over.

She went about this phase of the bath with the same discretion as before, folding back the sheet only as much as necessary as she slowly made her way around the bed again, with the silent maid in attendance at her elbow. From time to time uncorking the bottle in her hand the younger woman shook a drop or two of the oil into Rosalie Parvay's outstretched palm, and without being asked she occasionally passed her mistress a hand towel she had draped over her arm for her to wipe the perspiration from her forehead—the two of them joined in a single rhythm which made it seem that the rubdown, like the bath, was something they were long used to doing.

And Rosalie Parvay wasn't content just to oil Avey Johnson's body. She was also lightly kneading the flesh across her shoulders and down her back and sides between her small hands. And when she turned to the limbs—which came in for most of her attention—she not only oiled and kneaded them thoroughly, but afterwards proceeded to stretch them by repeatedly running her hands down from a shoulder to a wrist or from a knee to an ankle, gently yet firmly pulling and stretching the limb before she finally drew back and covered it again with the sheet.

It was the way Avey Johnson used to stretch the limbs of her children after giving them their baths when they were infants. To see to it that their bones grew straight. Putting them to lie on the kitchen table in Halsey Street, she would first rub them down with the baby oil, and afterwards taking each puffy little arm in her hands, then the legs that were still partly curled to fit inside her, she would repeatedly stroke and pull on them in the same gentle yet firm manner—stretching, straightening the small limbs. At the end, grasping them by the ankles, she would dangle them briefly head down, then hold them high in the air for a second by the wrists as if to show off their perfection to the world.

Meanwhile, Rosalie Parvay had turned her attention to the upper half of her legs which she had left for the last. And her touch, Avey Johnson realized, her body stiffening momentarily, had changed. As if challenged by the sight of the flesh there, which had grown thick and inert from years of the long-line girdle, she was vigorously kneading it between hands that felt as strong suddenly as the maid's beside her looked to be.

And she was utterly concentrated. Her little ruminative sing-song died. She ceased using the oil, so that Avey Johnson, who knew it was futile to protest, felt the roughness of her small palms along the entire length of her thighs. And when the maid reached over from time to time to offer her the towel she took no notice. She was oblivious to everything but the sluggish flesh she was working between her hands as if it were the dough of the bread she had baked that morning or clay that had yet to be shaped and fired.

Until finally under the vigorous kneading and pummeling, Avey Johnson became aware of a faint stinging as happens in a limb that's fallen asleep once it's roused, and a warmth could be felt as if the blood there had been at a standstill, but was now tentatively getting under way again. And this warmth and the faint stinging reached up the entire length of her thighs. (Their length and shapeliness would excite him even when she was dressed and he couldn't see them, Jay, talking his talk, used to say.) Then, slowly, they radiated out into her loins: When, when was the last time she had felt even the slightest stirring there? (Just take it from me! Jerome Johnson used to say.) The warmth, the stinging sensation that was both pleasure and pain passed up through the emptiness at her center. Until finally they reached her heart. And as they encircled her heart and it responded, there was the sense of a chord being struck. All the tendons, nerves and muscles which strung her together had been struck a powerful chord, and the reverberation could be heard in the remotest corners of her body.

"*Bon.*"

It was Rosalie Parvay. Avey Johnson heard her over a long pleasurable distance. Saw her through a haze of feeling she had long forgotten. The sheet in place, she had stepped away from the bed and was wiping her forehead with the towel the maid had just handed her.

"Is time now," she said smiling, "for you to put on your clothes and come get little something to eat."

In a matter of seconds she and the maid had gathered together the bath things and were headed toward the door. And they left the room in the same order they had entered, Rosalie Parvay leading the way with her father's brisk step and the maid carrying the washtub a few paces behind.

"*. . . the first thing I do the minute I reach home is to roast an ear of corn and put it on a plate for them. And next to the plate I puts a lighted candle. Everybody does the same . . .*"

She had grown uneasy yesterday when he had started talking of such things. Senile, she had thought to herself, or even slightly demented, and had glanced toward the door of the rum shop, thinking to make her escape. Today, presented with the candle and the innocent ear of corn on the buffet in the main room where she had been brought after getting dressed, she found nothing odd or disconcerting about them. They were no more strange than the plate of food that used to be placed beside the coffin at funerals in Tatem. She had seen it once at the funeral of an old man her great-aunt had taken her to, a plate prepared with meat, greens and the inevitable rice and a side-dish of sweet potato pudding which had been the dead man's favorite, resting on a small flowerstand of a table next to the open coffin in the front room. Would they bury the food with him she had wondered. Another long-forgotten fragment drifting up to imprint itself with the sharp-ness and immediacy of something that might have happened only moments ago on the empty slate of her mind.

She turned her attention to the food which the silent maid, whose name she had learned was Milda, had placed on the dining table where she was sitting. Before her lay a bowl of strained vegetable soup, sliced chicken on a plate, bread from the loaf baked that morning, and to complete the meal, half of a flawless avocado which Rosalie Parvay sitting chatting with her at the table called a pear.

The avocado was a gift from her elderly neighbor on the schooner, the one with the shawl. She had brought it over that morning, along with three others, when she came to inquire after Avey Johnson and to collect the shawl. The other woman had also paid her a visit while she slept. And she too had left a gift, this one a packet of herbs to be made into a tea that would restore her strength.

And Lebert Joseph had been there, Rosalie Parvay in-formed her. "He spent the whole night sitting up in one those chairs you see yonder," she said, pointing to the other half of the large room, the section nearest the door to the veranda,

225

which served as the parlor. The heavy, old-style wooden sofa and chairs to be seen there, which looked as if they were seldom used, were similar to the furniture in the bedroom. The bare walls were hung with framed photographs of Rosalie Parvay's five children and their families—children and grand-children—all of whom lived in Canada. *Grands and great-grands I has never seen he had cried out bitterly, sitting angry and bereft across from her at the small table.*

"He never so much as closed his eyes the night, oui," Rosalie Parvay was saying. "He sat up the whole time." And those times when she nodded off she confessed he would rouse her to go and check in the bedroom, although he never ventured near the room himself. Only toward dawn, when she reported that Avey Johnson had finally slipped into a deep sleep, did he get up and leave, to go and sleep himself and to prepare for the Big Drum. That had been over six hours ago, so that she was expecting him back any minute now.

Then, in an aggrieved voice: "Is the first time, oui, that old man has ever spent a night in this house! Each time he comes home on the excursion I does try and get him to stay here. It would be more comfortable for him. I has done everything but get down on my knees and beg that man. Oh, he'll take his meals here, oui, and have his bath, but he wun' sleep anyplace but in the old house belong to the family up on that hill you see yonder . . ."

The hand with the wedding ring on the middle finger directed Avey Johnson's gaze out of a large window next to the buffet opposite where she sat. There, some distance beyond the neat yard outside the house and the road running past it, was to be seen a low hill with a scattering of trees and small wooden houses on its depleted-looking slopes. In the foreground, between the hill and Rosalie Parvay's bungalow, she

also saw a newly harvested field lying stripped and drying
under the afternoon sun, and for a moment, her mind swinging like a pendulum back in time—as it had been doing ever
since she awakened—it was the ruined field of sea-island cotton she and her great-aunt used to cross on the way to the
Landing.

". . . He needs to give up that grog shop anyway and come
home for good," Rosalie Parvay was saying, caught up in what
obviously was a long-standing complaint with her. "He's too
old to be bothering up with a shop and running back and forth
each year on the excursion. Is time for him to leave off all that
and find himself home. All those old-old Carriacou people
you see on those boats need to do the same . . ."

She paused, and with a sad encompassing wave of her hand
took in the room, the house. "Here it 'tis my one only in this
big house. He could come live here. I could care for him, do
for him, 'cause he can't have that much time left. We would
be company for each other. If he feels he must keep a blasted
grog shop he could keep one here in Carriacou. But, no, he
wun' hear to me. Is years now I been trying to reason with
him, but he wun' hear . . ." Finally, in disgust: "He's a man
gets on like he and death had a wager and he won."

Then, in an abrupt change of mood that recalled her father,
she was suddenly telling Avey Johnson in a happier vein of
the trip she had made to Canada some years ago to visit her
children and their families. It had been winter during most of
her stay and the first time she had seen snow. "Snow!" she
cried, lifting her head and small arms dramatically, "is a thing
I never want to see again in this life!"

In the midst of the laughter this provoked Lebert Joseph
came in. The two at the table heard the scrape of his uneven
footsteps on the veranda and the sound of the door being

227

cautiously opened, and turning found his contrite and anxious figure in the doorway.

To aid him perhaps in negotiating the climb up and down the hill he was carrying a walking stick—something Avey Johnson had never seen him with before. It was simply the gnarled slender limb of a tree that had had the bark removed and been cut down to his size. With it he looked older and more stooped, and the little nervous side-to-side movement of his head that afflicted him occasionally, calling to mind the wand of a metronome or a hypnotist's finger in its steady rhythm, was more discernible.

In an abashed salute he raised the stick and made as if touching it to the brim of a hat. But he said nothing. Nor did he move from the doorway. He would not move or venture into the room it was clear until there was some word or sign from her. Either she would heap abuse on him for having deceived her about the channel, or somehow find it in herself to forgive him. And so she said—the anger she should have felt vanishing at the sight of the walking stick and his tremulous head—"I'm afraid I turned out to be the world's worst sailor. I'm so ashamed of myself."

Slowly then, aided by the stick, he crossed the room and sat down at the dining table, although he carefully chose a seat that did not face her directly. He even managed a wan smile in response to hers. He remained silent, cautious, not quite trusting her gestures of forgiveness, still expecting her anger, her abuse.

"Is a thing I told her could of happen to anybody their first time on the excursion." Rosalie Parvay spoke for him finally. (She had gotten up the moment he sat down to set a place for him and had called to the maid to bring him food.) "That old channel does some people so their first time. We in Carriacou is so accustomed to it we forget everybody can't take it the way we do."

"Is true. We forget everybody ain' use to it like us." He was speaking at last, in a low chastened voice, his eyes lowered. Only after a long minute did he raise them to inquire anxiously, "But you's all right now, oui . . . ? You must tell me you's all right . . ."

She nodded. "A little unsteady on my feet still but otherwise fine. Your daughter has been putting me back together again." Then, with a laugh to reassure him: "One thing though, I'm definitely taking the plane back tomorrow even if I have to ride on one of the wings. No more boats big or small for a while."

"Oh, oui, I has already seen to that. Your name is down for a seat on the first flight in the morning. You'll be back in Grenada and on your way home in no time.

"And what about tonight . . . ?" It was some time later when he asked this. He had eaten by then and had just tossed down a long neat finger of Jack Iron, to give him perhaps the courage needed to put the question to her. "Do you think you might still like to come to the Big Drum? See what it's like? Or you don' feel strong enough yet to be going to no fete? Or you don' wish to bother anymore 'cause of what happen . . . ?" He had grown cautious and uncertain again.

She held up a hand to stop him; spoke strongly. "Of course I'm going! That's what I took the trip for!"

It was the proof he had been waiting for, so that he was suddenly his old animated self again. "You see," he cried, turning to Rosalie Parvay with a smile of relief and triumph. "I was right. Remember I said to you this morning how one mind tried to tell me she wun' be up to the fete because of her condition. Or that she'd be too disgusted with me to want to bother. Din' I say that this morning . . . ?"

"Is true, oui," Rosalie Parvay confirmed it for her. "This morning-self."

"But a next mind said 'no,' she's not the kind to let a little rough water get the better of her. She might still want to come. Din' I say that . . . ?"

"Is true."

"Well, your *next* mind was right," Avey Johnson declared with a laugh. "I'm not the kind." She loved the way he used the word 'next.' It was true she no longer trusted him. He had lied, deceived and tricked her into coming on the excursion. Yet to her amazement she found herself all the more fond of him for having done so.

He left shortly afterwards to finish the preparations for the fete. They were to come up to the house around nine. He would wait for them at the crossroads halfway up the hill and escort them the rest of the way.

2

Nine o'clock, the hill that was scarcely a hill its elevation was so slight, and the three of them—Rosalie Parvay, Avey Johnson and the maid, Milda, still wearing her cap—climbing it under a starless, overcast night sky.

Beyond the beam of the flashlight Rosalie Parvay was using to clear a path for them, there was no distinguishing the land from the sky except for the occasional flame of the ritual candles burning in the houses scattered over the slopes.

Avey Johnson hadn't experienced darkness like this since Tatem, since those August nights when she would accompany her great-aunt along the moonless roads to visit a sick friend or to stand with her across from the church when the Ring Shouts were being held. Walking the blacked-out countryside with the old woman it would seem to her that every ha'nt in Shad Dawson's wood of cedar and live oak had escaped and was following hard on their heels. She would feel them reaching for her with their ghostly arms; hear them whooing like Halloween owls in her ears.

They were almost halfway up the hill, nearing the crossroad, before her eyes adjusted enough for her to discover that the darkness contained its own light. She was able then to separate the sky from the land and to make out the vague shapes of the houses and trees she had seen from the dining room window earlier. The island once again had solidity and form. Yet, with her mind continuing to swing like a pendulum gone amok from one end of her life to the other, she felt to be dwelling in any number of places at once and in a score of different time frames.

". . . What business, I ask you, an old-old man like that got living alone in the back of some grog shop, without anybody to do for him . . ."

For most of the brief climb in the darkness, Rosalie Parvay had been complaining again about her father's intransigence. But she broke off now as the strong beam of her flashlight picked out the spot a short distance ahead where another road could be seen crossing the one they were on. She paused upon reaching the spot and slowly panned the far side of the intersection with the yellowish light, until it singled out Lebert Joseph standing quietly waiting for them at the place where their road continued up the hill.

It was unmistakably him. There in the light was the head with its bald shiny crown and faint rocking motion. And the wrinkled gnome's face. And he was still wearing the frayed dress shirt and ancient pants from yesterday and carrying the stick he had shown up at the door with earlier. Yet for a moment Avey Johnson failed to recognize him. Her eyes must be playing tricks on her again she told herself, as they had

done that last day on the *Bianca Pride,* because the man suddenly appeared older (if such a thing were possible!), of an age
beyond reckoning, his body more misshapen and infirm than
ever before. He would have been unable to stand without the
aid of the walking stick. Another eighty or ninety years might
have been heaped on his back since she had seen him a few
hours ago, and the weight of those added years had bent him
almost double over the stick and turned him into an appari-
tion that had come hobbling out of Shad Dawson's wood to
frighten a child on a dark country road.

That was one moment. The next—as if to confirm that she
had been indeed seeing things—the crippled figure up ahead
shifted to his good leg, pulled his body as far upright as it
would go (throwing off at least a thousand years as he did),
and was hurrying forward with his brisk limp to take her arm.

Baffled, the woman spent the rest of the climb wondering at
their strangeness, her own of the past few days and the man's.

It wasn't long before a ragged fence of saplings appeared off
to their left in the flashlight's bright cone, and farther along
they came to a sapling gate in the same decrepit condition.
Here they stopped and while the others stood back, Lebert
Joseph, bent double again over the stick, hobbled forward into
the light. As he unlatched and opened the gate and then with
great ceremony ushered Avey Johnson through it, he was
once again the ageless, misshapen creature she thought she
had seen on the road below. But only for the moment or two it
took her to step inside. Then, his normal self, he was guiding
her across a dark moat of a front yard toward a small, lopsided
house, a candle burning in one of its windows, which stood
silhouetted against the sky by a banner of light behind it.
Voices could be heard coming from that direction and he

quickly steered her around the house toward the sound and the light at the back.

There, behind the house, she was met by the harsh, acety-lene-torch glare of two gas lamps, and for a moment blinded by all that light after the darkness of the hill she could see nothing. Then, gradually, her eyes adjusting, she made out a large denuded dirt yard that appeared to continue beyond the reach of the light, a lone calabash tree with one of the gas lamps and a few gourds hanging like forgotten Christmas dec-orations from its leafless branches, and a thin crowd of perhaps thirty mostly elderly folk standing around chatting or seated on the few chairs in evidence.

Over against the wall of the dilapidated house, which seemed about to collapse in a heap of dust and gray rotted boards, stood a table with soft drinks, two or three bottles of the rum they called Jack Iron and the second gas lamp. Most of the men were congregated there.

To one side of a clear space in the center of the yard sat three drummers. One was a boy of about sixteen wearing sneakers and the other two were men Avey Johnson's age or older, with stiff, work-swollen hands that looked as if they had lost all their suppleness long ago. The oldest of the two had a large white handkerchief tied around his head. The drums which they held cradled between their knees were simply small rum kegs with a swatch of cured goatskin lashed over the top.

DeGale Clement. Edmund Joseph. Antoine Vespry. Clarice St. Hilaire. Cedros Joseph. Fifi Munday. Josiah George. Ophelia Joseph. John-John Placide. Names euphonious and lyrical. They belonged to the oldest among Lebert Joseph's friends and rela-tives gathered in the yard. Moving among them introducing her, he called them out as if each was a poem complete in

234

itself. *Bel Louise Albert. Zabette Bartholomew.* Above their wreathed faces the women wore versions of Rosalie Parvay's fanciful headtie, and the skirts of their homemade dresses were long and gathered full at the waist. Juba skirts. *"Is the skirt in the Juba gives it beauty!"*

Blackie Sammerson. Julien L'Esterre. The eyes of the men were already mystical with Jack Iron.

"So you's come on the excursion to see the Big Drum, oui," they said, speaking with the easy familiarity she was used to by now, regarding her with those eyes which refused to see any differences. "And how you like Carriacou?"—taking her hand in theirs for a moment with Old World courtliness . . .

The introductions over, a chair—a loose-jointed affair with a rush bottom—was quickly found for her and placed over near the lone tree which held the lamp. Did she wish something to drink? Was the chair comfortable? Could she see good from there? Was she all right? Both father and daughter fussed over her. If she needed anything she was to ask Milda whom they had told to remain at her side. (The maid, tall and silent, had already taken up a sentry's position beside her chair.) And they would be back to check on her every moment they got. Then, "begging for an excuse" as he put it in the formal manner of the old people there, he hurried away, taking Rosalie Parvay with him.

The next time Avey Johnson caught sight of him he had abandoned the stick and was down on his knees inside the clear space at the center of the yard. And behind him, on their knees also, were to be seen the elderly relatives she had just met, along with Rosalie Parvay and two or three middle-aged kin. They were eight in all behind him on the hard-packed ground which looked as if it had been tamped smooth by an endless procession of dancers over the years.

Outside their kneeling circle the other guests had fallen silent. All movement had ceased in the yard. And in the silence, the stillness, Lebert Joseph slowly opened his arms, raised his tremulous head to the sky and, abruptly, like a shock wave on the air: *"Pa'doné mwê . . . !*

"Si mwê mérite/Pini mwê/Si mwê ba mérite/Pa'doné mwê . . ."—singing in his quavering yet piercing falsetto.

"Is the 'Beg Pardon,'" Milda whispered and bowed her head.

Avey Johnson nodded, remembering. It was the first song he had sprung on her yesterday, no more than twenty minutes after she had entered the rum shop. All of a sudden he had dropped onto his game leg so that he appeared to be kneeling there across the table and had started singing. She had judged him to be either senile or lunatic or both, and had wanted to leave.

Following Milda's example she bowed her head. *Pa'doné mwê.*

Once Lebert Joseph offered up the opening statement of the song, his relatives behind him on the ground quickly joined in the singing. And the makeshift drums that had been silent all along began a solemn measure. Arms opened, faces lifted to the darkness, the small band of supplicants endlessly repeated the few lines that comprised the Beg Pardon, pleading and petitioning not only for themselves and for the friends and neighbors present in the yard, but for all their far-flung kin as well—the sons and daughters, grands and great-grands in Trinidad, Toronto, New York, London . . .

". . . when you see me down on my knees at the Big Drum is not just for me one . . . Oh, no! Is for tout moun'." And his little truncated arms had opened in a gesture wide enough to take in the world.

He raised his hand now and abruptly the singing ceased and the keg drums fell silent. Two of the younger men on their knees behind him quickly rose and came forward to help him to his feet; and the other family members, the Beg Pardon over, withdrew from the circle to mingle once again with the crowd.

Over by the tree Avey Johnson slowly lifted her head. And for an instant as she raised up it almost seemed to be her great-aunt standing there beside her in the guise of the big-boned maid. *Pa'doné mwê.*

What next was to come? She was wondering this to herself during the lull which followed the Beg Pardon when suddenly, startling her, a voice rose above the talk and laughter that had resumed in the yard. An old woman's voice. Frail, hopelessly raveled yet piercing, rising without warning from somewhere among the thirty-odd guests gathered behind the house. In an imperious manner it offered up the first line or two of a song. And once again the yard fell silent. But only for as long as it took the singer to state her theme. Then, as if to shore up the voice in its frailty, other voices rushed in, singing with her. The rum kegs followed suit.

And from out of the crowd came a gaunt old woman, two thick iron-gray braids showing beneath a dowdy felt hat. Along with the hat she was wearing a sweater to protect her from the night dew, although her feet under the long skirted dress were bare. Slowly she made her way over to the unmarked circle Lebert Joseph and his relatives had just vacated, and alone on the hardpacked dirt she began a grave, stiff-jointed dance (a non-dance really)—her bare feet scarcely leaving the ground—to the accompaniment of the drums and the voices of those looking on.

237

"The nation dances starting up," Milda bent over her to whisper. "Is only the old people dances them."

"She's a Temne, oui. The one you see dancing there is of the Temne nation." It was Lebert Joseph speaking moments later from the other side of her chair. He had returned to name the various dances for her.

("What nation you is?" he had shouted across the table at her and she had looked in panic toward the door.)

"Is the Banda people turn now," he informed her sometime later as an elderly man accompanied by two women his age sang their shrill way out to the center of the yard and there performed another version of the flat-footed non-dance. Then: "Arada, oui"—and this time the singing and drumming and even the movements of the aged dancer—a woman— were slightly more spirited. Then: "Moko. Is the song of the Moko nation you're hearing now." All the names he had flung at her yesterday in his relentless interrogation. *What nation you is?* Shouting it in her face.

As the dances continued to unfold she discovered they followed a set pattern. First, from around the yard would come the lone voice—cracked, atonal, old, yet with the carrying power of a field holler or a call. Quickly, to bear it up, came the response: other voices and the keg drums. And the one or two or sometimes three old souls whose nation it was would sing their way into the circle and there dance to the extent of their strength. Saluting their nations. Summoning the Old Parents. Inviting them to join them in the circle. And invari- ably they came. A small land crab might suddenly scuttle past the feet of one of the dancers. A hard-back beetle would be seen zooming drunkenly (from all the Jack Iron imbibed ear- lier) around their heads. Sometimes it was nothing more than a moth, a fly, a mosquito. In whimsical disguise they made their presence known. Kin, visible, metamorphosed and in-visible, repeatedly circled the cleared space together, until the visible ones, grown tired finally, would go over to the lead drummer—the older man with the handkerchief around his head—and lightly touch the goatskin top of his drum, and the music would instantly come to a halt.

"Cromanti. Is Cromanti people you see in the ring now." Later: "Congo, oui. They had some the prettiest dances . . ." Lebert Joseph continued to instruct her.

And then during one of the long intervals which followed each performance, he suddenly while standing beside her drew himself up on his good leg, raised his head, and his threadbare yet piercing voice offered up the opening verse and chorus of his nation's song.

"He's a Chamba, oui," Milda spoke after some minutes. By then he had already been swept across to the circle by the tide of other voices joining his and by the drums, and could be seen forcing his stooped frame and uneven legs through the rigors of the dance. (*"I's a Chamba!"* he had declared out of the blue, and in his pride his shoulders had almost come straight.)

With him gone from her side Avey Johnson tried sorting out her impressions and ordering her thoughts. For close to three hours she had listened to the stark, high-pitched songs whose words she could not understand. She had been startled, shocked yet thrilled by the voices that had erupted without warning during the lulls—the keening trembla of the women's voices; the hoarse, penetrating field hollers of the men's. From her seat near the tree she had watched the often feeble efforts of the elderly folk to dance their nation out in the circle of beaten earth, and at times had feared for their balance, some

239

of them looked so fragile. Her eyes had been drawn repeatedly
to the rum kegs that served as drums . . .

The bare bones. The Big Drum—Lebert Joseph's much
vaunted Big Drum—was the bare bones of a fete. The burnt-
out ends. A fete in keeping with the depleted-looking slopes
she had seen from the dining window earlier, the leafless tree
and the wreck of a house before her now, and the faces of most
of the guests which attested to the long trial by fire.

She should have been disappointed, and she had felt a
momentary twinge of disappointment when she first entered
the yard and had seen what little was there. She should be
silently accusing Lebert Joseph of having deceived her again.
Had she risked her life on the decrepit boat, disgraced herself
to her permanent shame for this?

To her surprise though she felt neither disappointment nor
anger. Rather she found herself as the time passed being
drawn more and more to the scene in the yard. The restraint
and understatement in the dancing, which was not even really
dancing, the deflected emotion in the voices were somehow
right. It was the essence of something rather than the thing
itself she was witnessing. Those present—the old ones—understood this. All that was left were a few names of what they
called nations which they could no longer even pronounce
properly, the fragments of a dozen or so songs, the shadowy
forms of long-ago dances and rum kegs for drums. The bare
bones. The burnt-out ends. And they clung to them with a
tenacity she suddenly loved in them and longed for in herself.
Thoughts—new thoughts—vague and half-formed slowly beginning to fill the emptiness.

"Ah, the music turning brisk!"

It was Milda speaking with sudden animation, and with a
start Avey Johnson came to herself to hear a different sound in

the yard. Lebert Joseph and whoever else had followed him to dance their nation had departed from the circle, and a somewhat younger-sounding voice raised in a livelier, more festive song had mounted the air. Other voices and the drums had already joined in and from all over the yard many whom the woman had not seen dance before, young and old alike, were moving eagerly toward the space at the center. Among them was Rosalie Parvay, who like her father had been keeping a constant check on her all evening.

"Is the creole dances starting up, oui," Milda said. She had begun to sway lightly to the music without being aware of it. "Anybody that feels to can dance now."

Avey Johnson felt the subtle movement beside her and looking up said, "And what about you? Wouldn't you like to go and dance?"

Milda abruptly stopped swaying and looked off. "Miss Rosalie say I must stay right here in case you wish anything."

"She only meant until everybody started dancing. I'm sure of that. Besides, I'm a big girl and really don't need a bodyguard."

Milda laughed and turned back. In the harsh light of the gas lamp on the tree nearby, her eyes were a golden, see-through brown.

"Go ahead."

She kept on urging her until finally Milda, with a big-boned gracefulness, slowly reached up and began unpinning the maid's cap on her head. "I gon' dance just this one then and come right back," she said. Carefully folding the cap so that it lay flat, she tucked it into the belt at her waist, and turned to leave: "Well, then, I gon' beg for an excuse."

Her stride as she swiftly crossed to the dancers was that, Avey Johnson thought, of her great-aunt striking out across the fields toward the Landing, and of the taxi driver two days ago as he came hurrying to rescue her from the crowd on the wharf. A stride designed to cover an entire continent in a day.

With the shift to the creole dances the mood in the yard changed and it began to fill up. From around the corner of the house came a number of new arrivals, most of them young people Milda's age. They might have been standing all along in the dark moat of yard front or on the road beside the straggly fence, waiting for the music to "turn brisk." The moment they rounded the corner of the house they invariably headed for the center where the dancing was taking place.

The drumming meanwhile, in keeping with the changed mood, had grown more spirited. Where the hands of the older players had looked too stiff and work-scarred to even bend before, they were racing now over the goatskin with a dexterity and speed the youth drumming with them was hard-pressed to equal. As if the sound of the roused drums wasn't enough, a group of young men from those newly arrived in the yard had gathered to one side with an array of maracas and shak-shaks, bottles, cowbells and hoeblades which they were either shaking or beating with spoons. The bottle-and-spoon boys. One muscular fellow in a red T-shirt had appeared carrying the heavy iron hub of a car wheel in the crook of his arm. And this he was striking with a thin metal rod that became a blur in his hand each time the tempo of the music increased. Iron lending its authoritative voice.

The presence of the younger people brought a heightened note to the fete. Nevertheless those in charge remained the elderly folk, and chief among them Lebert Joseph. He was an indefatigable host, appearing to be everywhere at once. One minute Avey Johnson glimpsed his diminutive figure amid the dancers. The next he was chatting, laughing, drinking with those who like herself were watching from the sidelines. And he was constantly darting over to her with the string of solicitous questions: Was she all right? Was she enjoying herself? Did she wish another soft drink? Wasn't she tired just sitting and would maybe like to take a turn out on the floor?—this with a sly smile, his head performing its trickster's dance. Then, before she could reply to any of it he would be gone, his mismatched legs bearing him swiftly, comically someplace else.

Where was the walking stick? It had not reappeared since he had abandoned it to sing the Beg Pardon on his knees. And what of the crippled dwarf of a thousand years she had seen or perhaps not seen at the crossroads earlier? Not a trace of him was evident. He had been packed away for another time in the trunk containing the man's endless array of personas. Another self had been chosen for the fete, one familiar to her, because he was once again the Lebert Joseph she remembered from the rum shop, who had amazed her by dancing the Juba over in the sunlit doorway with the force and agility of someone half his age. Out of his stooped and winnowed body had come the illusion of height, femininity and power. Even his foreshortened left leg had appeared to straighten itself out and grow longer as he danced.

"*Hélé, hélé, mwê pléwé . . . !*"

There it was again, his shaky, high-pitched falsetto sending aloft another song from somewhere in the yard to end a lull that had fallen. She recognized the voice at once. Quickly the singing and drumming, then the dancing got under way, with him at the center of it all. He was the hub, the polestar. Even when, in his restlessness, he left the circle of dancers to join the lookers-on or to check on her, the fete continued to wheel and eddy around him. And once the dance had gone through its interminable round, it was his hand coming to rest briefly on the lead drum which brought all movement and sound to a halt.

Then, alone in the empty circle with a bottle of Jack Iron, he would sprinkle rum in a wide, bright arc over the trampled earth. Making libation. Wetting the ring. Preparing it for the dance to follow. And he always made a point of wetting the keg drums as well. Even the drummers came in for a fine misting as he wielded the bottle over the goatskin.

And following each wetting the drumming became more extravagant and complex, more joyous. The hands racing over the kegs were soon as blurred as the metal rod the young man in the red shirt was using on the hub of the car wheel. Setting the pace was the lead drummer. The old man, the handkerchief around his head soaked with perspiration, was playing as if he and his instrument were one, his face transfixed and his eyes staring unseeing ahead under an amber film of rum. Hands flashing, he spurred the drumming on. Yet every so often in the midst of the joyousness and speed he would pause, and placing his left elbow on the drumhead he would draw his right thumb across the top. While his companions continued playing to the noisy accompaniment of the bottle-and-spoon boys and the singing iron of the wheel hub, his great swollen thumb would knife across the goatskin at an angle.

And the single, dark, plangent note this produced, like that from the deep bowing of a cello, sounded like the distillation of a thousand sorrow songs. For an instant the power of it brought the singing and dancing to a halt—or so it appeared. The theme of separation and loss the note embodied, the unacknowledged longing it conveyed summed up feelings that

were beyond words, feelings and a host of subliminal memories that over the years had proven more durable and trustwor-
thy than the history with its trauma and pain out of which
they had come. After centuries of forgetfulness and even de-
nial, they refused to go away. The note was a lamentation that
could hardly have come from the rum keg of a drum. Its source
had to be the heart, the bruised still-bleeding innermost
chamber of the collective heart.

For a fraction of a second the note hung in the yard, knifing
through the revelry to speak to everyone there. To remind
them of the true and solemn business of the fete. Then it was
gone.

Where had she heard that fleeting sound before, Avey
Johnson asked herself. Then: On the wharf. Underscoring the
festive voices when she landed two days ago had been the
same solemn note, like the muted ringing of a church bell to
both summon and remind them.

The dancers, perhaps fifty in all, had long since spread
beyond the space provided for them and were threatening to
take over the entire yard. Only a handful of spectators were
left besides herself. One by one the others had either joined
the moving circle or had simply allowed themselves to be
swept in once it reached where they were standing. She would
have to move soon if she was not to be engulfed also. She
looked around. Only the area near the drummers remained
free, the dancers steering clear of it as though it was somehow
sacrosanct. She would go there.

At the heart of the revelers were the young people, Milda
among them, her shoulders and bared head visible above the
others. There the dancing was at its liveliest. Arms raised,
forefingers pointing in a carnival salute, singing full voice,

Milda and those her age were turning the Big Drum into a Trinidadian jump-up.

Had Thomasina Moore been present that was where she would have been. At the center, with Milda and her group. *"Girl, those drums got to me!"* That time in Cartagena. And for the first time ever Avey Johnson found herself thinking of her with something akin to affection.

To restrain the young people perhaps, the older folk—those who had dominated the fete earlier—were dancing on the perimeter. Lebert Joseph, Rosalie Parvay, the barefoot woman with the braids who had opened the nation dances—all were there. And in sober counterpoint to the jump-up, they were performing the rhythmic trudge that couldn't be called danc-ing, yet at the same time was something more than merely walking. A non-dance designed to conserve their failing strength and see them through the night.

Occasionally, even they forgot themselves and a hip for all its stiffness would swing out. A bent shoulder would flicker in time to the music. An old woman might suddenly swirl in a graceful turn, her Juba skirt flaring. Trudging past the lead drummer they directed a sweeping bow his way in acknowl-edgment of his mastery. Their outstretched arms hailed the sound of the struck iron, which by now was on a par with the voice of the drums.

Clangorous, insistent, soaring, the iron was sending out a call loud enough to be heard from one end of the archipelago to the other. Iron calling for its namesake and creator. Until after a time the call was answered. Those among the elderly who, like Lebert Joseph, possessed *connaissance* could tell. They sensed a presence squatting in the darkness beyond the reach of the gas lamps. Ogun Feraille. Taking his nightly stroll around the islands he had heard the sound of the gong-gong and dropped in.

"If it was left to me I'd close down every dancehall in Harlem and burn every drum!"

Slowly Avey Johnson stood up. She unhurriedly picked up her chair and, holding it easily with one hand against her side, began walking over to where the musicians were playing, away from the voice in her ear.

Once there, she set the chair down close to the bottle-and-spoon boys standing beside the drummers.

And then she did an odd thing. Instead of sitting down she turned and slowly retraced her steps to her old place beside the tree, and stood there. Her face was expressionless, her body still and composed, but her bottom lip had unfolded to bare the menacing sliver of pink.

The dancers in their loose, ever-widening ring were no more than a dozen feet away now. She could feel the reverberation of their powerful tread in the ground under her, and the heat from their bodies reached her in a strong yeasty wave. Soon only a mere four or five feet remained between them, yet she continued to stand there. Finally, just as the moving wall of bodies was almost upon her, she too moved—a single declarative step forward. At the same moment, what seemed an arm made up of many arms reached out from the circle to draw her in, and she found herself walking amid the elderly folk on the periphery, in their counterclockwise direction.

For a time she did nothing more than follow along in their midst. So as not to throw those behind her out of step, she was careful to move at their pace, although she did not attempt their little rhythmic tramp. She was content to simply be among them and to return the smiles and approving nods that came her way. By the time she had completed one full turn of the yard though and was back near the tree, she had slipped without being conscious of it into a step that was something more than just walking.

Her feet of their own accord began to glide forward, but in such a way they scarcely left the ground. Only the broad heels of her low-heeled shoes rose slightly and then fell at each step. She moved cautiously at first, each foot edging forward as if the ground under her was really water—muddy river water— and she was testing it to see if it would hold her weight.

After a while, by the time in fact she reached the tree again, she was doing the flatfooted glide and stamp with aplomb. And she was smiling to herself, her eyes screened over.

"Ah, din' I say she wasn't the kind to let a little rough water get the better of her!" Lebert Joseph. Jubilant. A proud father.

"And look, she's doing the 'Carriacou Tramp' good as somebody been doing it all their life!" Rosalie Parvay exclaiming in astonishment as the two of them discovered her among the dancers.

Avey Johnson smiled but she neither heard nor saw them clearly. Because it was a score of hot August nights again in her memory, and she was standing beside her great-aunt on the dark road across from the church that doubled as a school. And under cover of the darkness she was performing the dance that wasn't supposed to be dancing, in imitation of the old folk shuffling in a loose ring inside the church. And she was singing along with them under her breath: *"Who's that ridin' the chariot/Well well well . . ."* The Ring Shout. Standing there she used to long to give her great-aunt the slip and join those across the road.

She had finally after all these decades made it across. The

elderly Shouters in the person of the out-islanders had reached out their arms like one great arm and drawn her into their midst.

And for the first time since she was a girl, she felt the threads, that myriad of shiny, silken, brightly colored threads (like the kind used in embroidery) which were thin to the point of invisibility yet as strong as the ropes at Coney Island. Looking on outside the church in Tatem, standing waiting for the *Robert Fulton* on the crowded pier at 125th Street, she used to feel them streaming out of everyone there to enter her, making her part of what seemed a far-reaching, wide-ranging confraternity.

Now, suddenly, as if she were that girl again, with her entire life yet to live, she felt the threads streaming out from the old people around her in Lebert Joseph's yard. From their seared eyes. From their navels and their cast-iron hearts. And their brightness as they entered her spoke of possibilities and becoming even in the face of the bare bones and the burnt-out ends.

She began to dance then. Just as her feet of their own accord had discovered the old steps, her hips under the linen shirtdress slowly began to weave from side to side on their own, stiffly at first and then in a smooth wide arc as her body responded more deeply to the music. And the movement in her hips flowed upward, so that her entire torso was soon swaying. Arms bent, she began working her shoulders in the way the Shouters long ago used to do, thrusting them forward and then back in a strong casting-off motion. Her weaving head was arched high. All of her moving suddenly with a vigor and passion she hadn't felt in years, and with something of the stylishness and sass she had once been known for. *"Girl, you can out-jangle Bojangles."* Jay saying it with amaze-

ment at the Saturday night pretend dances when he would
turn the floor over to her.

Yet for all the sudden unleashing of her body she was being
careful to observe the old rule: Not once did the soles of her
feet leave the ground. Even when the Big Drum reached its
height in a tumult of voices, drums and the ringing iron, and
her arms rose as though hailing the night, the darkness that is
light, her feet held to the restrained glide-and-stamp, the
rhythmic trudge, the Carriacou Tramp, the shuffle designed to
stay the course of history. Avey Johnson could not have said
how long she kept her arms raised or how many turns she
made in the company of these strangers who had become one
and the same with people in Tatem. Until suddenly Lebert
Joseph did something which caused her arms to drop and her
mind to swing back to the yard and the present moment. He
had remained at her side all along, watching her dance with
the smile that was at once triumphant and fatherly, and dancing himself, the slow measured tramp. But as her arms went up
and her body seemed about to soar off into the night, his smile
faded, and was replaced by the gaze that called to mind a
jeweler's loupe or a laser beam in its ability to penetrate to her
depth. His eyes probing deep, he went to stand facing her in
front. His oversized hands went out, bringing to a halt for a
moment the slow-moving tide around them. And then he
bowed, a profound, solemn bow that was like a genuflection.

Rosalie Parvay nearby quickly followed her father's example. Taking his place in front of Avey Johnson she swept
down before her in an exact copy of his gesture.

To her utter bewilderment others in the crowd of aged
dancers, taking their cue from him also, began doing the
same. One after another of the men and women trudging past,
who were her senior by years, would pause as they reached her

and, turning briefly in her direction, tender her the deep, almost reverential bow. Then, singing, they would continue on their way.

One elderly woman not only bowed but stepped close and took her hand. Cataracts dimmed her gaze. The face she raised to Avey Johnson was a ravaged landscape of dark hollows and caves where her wrinkled flesh had collapsed in on the bone. Her chin displayed the beginning of a beard: a few wispy white hairs that curled in on themselves. An old woman who was at once an old man. Tiresias of the dried dugs.

"Bercita Edwards of Smooth Water Bay, Carriacou," she said, and holding on to Avey Johnson's hand she peered close, searching for whatever it was she possessed that required her to defer despite her greater age. "And who you is?" she asked.

And as a mystified Avey Johnson gave her name, she suddenly remembered her great-aunt Cuney's admonition long ago. The old woman used to insist, on pain of a switching, that whenever anyone in Tatem, even another child, asked her her name she was not to say simply "Avey," or even "Avey Williams." But always "Avey, short for Avatara."

3

"You know," he said, "I watched you good last night at the fete and I can't say for sure but I feels you's an Arada, oui. Something about the way you was doing the Carriacou Tramp there toward the end put me in mind of people from that nation."

"Is true," Rosalie Parvay agreed. "Is the same thought came to me."

It was seven o'clock the following morning, mist blanketing the ground, the sun already high although partly obscured by scattered clouds, and the three of them were standing waiting at the tiny airport, along with a handful of out-islanders who were also flying back to Grenada. Nearby, on a dusty patch that served as an apron, the small plane was being readied.

"And there's the height of you for another thing," Lebert Joseph was saying. He had resumed carrying the walking stick this morning and he raised it now to indicate her height, making her out to be far taller than her five feet eight from the way he held it up. "The Aradas are mostly a tall people—especially the women. You even carries yourself like one them now that I think of it."

Avey Johnson laughed. The man refused to give up on her. He saw (and insisted that others also see) things about her which could only be of his imagining. She was thinking of the strange bowing that had gone on last night. "I'll have to take your word for it," she said. "You're the expert in such matters."

On sudden impulse she bent and took his face between her hands. It was something she had wanted to do ever since they had become friends, to bring to a halt the exhausting rocking motion of his head which she sensed there rather than saw. She then brought her face to rest against his for a long moment, forgiving him his duplicity, thanking him, saying good-bye.

Turning to Rosalie Parvay she embraced her also. In her pocketbook she carried letters to her children in Canada to be mailed from the States. They would reach them faster that way. She promised she would mail them off as soon as she reached New York.

To fix their image in mind she kept her eyes closed for a long minute after the plane was airborne. At takeoff, while Rosalie Parvay waved from the receding ground, he had simply stood on his good leg, the stick raised. Hail and farewell. They had looked in the growing distance more like sister and brother rather than father and child.

The plane, bearing north, was taking her over the center of the island. Little could be seen because of the mist on the ground and the thin, scattered clouds through which they were climbing.

She made out a few low-lying hills. Was the one she had climbed last night among them? There was a passing glimpse of a large tin-roofed house. Could it have been Rosalie Parvay's bungalow? Along the coastline at the northern end she spied a tranquil bay sheened with sunlight. The Smooth Water Bay of the bearded old woman last night? Everything fleeting and ephemeral. The island more a mirage rather than an actual place. Something conjured up perhaps to satisfy a longing and need.

She was leaving Carriacou without having really seen it.

"Is only this excursion business I don' understand!" His face in the rearview mirror of the taxi had been filled with angry bewilderment.

Perhaps he would come to drive her to the airport later today. The desk clerk at the hotel might have told him the time of her new flight. If so, if he appeared, she would sit him down, take off his mirror sunglasses and the straw cowboy hat and explain it to him in her way.

She would tell him—she didn't know why but she would—about the living room floor in Halsey Street: of how when she would put on the records after coming in from work, the hardwood floor, reverberating with the music, used to feel like rich and solid ground under her. She had felt centered and sustained then, she would tell him, restored to her proper axis.

And another thing. She would quote him the line from the story that had been drilled into her as a child, which had been handed down from the woman whose name she bore. "Her body she always usta say might be in Tatem but her mind, her mind was long gone with the Ibos . . ."

Crazy. The American black woman gone crazy he would think to himself, and blame it on the excursion.

Nor would she stop with the taxi driver, but would take it upon herself to speak of the excursion to others elsewhere. Her territory would be the street corners and front lawns in their small section of North White Plains. And the shopping mall and train station. As well the canyon streets and office buildings of Manhattan. She would haunt the entranceways of the skyscrapers. And whenever she spotted one of them amid the crowd, those young, bright, fiercely articulate token few for whom her generation had worked the two and three jobs, she would stop them.

"It is an ancient mariner/And he stoppeth one of three." Like the obsessed old sailor she had read about in high school she would stop them. As they rushed blindly in and out of the glacier buildings, unaware, unprotected, lacking memory and a necessary distance of the mind (no mojo working for them!), she would stop them and before they could pull out of her grasp, tell them about the floor in Halsey Street and quote them the line from her namesake . . .

She would enlist Marion in her cause. Marion whom she had tried to root from her body by every means possible, repeatedly throwing herself one day down the five flights of stairs. *Pa'doné mwé.* Of her three children, Marion alone would understand about the excursion and help her spread the word.

Once, years ago, when she had been telling someone about

her days as an organizer for the union on her job, Marion, overhearing her, had cried—she had been no more than twelve at the time—"Oh, how I wish I had known you then!"

Tatem. Avey Johnson found herself thinking of the house her great-aunt had left her. By the time the plane touched down in Grenada she had made up her mind to fix it up. Or if it was beyond repair to build a new one in its place. Sell the house in North White Plains as Marion had been urging her to do for years and use the money to build in Tatem.

It would be a vacation house, and once she retired she would live part of the year there. And each summer she would ask that her two grandsons be sent to spend time with her in Tatem, especially the youngest one, who had known the value of a dime-store xylophone. If forced to, she would be as tyrannical in demanding that they be sent as her great-aunt had been with her.

And Marion could bring some of the children from her school, her "sweetest lepers," as she called them. The place could serve as a summer camp.

And at least twice a week in the late afternoon, when the juniper trees around Tatem began sending out their cool and stately shadows, she would lead them, grandchildren and visitors alike, in a troop over to the Landing.

"It was here that they brought them," she would begin—as had been ordained. "They took them out of the boats right here where we're standing . . ."